NOWHERE

to

HIDE

ANASTASIA SMITH

First Deep Rose Press trade paperback edition November 2018

For information about special discounts for bulk purchases, please contact Deep Rose Press at the email listed above.

Manufactured in the United States of America

10 9 8 7 6 5 4 3 2 1

ISBN: 978-1-64467-492-5

ISBN: 978-1-64467-492-5

For Eileen, the one who gave me my spark.

1

"Remember what's at stake," he said. And he was right. I needed to remember why I had to do this; what would happen if I didn't. But damn, how it hurt so much. I glanced at my phone; I knew how badly this would hurt her. And yet, here I am, still willing to do it. But if I didn't, I would be putting her life at risk. This is what's best. And whether I want it or not, this is my truth; this is what I have to do.

———— ⬡⬡⬡ ————

As I rolled heavily out of the bed, a wave of nausea flooded over me. Everything ached, not to mention the raging hangover. Stumbling to the bathroom, I massaged my temples in an attempt to ease the pain. The bathroom seemed a mile away. I gripped the counter for balance. Looking down, I noticed the bruises that littered my hands and arms. My nails were chipped and dirty. I waved it away with disregard, thinking nothing of it; I was always a little beat up after a night out. But once looking into the mirror, I felt my heart skip a beat, and I jumped back into the corner, startled.

I barely recognized my own reflection. A slit that started small above my left brow grew into a gash, the color deepening as it stretched over my nose and ended in a jagged, abrupt twist at the opposite corner of my mouth. It rested over a color varying bruise that ran in patches across my jaw. The bridge of my nose laid crooked, worse than a witch's even.

A sharp sting shot through my ear, drawing my hand's aid. I pulled it away to see the red that dampened my neck, dress, and now fingers. Following the trail of blood to my shoulders and neck, my eyes widened at the discoloration overlaying my throat. The woman looking back at me was unrecognizable, mutilated. After a moment of pure numbness, a thought ran through my head; *what happened?*

Looking down, my wrist was just a smudged patchwork of entry stamps. Small bits and pieces of the night before flashed through my head. Dancing on a club floor. Shots with a group of unknown men and women. Walking the streets of Chinatown. That's where it changed. First we were all together; a loud, drunken group of 22-year-olds making their way obnoxiously through the streets.

"Hey, what's down this way?" I ask. The guy, whose sister took charge as the head of the pack, is standing next to me and seems to know his way around the city. I, again, look down the alleyway, drawn to the narrow beam of light peering from an open door.

He raises his eyebrows, almost in a disapproving way. But his face changes soon afterwards, showing his weighing of decisions. Then he smiles, "Are you ready to have the best time of your life?"

I take one final glance at the group as they make their way down the street, our absence unnoticed. I follow my guide down the dark, narrow path. The pavement is wet under my feet. There is a heaviness in the air that can be felt after the first step into the empty road and I begin to rethink my decision, "Are you sure this is safe? I mean, we aren't going to be mugged, are we?"

A small chuckle is the only answer I receive before we reach the door, "Don't act suspicious, got it?" His hand pushes the slab of metal, and the atmosphere instantly comes to life.

I ran to the nightstand and ripped my phone from the charger. Scrolling through the notifications, I noticed a dozen panicked messages, along with three missed calls from Josh.

"Allison? Oh, thank God. What were you doing in a joint in Chinatown at three in the morning?" Josh asked, "I mean, we've been through tons of shit together, and I've gotten you out of tons of shit, but this? I don't know what the hell I can do about this."

I tried to speak, "Yea-"

"What was that?" Josh asked.

The words were right there on my tongue, but nothing but a breathy, whistling attempt at words came out. I coughed in effort of clearing my throat, but almost died from the pain. I mistook swollenness for something blocking my airway. Gripping my throat, I tried to swallow, and winced at every movement. I took in a breath and tried to speak again.

"I-Don't-Know." The words came in a patchy, foreign version of my voice, "Josh, I'm scared."

I hear Josh's breathing over the line, "Are you alright?" he asked, "What happened?"

"I really messed up." The words barely escape my mouth as the tears that choked me up closed off my throat completely. I was going to speak again, but something by the door caught my eye.

A folded, matte black envelope with a flap lined in gold set barely under the door. I tore open the flap of the red-streaked envelope, the blood seeping from the thin paper onto my hands. I took a second before speaking again, "But now it's worse, Josh. Way worse."

"Jesus, Allison! What did you do?"

But as soon as they notice the door creep open, everyone freezes. But he just raises his hand, "Guys, she's with me." Everyone goes back to what they were doing as if nothing happened. A tall man with shaggy, dirty blonde hair walks up to my escort, gripping his hand and handing him a drink.

"Dude, it's gonna get lit here tonight. I've already had six drinks and smoked more in two hours than I had all year," his friend said with a kind of proudness of his actions. He pushes his drink into his friend's hand and stumbles over to me. I am backed into a wall, and this man's arm stretches over my head, gripping the wall for balance. He takes my chin in his hand, examining my face, eventually locking our eyes intense gaze; a smile creeps onto his lips, "Who's your friend?" he asks, never breaking eye contact.

I dive under his arm and hurry back to the only person I know, "A friend of a friend. Or the fiancée of a friend, I should say. She's engaged, Mick, stop staring at her like that," he says and I hide my left hand in my pocket

"Okay. Yeah, sure," Mick says. I can feel every inch of my body tighten as his eyes graze over it and a smile creeps onto his

lips.

"Mick, I'm serious."

"Yeah, yeah, off limits. I'm not looking," Mick says as he finally rips his gaze away and faces his friend, "Anyway, dude, you ready to have fun?"

"Yeah, what do we got tonight?" We start walking towards the center of the room. There are tables and tables of people gambling away their entire paychecks and not even caring. People carry around drink, and women throw themselves upon men. A dark man with an accent - Fijian? - walks up to us and hands us drinks off of a tray.

"Okay we got the ush - baccarat, craps, roulette - and tonight we have Classic, Switch, Spanish 21, Pontoon, and Super Fun 21," Mick says, throwing his arm around me, raising his eyebrows up and down. I push his arm off, stepping two to the left.

We sit down at a table of Classic Blackjack and after so long I start to relax. My days at Harvard start coming back to me, and winning comes naturally. I play for hours and hours and as the night goes on my winnings increase. Mick wandered off around 10:30, almost an hour and a half ago. But my new acquaintance stayed by my side all night, and is still there, "Thanks for saving me back there. When Mick wouldn't give it up."

"It was nothing. He doesn't meet many women; he just sticks here with the men," he says.

"Yeah that was quick thinking, the whole 'fiancée' thing. Very clever," I say. His eyes are beautiful, like ice that has the slightest tint of blue. And they are so bright. His jaw is firm, strong. And his hair is that perfect mix of blonde with brown

flecks.

"Yeah, well I try to be clever in front of an attractive woman; I've heard it makes me more attractive," he says, his face closer now.

I can feel my heartbeat quicken until it's almost a flutter, "Well, I think what you've heard is very true," I say. But as I do I glance over his shoulder. Mick is sitting there watching us. His eyes are narrowed and his jaw clenched. But before I can say anything, the man in front of me leans in closer and I know what he's going to do.

We are centimeters apart when we hear loud voice address the room, "Everyone! We've got 30 seconds!" Mick shouts. He looks down at us, and the look on his face tells the story. His grin couldn't be wider, and he couldn't be happier with himself.

I look back over at this man I almost kissed, expecting him to be as pissed as I am. But he isn't. He's smiling the way you would if someone thought they ruined your plan, but they instead made it better. And now I realize, that's exactly what has happened.

I sit there, staring into his eyes, and I can hear the people around us start the countdown. He smiles, and I can't help but do the same. When the crowd finally hits one, we dive at each other, as if we have waited our entire lives for this second.

It feels like time has frozen around us. His hand is soft on my cheek. I pull him in even closer so our bodies touch, and I wrap my hands around his neck. I feel so safe in his arms. His warm body and his firm yet soft grip. The way his hand pulls me in by the waist. His soft hand through my blonde hair.

"I've wanted to do that all night," he says, his finger stroking my cheek.

"Me too."

But something starts to pull me back from this moment, back to reality, "Hello?" the dealer says. I look down at my phone. 12:08. We have been here for eight minutes. We turn to face the table, and I set two red chips by the cards.

"So, am I ever going to see you again?" he asks, "Or are you just here for the holiday?"

My heart sinks when I think about this, about going home. About never seeing him again. Then I think about what's going to happen when I get home, how pissed my aunt's going to be for kissing a guy when I don't even know his name, "No, I'm just here until tomorrow. I leave at ten."

"Oh. So where are you running to so early?"

"LA," I say collecting yet another win. I glance to my right to see Mick coming towards our table. I roll my eyes and set my chin in my hand.

"Ah, that explains it," he says and throws three chips into the middle of the table.

"Explains what?"

"The deep tan in December, well I guess now January, the long beach waves, and not to mention the perfect beach bod," he says raising his glass before taking a drink. I smile and look down at my arms then start to look around the room. They were significantly darker than anyone else's. I look back at him and you can just see what I'm feeling on my face. I am surprised and flattered and happy. My soul is genuinely happy. Something it hasn't been in a long time.

I take one last glance at my arms but freeze when I see a familiar pair boots on the floor. I flick my eyes up and the feeling completely dissipates. Mick sits in the seat next to me. I roll my neck and look over to my partner for the evening. He looks just as thrilled to see Mick as I am.

"You seem to be having lots of luck tonight, little lady," Mick says, folding his hands. He throws wads of cash on the table; the amount of money I've won.

And I don't know if it's the beer or just the annoyance of Mick's constant suffocating manner and presence, but whatever it is, it causes me to say the worst thing I possibly could.

"Yeah, well I guess I'm just really good at keeping track of numbers."

Yeah, well I guess I'm just really good at keeping track of numbers; the line that ruined me.

As soon as the words leave my mouth I freeze. My stomach twists into a pretzel and my heart pounds as though it's trying to flee from my chest. But I don't blame it. I don't want to be here for the aftermath either, "I mean," I look over to the man I've kissed. The man I've talked to for hours. The man I might even love. But he just stares back and I can see he knows how this is going to end.

"You're what?" Mick asks.

I look around and see two men creeping up behind Mick. One is slightly taller than the other, but they both look equal in strength; a level of which is not in my favor. That's when I get up, grab the cash, and bolt.

My shaking hand pulled on the flap of the gold-lined envelope. The first piece of paper felt thick - a picture. I flipped it over.

A paralyzing pain ran through my spine and sent me to the ground. I grip my back, holding the place where the dresser's corner made its mark. The picture lay on the floor next to my hand. I reached for it and my eyes began to burn. I wiped the red fingerprint from the right-center of the photo. His body lay limp on the ground. His perfect blonde hair was red and matted. And his beautiful eyes were closed; they would never see the lights of the city again.

"Allison, what the hell happened?" Josh shouted through the phone. I did not answer. How could I? My mind was buzzing yet blank. I was in pain yet numb. I couldn't make sense of it, and it was maddening.

"Allison!"

I set the phone down beside me. The reddened envelope that I had set beside me was not yet empty. I lifted it off of the ground. My fingers ripped at the bloody flap once again. My hand sifted through the envelope and I pulled out a waxy, thin piece of paper; a flyer from the Walmart Photo Center. My hands shook as I slowly turned over the piece of paper.

This is what happens to people who count.

2

"Wait, so who is the guy in the picture? Like, what's his name?" Josh asked.

"I don't know." I fumbled with the locket around my neck.

"Okay, let me make sure I have this right. You get cold, so you go into a club. Alone. You sit there alone, and a guy comes over to you. You walk with him to a group which consists of his sister her two girlfriends and their boyfriends. You all start drinking and dancing, then this guy's sister gets bored, so you all start walking around the city. You make your way to Chinatown and get curious and walk down a dark alley with a man you don't know, kiss him, then get caught counting cards."

"Yes, that's right," I said staring at the wall, the heart-shaped silver still clutched between my fingers. Hearing Josh say it, explain the evening, made me realize how ridiculous it was. How stupid I was.

"Nina's gonna kill you," Josh said. And he was right. Aunt Nina was going to kill me, "She didn't even want you to go on that trip in the first place."

"I know," I said. I was completely numb. I couldn't say

anything else. All I could do was think about him. How he had to pay for my slip-up. How he was dead. Because of me. My eyes welled up with tears again and I pulled my legs closer to my chest, "Josh, should I go to the police?"

"Um…" His voice trailed off, "I don't know. Did they threaten you?"

"No."

"Then I'd hold off," he said, "Wait and see what happens. Anyway, you said when you looked in the mirror, you were beat up. How badly? I mean, is she gonna notice?" Josh asked. I wished he would just shut up; I didn't feel like talking, like answering questions. But I knew he was just trying to help.

"Josh it's bad," I whisper, "With the way she notices everything… Even if she didn't, she'd have to be in a coma not to notice."

"Ugh, Allison," he replied, "I mean, I could do it if you really need me to."

"Very funny," I muttered. There was no emotion in my voice, and I just continued staring at the wall. A small crack ran down from the windowsill to the floor. It was just a small white line that twisted and turned through the drywall. One little stress fracture that, over time with weathering, could grow larger, become a bigger hole, even cause the entire building to collapse. An entire building collapse because of one small crack.

"Come on. I'm just trying to lighten the mood," Josh said. I could hear him sigh over the phone and lean back in his seat. I could hear the fans fire up as the computer sprang to life, "Allison? What time are you supposed to catch your flight?"

"Ten."

"Allison, it's 11:30. If you're trying not to make Nina

suspicious, you're not off to a good start," he said.

"That sucks."

"I'm on my way over. Hurry and see what flights you can catch. I don't know what luck you'll have, but I'd hurry. I mean, that is if you don't want your aunt to kill you." The phone line cut off with a beep and I just threw it on top of my bag. Josh was right; I needed to see what flights I could catch to get home.

I picked myself up off of the floor and started towards the small coffee table in front of the sofa. The rays of sunlight peeking through the curtains were too much to handle, and I reached for one and yanked.

I toppled down with the curtains and lay buried on the floor. I ripped the heavy curtain off of me and the light from the rising sun illuminated the room. I just sat there staring out to the distance, to the morning awakening over the sea. The waves crashed over each other and the birds swooped down over the vast blue water. Ships left the ports and snow covered their sails.

I fought to peel my eyes open; the light was so bright. After what seemed like years, I pried my gaze from the ocean and crawled back to the sofa. My computer was also pulled down by the curtain, and I grabbed it from the bedside.

While on the floor, I froze. My arm reached for the shoe that lay a few feet under the bed. When I pulled it back, my fears were confirmed. I dropped the shoe and pushed it away, but it was too late. The blood that stained the heel of the shoe already covered my hands. I started screaming, and I could feel the tears falling helplessly from my face. I curled up in a ball.

After the several minutes it took to reel it in, I made a third attempt to sit on the sofa and book a flight. I took a deep breath as I entered the web address and scrolled through the page. *11:30 p.m.* That was the earliest flight.

My heart fell to the floor. No, it fell through the floor, the twelve floors below me and to the lobby. I was going to be in so much trouble. I had about six hours until I was expected in LA. Then what? Josh was already there, but Lord only knew what he was saying. His cover-ups had never been the best. When we were at the beach the summer after eighth grade, Aunt Nina caught him looking at me. What was his excuse? The sun was bright, and I was blocking it. He was covering for me, making sure that Aunt Nina didn't see the guy I was with, or that we were a little more than friends.

I tried to think of an excuse, something I could tell her.

I couldn't think of anything.

But it was because that woman saw through *everything*. You could have a sad look on your face because you forgot your charger and she will pry the fact that you had depression, your parents died, and you self-harm out of you. All because you forgot your phone charger. I've seen her do it. That's why this excuse had to be good.

I tried to think of something but nothing added up. *I slept in;* doesn't explain why I got beat up. *I got in a fight;* she wouldn't believe it, and even if she did, I would've been in trouble. *I was in an accident;* I would be in the hospital.

I tried and tried for hours to come up with an excuse, a plan. But when I looked at the clock, two o'clock had come and I had nothing.

I ran my hands over my face, and through my fingers I caught a glimpse of my reflection in the mirror above the sink. A layer of blood lay dried, crusted over the length of my face. A blood-soaked goose egg protruded from my forehead.

My phone rang, and I answered it, "Allison, hey, did you get a flight?"

"Yeah, I booked one. Josh, is that music?" I asked. Why would there be music playing that loudly in the house?

"Yeah, we're at the Pier," he shouted over the bass, "I said it was just a thank you for taking care of you when your parents died and not letting someone else move you away." I let out a sigh, and I knew Josh could feel my eyes roll, "Listen, it was the best I could come up with, but Nina's having a blast, so you don't have to worry about her." A pause stretched, and I could hear the music and Aunt Nina's loud voice over everyone else's. I remembered the many times in school when everyone knew when Aunt Nina was coming down the hall just by the volume of her voice, "So what time will you land?"

"Um, six."

"Well, that's not bad at all. That's only one hour later," Josh said. He was out of breath, but I wasn't concerned. That woman could disappear in the blink on an eye, "Shit, I lost her. Again. How many people does she know? She's like a twenty-one year old trapped in a 49-year-old's body. And she's so fast."

"Freakishly," I said.

"So I'll just stall her until five-ish, then we'll come get you."

"Well, you see, I land at six a.m." Another sigh stretched through the silence, "I'm sorry."

"I'll see what I can do. Am I a bad person if I intoxicate her, or at least strongly encourage it? Because that's something I can work with. Listen, I have to go, I actually can't find her now. Bye." And with that the line went dead.

In a rush, I packed my things and left the room. If I got the letter under my door, that means they knew where I was; and that was something I was not comfortable with. I threw my stuff into the rental and drove out of the parking lot. I slammed my finger on the power button, and the radio sprang to life, *"...And next we have news of a homicide. The body of twenty-two year old Leo Kutsikovich was found in an alley outside of what seems to be a nightclub in Chinatown at six-thirty this morning."* I looked at the picture sitting on the passenger seat, *"At a first glance, police thought the cause of death to be blunt-force trauma to the head from being thrown into a nearby brick wall. But after further examination, it was confirmed he was strangled until inches away from death when he was shot twice in the chest, one bullet going straight through his heart. It was also-"*

I turned the radio back off as a tear crawled down my cheek. Gripping the steering wheel, I took deep breaths as traffic stood still. I propped my arm up on the door and let my head fall into my hand, looking out the window. The city was buzzing. Shops and restaurants lined the streets. People hurried in and out, sunglasses covering their eyes.

I push past people and throw myself against the door. The door flies open and I am shaken to the core by the chilled air I am greeted with. I am barely fifteen feet from the doorway when strong hands grab my arms and lift me off of the ground. I feel the blood trickle down my neck. My hands grip the brick wall as I am lifted off of the ground once more. I scratch and rip at the hands around my neck; they do not budge, but get tighter. The corners of my vision begin to darken as I gasp for air. The burning in my chest continues to grow and I fear I am not making it out of here alive.

The man in front of me is massive. He has strong arms that look like they'll burst from his shirt at any minute. A small blue vein sticks out of the side of his neck. His face is squared, his jawline intense. I can't see his eyes through the dark sunglasses that sit over them. He is standing completely still, as if he is made of stone.

As the sound of footsteps approaches, his grip loosens, but still remains firm; I'm not going anywhere. A small click is enough to draw my attention to the left. The silver shines in the streetlight and the sharp edge sends a chill through my entire body. The knife's owner could be the twin of the man who holds onto me.

I try to cry for help as the pointed edge creeps towards my face. But nothing comes out. The man runs the dull edge along my cheek and down to my jaw. The green of his eyes becomes clearer the longer I look into them.

"Such a pretty face," the man says. He shifts the blade and in a second my jaw radiates with a stinging pain, "Too bad you won't get to keep it." He lifts the blade from my face and drives the point into the skin above my eyebrow. A small, rasp, squeal escapes my mouth as the biting sting continues.

I feel the tearing of my skin as the knife is slowly pulled down my face. It seems with every wince, the pressure with which the blade is applied increases. I look to the man as the smile on his face twists and his satisfaction grows with every centimeter his knife gains.

The coppery taste of blood slips into my mouth as the ongoing gash on my face continues to grow. I lick my lip and the searing pain is almost unbearable at this point. The blade crosses over the corner of my mouth with agony, but the tearing of flesh ceases with one last jerk of the blade.

The crack rings out, and the pressure on my throat is released. I gasp for air, sitting up. A few feet from me, the man whose hands were wrapped around my neck lies unconscious. The man with the knife not far from him. The kind man that I spent the evening with stands behind them. A bloody baseball bat hangs from my hero's hands as he stands there heaving.

But my gaze is soon shifted to Mick marching up to him from behind. One swing is all it takes to knock my hero to the ground, "Run!" he shouts from the ground. He rolls over onto his stomach, and his eyes meet mine, "Run!"

And I do. I take off running, only stealing one-second glances back. When I turn to see a gun in Mick's hand, I am met by a forcing impact that sends a jolt through my body. I look up and find a large pole standing tall, and proud, and in my way. I scramble to my feet and fly through the dark streets of the city.

I had around nine hours before my flight took off. If I got there two hours early, that left seven hours I needed to kill. A pang of hunger reminded me that I hadn't eaten since seven the previous day. Looking around, I decided to pull into a parking space that a car had just pulled out of. I swerved through the lanes and cut across the road. Horns blared and words were exchanged.

But I was instantly filled with relief when I read the chalkboard sign outside of the Handcraft Kitchen and Cocktails. I pulled on the door handle and made a beeline straight for the bar. I dropped myself in a bar stool, and slammed my hands on the bar top a little harder than I originally had intended, "Can I really get a 'hangover plate' *and* a bloody Mary for only fifteen dollars?" I said looking up at the bartender. But he just stared back at me, horrified.

What is his problem? Then I remembered; my face, "Listen, it's a long story," I said, then repeated my question. The bartender nodded and turned to make my drink. I watched as he mixed in the vodka, and couldn't wait to drink it. Setting the drink down in front of me, the bartender took one last, long look at my face, and then turned away.

Swirling the celery around in the vodka and tomato juice mixture, I looked around the place. A tall stone pillar stood directly behind me, and tables filled with people lined the walls. But every person I made eye contact with stared back, appalled. Groups of people whispered among themselves, "You know what," I said to the bartender, still looking at all of the dismayed faces around me. I turned back the face the bar, "May I have that food order to go?"

Raising my hand in front of my face, I hurried back to the car and avoided eye contact with anyone on the street. When I reached the safety of my car, I felt at peace for the first time that day. I looked down at the radio; *3:15 p.m.* I still had around six hours to kill.

Traffic in New York on New Year's Day actually isn't as terrible as you'd think. Everyone is too hung-over to even leave their bedrooms let alone drive. So naturally, being from California, I drove to the one place that I knew would kill a few hours and be relaxing at the same time.

But let me tell you, the Rockaway Beach in January is not the same as the Hermosa in LA. But with the fleece blanket from the trunk, the warm fleece I wore under my sweatpants and hoodie, and my hat and gloves, it wasn't too bad. I closed my eyes and listened to the waves, the stress breaking away with every crash.

I pulled my phone out of the small, brown, over-the-shoulder purse that hung around my body. Opening Snapchat, I plugged the phone into the portable charger in my purse. I videoed the waves, smiling as everyone folded over itself. I saved the video to My Memories. What would I remember when I watched this video next? The feeling of the bitter cold nipping at my nose? The feeling of love that filled the air the previous night? Or the horror of seeing a picture of a dead man I had kissed? My mind started buzzing, and my heart started racing. I took a deep breath in, then a deep breath out, and cleared my head.

I lowered myself backwards until I lay completely nestled in the sand. I closed Snapchat and opened Face Time. In my recents, I tapped on the 'Bro' with the red heart beside it. The phone rang, and I waited patiently as it did. When I heard the *swoosh* that showed he answered, I looked back at the screen.

Josh's face had that suspicious look, as he kept his eyes closely on something off to the side, "Okay I have the perfect pla-Jesus Christ Allison!" His eyes widened.

"I told you it was bad, Josh," I said, raising my brows.

"Yea, but I didn't think it was *that* bad," he said and ran his hand through his hair, "Well, I was going to tell you about my perfect plan before you scared the daylights out of me with your face." I just gave him the bird and let out a goofy laugh, "So you know how after your uncle left, and Nina took a hot minute to get it together, she stopped drinking almost entirely because she had you?"

And I did.

My heart is beating out of my chest, and I hold the packet of papers in my hands. We haven't really spoken much since that night. But it still early, and she hasn't had that many drinks yet. I really needed help, and she was the only place I could get it, "Aunt Nina?"

She sits at the counter, a glass of whiskey in front of her on the counter. She looks at me out of the corners of her eyes, "What?"

The word is cold, and I almost turn around and go back to my room. No, you have to, *I think,* "Well, um, I have this paper-project thing due tomorrow for school, and I haven't really even started it. I need an adult for it." *The words faded to a whisper, and I looked down at the ground, avoiding Aunt Nina's drilling glare,* "Here's the rubric."

She snatches the packet from my hands, "Why didn't you ask earlier?" *she spit in almost a snarl, flicking through the dozens of papers,* "Why would you wait until the last minute like this?" *Her breathing quickens, and I can feel the anger radiating off of her body,* "I don't know if we can do this. Is this worth a lot of your grade?"

I nod, "It's the end of the year project." *She stands up and opens her laptop,* "But it's not too hard. We're smart, I think we can do it. We just need-"

"What I'm still trying to get is why you didn't ask me earlier," *she says with one of her guilt-filled glance in my direction.*"

"I did."

The words barely squeak out and she looks up at me, horror-struck, "What did you say?" *She looks genuinely concerned.*

I repeat what I had mumbled, "I did." *I look away, but force my gaze back to her,* "You just don't remember."

Her eyes fall down at the counter then flick up to her glass. There's a fearful panic in her eyes, and she looks as if she has been snapped out of a spell. She hurries back to where she had been sitting. She grabs the glass and pours its contents, as well as the open bottles on the counter's, into the sink. She opens the pantry and pulled out bottled of water.

Cracking one open, she begins to drink as she grabs some of the dinner I'd had to make for myself. I'd left it out, like I have for the past few weeks, hoping she'd eat something.

She sits down next to me at the counter, and I am scrolling through a web page. I reach for the wireless mouse, and Aunt Nina grabs my hand.

I look up at her. There are tears in her eyes, and her hand lifts to my face.

And for the first time in weeks, she hugs me. She pulls me in close and nearly squeezes the life out of me. I feel her staggered breaths, and hug her back.

She pulls away, holding my hands as tears come flowing down her cheeks, "I'm so sorry," she whispers, "I-"

She struggles to find words, "It's alright," I say.

A smile comes on to her face, "No," she says, "it's not."

She looks me in the eyes and promises that it will never happen again.

"Well," Josh continued, "when you think about it, Nina rarely drinks and lets loose. But when she does, she gets wild." And he was right. But what adult doesn't let loose every once in a while? I mean, Aunt Nina drinking was as common as the Diamondbacks winning the World Series, "So what if we stay out here until a little later than planned because, oh I don't know, time got away from us, and by the time she would notice, she would be so into it, that she pretty much wouldn't. I'd make sure she got home safely, of course. Then while she sleeps in tomorrow morning, you sneak in." And it really wasn't that bad of a plan.

"That might actually work," I said as I thought it through.

"I know, I know. I'm a genius," Josh said and I just rolled my eyes. He laughed and I smiled. I missed him. And at that moment I just wanted to go home so he could hold me and give me one of his infamous, miracle-working pep talks like he always did.

"Who are you talking to?"

My heart pounded through my chest as fear flooded over me, and I froze. I could tell by the look on his face the same thing happened to Josh, "No one, Nina," he shouted.

"Mhm," I said with a guilty smile.

"Shut up and get out of here!" Josh yelled back, and he couldn't help but laugh, "Bye, love you."

"Love you too," I said then hung up.

The airport was a crowded mess. You could tell that it had been busy all night and day. Some people waited restlessly in stiff chairs. Flights boarded and others landed. I dragged my suitcase behind me. When I finally found where I'd be boarding, I realized I needed to use the restroom, badly. Hearing Aunt Nina's warnings in my head, I was hesitant to leave my suitcase with anyone. But I not only had my suitcase, but also a large duffle bag and a matching smaller one, and I wasn't taking them all to the restroom.

I looked around, trying to find someone trustworthy. Walking down the aisle I checked out the waiting passengers. A

Goth chick with black and pink hair. *Nope.* Two guys that wouldn't be able to pass for sober four hours from now. *Nope.* A preppy girl who just *had* to be a cheerleader in high school. *Nope.* I collapsed into a chair, losing all hope. But as I rubbed my face, I noticed an older lady sitting two seats diagonal to me. *Perfect.*

"Hi, I was wondering if you could watch my bags while I ran to the restroom very quickly," I said.

She looked up and smiled, "Sure dear, take as long as you need." I gave a quick thanks, grabbed my smaller duffle bag, and bolted for the bathroom. After I was relieved, I went to wash my hands.

I looked up into the mirror. My face was ruined. I touched the scabbing gash; green pus oozed onto my hand. I could hear Josh's 'doctor voice' in my head, "Well, that's not good." I reached into my duffle bag, pulling out the hydrogen peroxide and cotton pads I picked up on the way to the airport. I set them in the arms of the sink and turned towards the paper towel dispenser.

The water and soap sent a sharp, biting sting through my face as I scraped at the crusted blood. I threw away the bloody paper towels and reached for the peroxide. Pouring the acid onto the cotton, I sucked in a breath and went in.

A wave of pain that caused agony worse than the initial cutting of the gash washed over my face, and a small yelp escaped my mouth. But I continued until the blood on my face was gone, and the cuts were nothing but white, bubbling craters on my skin.

I pulled the mascara out of my bag. Right before the wand hit my lashes, a small and snorting laugh rang out, and I jerked my head to the side. A woman 35-years-old stood at a sink, shaking her head with a smile in her face. I looked at her. Our eyes met, and I arched a brow. The smile faded quickly from her face, and she left the bathroom without drying her hands. I took one last look in the mirror, shoving the mascara back into my bag, and took off.

The lady, along with my bags, was right where I left her. I sat down in the empty seat next to my bags, and my eyes hung heavy with the night, "Thanks again."

"No problem," The lady said, "but miss?"

"Yes?"

"Is your name Allison?" the woman asked.

"Yes, how did you know that?"

"Right when you walked away, two men, big men, came and handed this to me," she said as she pulled out an envelope. I sucked in a quick breath as I saw the same gold that lined the last, "They said to give it to Allison when she came back."

I took the envelope from the woman's hand. I slid one of my good, unbroken nails under the flap and tore the paper. Shaking the contents of the envelope onto my lap, I had completely forgotten that I was in public. Three pictures fell out first, followed by a piece of folded printer paper. I turned over the photos and a tear ran down my face.

A peaceful me lay on the beach in the first.

I unpacked my car in the second.

I walked through the airport terminal in the third.

Noticing the woman's eyes on the pictures, I shoved them forcefully back into the envelope.

I shifted away from the woman and unfolded the piece of paper. The rest of the tears that had built up in my eyes were released as I dropped the note on the floor and curled into a ball in the airport chair.

Did you really think you would get away that easily? And here, we thought you had to be smart to count. Oh yeah, and the police... I wouldn't if I were you. See you in LA, Allison.

3

I opened the driver's door of the Ferrari 488 and plugged my phone into the charger. Stepping into the car, I started the engine. My phone buzzed like crazy. Scrolling through the countless messages Josh had sent, I saw pictures of Aunt Nina dancing on the beach, smiling as she walked down the street, laughing in a convertible with friends, and passed out in her bed.

"Nice of you to call back," Josh said when he answered the phone, "So listen. As I assume you've seen, Nina is home, out cold in bed. We didn't get back to the house until four, so you're welcome for the bought time," he said then paused.

"Thank you, Josh," I said, "But I need to tell you something. Did you leave her there alone?"

"Yeah, I left," he replied. *Shit.* "But I locked the door and let the dog in, so I'm sure she'll be fine. Anyway, I came up to the hospital. I can get you in here and taken care of and probably have you out by eight if you get here within the next half hour. The joys of residency: you have all of the perks of the doctors without the schedule," Josh said, "What did you need to tell me?"

"Josh, they know where I live," I said.

"Wait, what? How?"

"I don't know, but they do," I said. I could already feel the pressure in my nose and the burning in my eyes, "What am I going to do? They're relentless." A thousand thoughts ran through my head. What if they knew *exactly* where I lived? Then what? Would they come and try to kill me like they did in New York? Would they go after Aunt Nina? "Josh, we have to do something. What if they hurt Aunt Nina? I could never live with myself…"

"Allison, you're spiraling. Just take a moment to calm down and breathe. We'll talk about it when you get here and taken care of because, as far as I can tell, you have a huge gash on your face that looks infected. And, you could have a concussion from being slammed into a brick wall. So just breathe, and we will worry about one thing at a time."

I walked through the hospital doors, and a million eyes followed me as I made my way to the front desk, "Hey, Patricia."

"Hey Alliso - whoa." Her eyes bulged and her head tilted, "Dr. Montgomery is down that hall," she said, pointing her pen towards a pair of doors behind her, "Third door on the left."

I pushed open the doors and ran down the hall, almost tripping as I flew into the room. On impact, Josh was knocked off of his feet, but caught his balance. His embrace was so warm, so comforting. It felt like home.

Josh pulled away, taking my face in his hands. Rubbing away the tears, he said, "It's okay. You're here; I'm here. You'll be okay." I gulped, pushing down a sob, and nodded my head, laying it on his chest.

I gripped the arm of the bed until my fingers turned white. The needle weaved in and out of my face, pulling together the torn skin. My eyes tighten with every prick of the needle, "Now that I'm here, what am I going to tell Aunt Nina, Josh?"

He looked up, "I don't know," he said, "But it needs to be something good." I said I know and told him how I thought for hours but nothing lined up. He told me to repeat my story, to let him hear it again, saying the most believable lies are just bent truths. And so I did, "Why don't you just tell her you fell down a flight of stairs?"

I rolled my eyes. That was the dumbest idea he's ever had, and I told him so, "No really, think about it. You still have the entry stamps from the clubs. Just tell her you were walking back to your room, and you were drunk and tripped. It backs everything up. The lump on your face; you hit your head *after you fell*. The stitches; you cut your face and went to the hospital *after you fell*. The bruising; it started to develop *after you fell*. See it's foolproof."

"Yes, but Aunt Nina's not a fool," I said, "She's a Criminal Defense Attorney in Los Angeles, Josh. She's a freaking genius. One who will figure everything out if you let her."

"Then don't let her." When I *really* thought about it, I started to see the possibility of it working, "You'll have a few hours to think about the perfect way to say it, so stop worrying, Miss Worrywart." He laughed and I couldn't help but join him. I took a breath and looked at Josh, "You can do this. It'll be okay," he said, "Anyways, where's the money?"

"What?"

"The money you ran with. Where is it?"

"Oh," I looked down at the floor, swinging my legs, "When I was on my way back to the hotel, someone took it."

"Wait, what?" Josh asked. He stopped mid-stitch.

"I was walking back to the hotel, and a man came up from behind me," I said, "He ripped the bag out of my hands and ran. I tried to chase after him, but he was too quick."

"Jesus, Allison. Are you alright?" Josh asked, "Did he do anything to you?"

Josh pulled the last stitch, "No, just took the money," I replied.

"Well, that's good." He helped me up, and I thanked him again, "Hey, what are friends for?" I smiled and Josh opened the door, "Now go home and get some rest. You've got a genius to lie to."

The drive back to my house seemed to last for hours. The lights took years to change, and cars took decades to pull out. All of which wore down on my patience, but in the end was bearable. One thing that I could not stand, though, was the silver Toyota Tundra that cruised in front of me in the passing lane.

When I was younger, Aunt Nina had, and still has, the worst road rage on the planet. She would try to keep her cool through slow drivers and the people that swerved in the lanes. But she absolutely *despised* people who cruised in the left passing lane. She would blow her horn and yell out the window as if the drivers in front of her could hear her. As I grew older and learned to drive, I adopted this pet peeve as one of my biggest as well.

I blew the horn as I drove down the highway. I couldn't get over into the right lane, and the truck in front of me had been moving slower than molasses for almost eight miles now. My temperature rose, blood boiling, with every passing opportunity the truck had to get over. Finally, miles later, I was able to get over.

When I pulled off of the exit, I ran the story though my head one more time. I fell down a flight of stairs. My head slammed against the steps as I went down, resulting in a gash and lump. Then I went to the hospital to get stitches.

By the time Aunt Nina woke up, I would've already put foundation over the bruising that covered my neck. It seemed to focus around the throat, and I didn't want to take any chances. I pulled into the long, stone driveway.

Light flickered through the palms that lined the driveway. Looking at the house, no lights shone through the big glass windows on either floor. The large columns that stood on either end of the semi-circle porch were still lined with the white Christmas lights we put up three weeks ago.

Putting up Christmas lights at our house was always so easy. We never had to untangle them; because of my control freak, OCD aunt, they were neatly wrapped and organized in boxes, all separated by room. They even had their own specific spot in the basement, with the lights and garland for the foyer on the top of the stack, and the outside lights on the bottom.

I smiled, remembering the day we put them up, and unlocked the front door and stepped into the thirteen thousand square foot mansion, the smell of fresh pine and peppermint filling my nose. The lights and garland snaked up the railing of the grand staircase. The stairs curved with the cream walls that stretched to the ceiling of the twenty-foot grand foyer.

The kitchen called me, and I felt the pang of hunger in my stomach. I left my bags by the door and walked through the opening underneath the staircase. The living room was completely dark as I rounded its corner, heading towards the kitchen.

Rays of the early morning light crept through the large, glass backdoor in the kitchen. As I passed through the cased opening, I stopped to look at the view, leaning against the doorway. The house rested on top of a hill, a priceless view of the mountains visible in every direction. Aunt Nina loved the mountains, said they calmed her.

I stood there a minute, taking in the beauty around me. Life moved so quickly here, and I never stopped to take in the beauty of it. Aunt Nina would sit outside for hours at a time after a long day, just staring at the mountains. And after what happened in New York, I understand why.

A light mist hovered in the air. The hills rolled into the distance. The branches of the palms rustled with the breeze, and the feathery clouds drifted with the wind. The lights of the city sparkled against the rising sun. I closed my eyes, letting the warmth of the sunlight encase my body.

"It's beautiful isn't it?"

Every muscle in my body tightened, and my eyes flew open, "Nice of you to come home." I whipped around. Aunt Nina sat in a white loveseat in the living room. I hadn't even noticed her sitting there in the dark.

With the early morning showing through the grand window covering most of the wall behind her, she looked regal, almost queenly. Her light brown hair was clipped back in a loose French twist. Her bangs laid hanging free on the right side of her face, not stretching longer than her ear. A brow was arched over one of her hazel eyes. Her head tilted downwards so that she looked up at me, and the silver locket around her neck, identical to mine, glinted in the sunlight. She folded her arms across her chest. They lay over a black silk robe, the one I have seen almost every day of my life since I was a child.

Her features were faint in the darkness of the room, but one thing was certain; she was not happy. When Aunt Nina got upset, she usually blew up, yelling and screaming, pointing and scolding. But there were the few times when she seemed calm, but those were the times you feared most. Because inside, she was a ticking bomb, just waiting to explode. The anger built up during the conversation and let loose when triggered.

"Well," was all she said. She shifted in her seat. I knew this all too well. This was Aunt Nina's way of saying 'explain yourself.'

"Well..." My mind suddenly went blank. I tried to play it cool, but when I looked at Aunt Nina, her chin had risen, and her brow arched even higher, "You see, I was in Times Square most of the night."

"Most?"

"Yes, well, I went into a club because it was freezing. Yeah, you were right, I should've packed warmer clothes," I said. She raised her brows, tilted her head and nodded with a smile. But it was fake; she wasn't buying it. She leaned over and reached for the lamp, the stand on which it sat separating the loveseat from the couch. *Oh no.*

The light flicked on, and I looked down and away. I shot my hand up and rubbed the back of my neck so that my arm covered the bruising, "Look at me," Aunt Nina said. I closed my eyes and my head hung low. I looked up at my aunt and just prayed that I lived to see tomorrow.

For a split second her eyes widened, but only for a second. Then they slammed shut and I knew I was done for. Her jaw clenched and she took a deep breath, "This better be good."

"Yeah, um, well I went out and, uh, I was partying with a group of friends. You know, Happy New Year and such," I said, which was true. All of what I had already said was true. She blinked at me and I went to speak again. Then I noticed the glass of dark drink on the coffee table.

Aunt Nina's brows furrowed, and she followed my gaze. She nodded her head, "Ah." She reached for the glass, "Diet Coke," she said then took a sip, "Continue."

"Yes, well by the time I got back to the hotel, I'd had a few drinks. And, um, well I was making my way up the stairwell, the steps were concrete by the way, and while I was walking up the stairs I lost my balance. And fell." And I knew that was probably the worst excuse I had ever given her in my entire life.

She nodded her head as if she were interested in my story, "Oh really?" In my opinion, I think she just wanted to see how far I'd go before I cracked and told the truth; I always did.

"Yeah. Then I went to the hospital and got these stitches."

"Mhm, okay," she started as she stood up out of the chair, "So, you're not telling me the truth. I know because you've blinked about thirty times in the past minute, and you always blink a lot when you lie." She was standing right in front of me now, and I could smell the Herbal Essence shampoo from her damp hair and the Diet Coke on her breath, "And those stitches," she said, reaching a hand out and touching my face. She pulled her hand back, rubbing the dots of blood between her fingertips, "are fresh; definitely not over twenty-four hours old. Josh, I'm assuming? So I am going to ask you again to tell me what happened, and this time you're not going to lie."

So I told her the truth. I told her about the club. I told her about the dark alley. I told her about the midnight kiss, about the counting, "I told you to stop doing that," she said shaking her head, "Doing it at school was fine, but not in the real world." And she did. And I should've listened.

"I know, I'm sorry," was all I could say, "But they aren't after me for only counting."

"*Aren't.* You just said *aren't.* So they're still looking for you?" Aunt Nina put her head in her hands and rubbed her face, "What did you do?" Her breathing was heavier now, and I could tell her anger was building up; the calm before the storm wouldn't last much longer.

"I, uh, I ran with the money I had won," I said.

"*You what,*" she said. And I knew. I was going to die, "*Are you kidding me?*" Her face turned bright red and her hands balled up into fists, "How much money was there?"

"Almost a million dollars." The words came out as a mumble, but Aunt Nina understood exactly what I said.

"*One million dollars?*" she asked, "I swear to God, Allison, you better be joking. We don't have that right now. You know that. You're such an *idiot!*" Aunt Nina was screaming now, and she started to pace back and forth, "Why wouldn't you just give it back?"

"Well, that's the thing. I don't have it."

"*What do you mean you don't have it?*"

"Well, that night, I was not thinking straight, and I was walking through the streets alone. A man attacked me and took it." The only sound was Aunt Nina's heavy breathing, "I know. I don't even know why I took it. I guess I knew we've been behind lately. I just thought-"

"Oh you thought!" Aunt Nina yelled. "Well, did you hear that? Allison thought, so that makes it all better! It doesn't matter that I now have to come up with the money that you lost, which is..."

"Eight hundred thousand."

"...*eight hundred thousand dollars!*" She threw her hands in the air and let them fall, hitting her sides, "You know we don't have that kind of money anymore! So, you obviously weren't thinking, or you wouldn't have even thought of doing something like this!" Taking the clip out and throwing it onto the couch, she ran her hands through her hair. I really screwed up.

"I know-"

"Don't you *dare* say I know," she said, still screaming. She whipped around, her finger in my face. Her voice was high pitched now for it always raised an octave when she yelled, "Because apparently you didn't know, or you wouldn't have done something so stupid! And if you did know, if you *knew*, that's just going to make me even more pissed than I already am!"

In that moment, I was more horrified than I had ever been in my entire life. I had never seen her act this way, "Aunt Nina, listen. I'm sorry-"

"Yeah, I'm sorry too. Sorry that I trusted you! I knew I shouldn't have let you go on that trip. But, you had never let me down. But now..." Aunt Nina had the most painful look of disappointment on her face, "I've lost a lot of respect for you, Allison."

"Aunt Nina-"

"No. Just shut up. Stop talking." And I should've. She was

so furious. A big ball of anger that could not be stopped. She turned, bending down to grab the clip that always held her hair up. But when I spoke… like I said, I should not have said another word, because what I said next…

"Aunt Nina, please. I really am sorry. I was just trying to help. I, you were just so uptight, and I missed the old you; the you that would play board games on Sunday's and sing Hamilton with me in the car. You've changed, and I could tell you didn't like it any more than I did. I just tried to think of what Mom would've done."

Aunt Nina froze, her hand hovering over the clip, "What did you just say?" she asked. She turned around, the clip now in her hand, "Don't you *ever* compare yourself to my sister, what you did to what my sister would've done. My sister *never* would've done this!" Something snapped in Aunt Nina, and I did not recognize the woman standing in front of me. The look in her eyes shot daggers deeply into me, and I could feel my heart pounding, my head reeling, my ears ringing.

"Aunt Nina, I didn't mean-"

"No! Do you know what you are?" she asked as she took a step towards me, "Do you? You're a naive, irresponsible child. That is all you are." I heard a crack, and when I looked down, I saw the pieces of the broken clip in her hand. With every word she said, she inched closer and closer until we passed under the staircase and I was pinned up against the front door, "You may be 22-years-old, but you act like you are ten. I've never met someone so immature and childish! So don't ever compare yourself to my sister like that again. Because right now, she would be so disappointed in you." I looked into my aunt's eyes. They were cold. Her face was not even an inch from mine, "I know I am."

I was mortified. The way she looked at me, the way she talked. It was the way she looked at people as she called them out on the stand; it was the tone she used as she attacked and pried information out of witnesses. A tone she would never use outside of court. It was then I remembered that my aunt was the best, most feared Criminal Defense Attorney in Los Angeles.

She stood there hovering over me. The morning sunlight poured through the windows around the door. A ray of gold shone directly into her eyes, but she still did not budge.

I didn't know who stood over me, but it wasn't my aunt. My aunt was loving and caring and kind. She lost sleep to help others. She gave pieces of herself to save others. Aunt Nina was the woman who brightened a room by simply walking in. Her heart was bigger than those of most of America put together. She touched the lives of others. And she lived life passionately and with a confidence that inspired others. She was the most remarkable woman that ever lived.

But in that moment, she was a different woman. I lay there on the floor looking up at her. She turned and stormed off, making her way towards the stairs, "I am exhausted. You know, because I woke up at seven o'clock after sleeping for only three hours, waiting two for my niece who was almost sixteen hours late. Do you know what my mom would've done if I was sixteen hours late from a flight with no call or message? I would've been dead." She grabbed the handrail and shot another look back at me, "I don't appreciate that by the way. Having Josh take me out when you know how badly drinking affected my life."

She marched up the stairs, and I called after her, "Aunt Nina!" But she just continued up the stairs, "Aunt Nin-" But I was cut off by the slamming of the bedroom door. I slid down the door. My hand covered my mouth and the tears ran down my face.

I waited before making my way up the stairs. I passed Aunt Nina's door, pausing. I stood in front of the door with my fist raised to knock. But what would I say? I dropped my hand to my side and finished the remaining distance to my room. Opening the door, the homely scent of orange escaped the room, and a smile crept onto my face. The fatigue that had been slowly taking over my body finally won, and I gave in. Dropping onto the bed, all I wanted to do was sleep, but my mind was still in a complete fluster. Still, I could feel the exhaustion falling over me. If Aunt Nina, the most compassionate and understanding person I knew, wouldn't speak to me...

4

Something hits me and I am awake. I sucked a quick breath in through my nose, lifting my head from the pillow. Whatever had hit me was buzzing, but that's not what I noticed. Aunt Nina stood in the doorway. But she was gone as quickly as she came, leaving without a word.

The buzzing stopped briefly, but came back seconds later. I sat up and yawned, rubbing my face. My phone lay buzzing near my leg, vibrating the whole comforter. I picked up the phone, "Hello, Josh."

"Well?" he said.

The haze of sleep was still over me, and I was not in the mood for his games, "Well what?" I threw off the coral comforter and walked to the bay window on the other side of the bedroom. The gray walls absorbed the afternoon sunlight that poured through the glass panes. The light shined through the waving leaves and covered my face.

"Well if you would've read my messages-"

"I was sleeping, Josh. You know, because I only almost died in New York City *and* flew overnight, which you know I can't sleep on planes. So, I'm sorry, Josh, for sleeping." I realized I came off a little harsh, but I didn't care.

"Oh. But, does she know?" he asked.

"Yes, Josh. She knows," I answered. I heard the water of the shower turn on down the hall, "And she's livid." I walked to the bedroom door. Laying my hand on the handle, I pulled it open.

"I'm sorry." Josh said.

"It's not your fault," I said. Walking down the hall, I looked at the pictures that hung in frames on the walls.

My first day of kindergarten.

High school graduation.

Eighth grade formal.

But none of those photos did I love as much as the one at the end of the hallway. The day I was accepted into Stanford Law. The day my dreams came true. The dream of being even close to how amazing my Aunt Nina was.

I remember the day I decided I wanted to be a lawyer like her. I was a freshman in high school. For my Freshman Seminar class, I had to job shadow someone, so naturally I shadowed Aunt Nina. But I didn't shadow for a day like the other kids. I followed Aunt Nina through the entire duration of a murder case.

"Hey, didn't you mention job shadowing me?" Aunt Nina asks as I walk into the room. My damp hair is clinging to my back, and I pull it back and clip it into a loose French twist. Just like Aunt Nina does after she showers.

"Yeah, but if you're busy, I can shadow someone else," I say.

Aunt Nina smiles, "Come here." She pulls out the stool next to her. I walk over and sit down. A huge mess of papers lays spread over the counter, but still they all are organized, each one having a place.

"Do you know what any of this means?" Aunt Nina asks. I pick up a paper and start to read, "A man was accused of killing his wife's sister. Apparently, they had a thing in college – I guess she went back and forth between two men – and she recently married the guy she had left him for," Aunt Nina says, "He was arrested, and now it's my job to get him off."

I set the paper down on the marble countertop, "Did he do it?" I ask looking up at Aunt Nina. She turned to face the counter, putting the paper I had just been reading back into her desired spot.

"I don't know," she says, then turns to me, "It's not my job to know. It's my job to make the jury believe he didn't." I look down at my hands. It was now I knew what my aunt did, or at least I thought.

"What do you think?" I ask, looking back to Aunt Nina. She tilts her head and looks at me, "I mean, do you think he did it?"

Aunt Nina nods and smiles, "Honestly, no," she says.

"Really? Or are you just saying that to make me feel better about shadowing you?"

Aunt Nina just laughs, "You always have been smart," she says, "But, yes, I really do think he is innocent. When I talked to him last, all he kept telling me about was how his wife was in shock - I mean do you blame her? - and how she wasn't talking to anyone, especially him. Said all he wanted was to lie next to her and hold her again." She pulled out her notes. She always took very detailed notes on every interview she has with a client.

"So, who do you think did it?" I ask. If his own wife wouldn't talk to him, how was my aunt supposed to convince

twelve strangers that he had nothing to do with it?

"To be honest, I think it was the husband. Mark, the client, told me about how the sister's husband has psychotic breaks - had them in college too."

I followed everything Aunt Nina did with the case after that. I didn't miss one interview, one phone call, one meeting. Nothing. But the day the case went to court was the best. The way she ran the victim's husband into the dirt, how she locked up the real murderer and kept an innocent man out of jail.

I sit quietly in the seat behind Aunt Nina's table, "The defense's witness," the judge says. Aunt Nina stands up from the table, straightening her papers. I know exactly what she was going to say, we'd rehearsed it a thousand times. But still, I am so eager to hear it. She takes in a breath before looking up, and I'm already sitting on the edge of my seat.

"Mr. Richardson, where were you, the afternoon of Mariah Richardson's death?" she asked. She tilts her head, and although I cannot see her face, I know the look that's on it. It's that accusing look that somehow says you're a liar, I know I'm right, and I don't believe you all at the same time.

"I was in the kitchen washing dishes after Sunday family dinner," Mr. Richardson says, "when I saw that filthy scumbag talking to my wife. He was there with his own car because he came from work."

Aunt Nina looks down at her client then back at Mr. Richardson, "Wow. You were very quick to point fingers, Mr. Richardson," she says. Mr. Richardson looks like he might speak, but Aunt Nina isn't finished, "So why don't you tell me about what you saw, about my client with your wife?" she asks, this time giving the witness time to speak.

"Well it was the second time I'd seen him with her, and he was being very forceful. My wife looked back at me, but she mouthed I'm fine. So I continued to wash the dishes. But at exactly four minutes past three, I heard a gasp come from my wife's mouth. I looked up just in time to see your client slit my wife's throat right there on the patio. And I know it was four minutes past three because I was looking at the clock on the stove when my wife gasped."

Aunt Nina had been looking down at the contents of the table, but looks up at Mr. Richardson when he finishes, "Well you seem to have your very detailed story straight," she says, "So can you tell me about the medication you take for your psychotic breaks?" There is a small reaction in the courtroom, but it is almost unnoticeable. Aunt Nina didn't think there would be a reaction too big to that, but I did. Now I have to do laundry for two weeks, no complaining.

"Yes, I take clamozine every day at three on the dot," he says, "It has to be three. Exactly three." Aunt Nina shifts her weight, all one hundred and thirty pounds of it, and straightens. She crosses her arms and walks around the table and towards the witness. But right before she reaches the stand, she turns away and starts pacing.

"Really?" she asks, seemingly unphased. And she wasn't, she already knew that. I look up at the clock; 3:32.

"Yes, I actually had to refill my prescription that day," Mr. Richardson answers, but as soon as he does his eyes widen a little.

Aunt Nina spins around on her heels, "You did?" she asks, "And around what time did you go out? To refill the prescription, that is."

"Around 2:30," he says.

"And you live how far from the pharmacy?"

"About 15 minutes."

"And, where did you take your medication?"

"I took it at the pharmacy, does this have any relevance?" Mr. Richardson asks. *His foot starts tapping and the pointer finger on his left hand starts tapping the seat next to his leg.*

Aunt Nina looks at him, "It does. So were you able to take your medication at the right time?" she asks.

"I was."

"Which was what time, on the dot?"

"Three."

"Okay," Aunt Nina says, "So then, what time did you leave the pharmacy that is 15 minutes from your house?"

"3:12," Mr. Richardson says. He rolls his eyes and looks at my aunt.

"But what time did you say you saw your wife murdered?"

"3:04."

This is when Aunt Nina and I get the reaction we want from the courtroom. She turns and walks back to her table, waiting for the room to settle. When I catch her eye, she smiles, and I know we have him. As if on cue, Aunt Nina speaks, *"I am going to ask you, Mr. Richardson, are you responsible for the murder of Mariah Richardson?"*

Mr. Richardson shifts in his seat and switches the hand that taps the chair to his right, *"No."*

"Why would you lie about the events of that day then?" Aunt Nina asks.

"I'm not," Mr. Richardson responds. But beads of sweat are gathering around his face and he has been playing with the

small string that hangs from the bottom of his blazer since he mentioned leaving the house.

"Did you or did you not just sit here and tell the courtroom that you saw your wife Mariah Richardson murdered at four minutes past three, but then go on the say that you did not leave the pharmacy until 3:12? And Mrs. Richardson had complained about violent behavior from you after you started taking clamozine, correct? And if it was indeed my client who killed Mariah Richardson at four minutes past three, why does the GPS in his car show him leaving the house at 2:48?

"The estimated time of death for Mariah Richardson was approximately 3:30 p.m. That is 45 minutes after my client left your house, but the same time as when you would've gotten home from the pharmacy at which you paid for your prescription refill at 2:57.

"And Mariah, did she or did she not leave you to get back with her ex, my client, in college? Did you fear that she was going to leave you again? That she was going to once again go back to the man that she loved, but had left her for another woman?"

"Your Honor, the defense is badgering the witness," the woman at the other table says over Aunt Nina's voice, "She-"

"Were you her second choice, Mr. Richardson?" Aunt Ina continues, "And when you saw them outside, together you snapped, like you often did when on your new medication. Did you kill Mariah Richardson?" I know Aunt Nina is a beast in the courtroom, but seeing her in action, it is amazing.

"I did not," Mr. Richardson says from the stand.

"You did, and you've pinned the blame on my client because he was the easy route. But you already knew that didn't

you?" Aunt Nina knows she's won this case. She's bit down isn't letting go until the rest of Los Angeles does too. Her biting tone cuts through the courtroom and her volume has risen significantly since the beginning of the trial, "You knew that if you killed her and pinned it on my client, he'd go to jail."

"Your Honor-"

"He'd finally pay for taking Mariah form you in college and for trying to now!" Aunt Nina slams her hands on the table, but Mr. Richardson is quick to react.

"What was I supposed to do?" Mr. Richardson yells from the stand, "Let her leave me again? Let him win again? I'm glad she's dead and-" But Mr. Richardson catches himself and ceases to speak

The courtroom becomes a pool of whispers, and Aunt Nina says, "And what, Mr. Richardson?"

He looks around until his eyes fix on his late wife's sister. She is sitting a few seats away from me. Her eyes are bulging out of her head and she looks as if her heart is being ripped up right in front of her. His finger taps the seat harder.

Then he looks at me and I can tell he recognizes me. I was there when Aunt Nina interviewed him, taking notes on the questions she asked the way he answered. His finger taps even harder.

And maybe it was the look in his sister-in-law's eyes, the sight of a fourteen year old girl, or the fierce accusation posed by Aunt Nina, but he mumbles, "And I murdered my wife."

"What was that?" Aunt Nina asks.

"I did it! It was me!" Mr. Richardson yells at the courtroom, "I did it! I did it! I did it." Mr. Richardson looks like he is about to have a mental breakdown on the stand. And he

does. He starts to cry and his face turns bright red. He pulls at his hair and his eyes are glued shut. He starts grunting, his jaw clenched and his teeth bared.

The room explodes and Aunt Nina sits down in her seat, "The defense rests." I stare wide-eyed at the man. I watch as Aunt Nina's client bends down and takes his kids in his grasp. His wife jumps into his arms, kissing him and apologizing. I smile, jotting down my notes.

I look back at the stand. The man that spoke not five minutes ago is in the midst of a complete breakdown. Police officers surround him, one latched to his waist, another holds his arms down.

He talks to himself as the officer's escort him from the courtroom. Sweat is rolling from his body and his hands still fidget in the handcuffs. He mumbles things that are illiterate and not in any way English. He looks at the officers and they just nod, repeating what he says. I am oddly intrigued by his behavior. He was composed for most of the trial, then he started fidgeting and it all went downhill from there.

Aunt Nina gathers her things then turns to face me, "3:51," she says. She gets up and walks towards the doors. I look at my phone to check the time. 3:51.

I think of what Aunt Nina had said. Then it hits me.

Aunt Nina looks at him, "It does. So were you able to take your medication at the right time?" she asks.

"I was."

"Which was what time, on the dot?"

"Three."

We walk outside, and Aunt Nina is hounded with reporters, "Ms. Schwartz, how did you know to call him in as a witness?"

one asks.

"How do you feel about the way you presented the case to the court with your niece watching?" asked another.

Aunt Nina walked down the long steps of the courthouse, not saying a word, but you could tell she was very proud with her performance. She smiled the whole way to the car, saying just before she got in, "I am very pleased with how today went. And with how I had the opportunity to show my niece why I do what I do."

And in this exact moment, I now realize what my aunt does. This is what I want to do with my life.

"No, it is my fault," Josh said over the phone, "But hey, she was bound to find out anyway. I mean she's only known to the whole world of law as the *Shredding Schwartz.*"

"Yeah," I replied, walking down the left staircase. A pang of hunger radiated through my abdomen.

When I reached the marble tile of the kitchen, I noticed a dirty plate and pan in the sink. The smell of seasoned meat filled the air, and my mouth waters at the heavenly scent. The stovetop was still warm and the microwave fan still blew. I opened the fridge to see what Aunt Nina had made. Nothing but the normal groceries. I opened the microwave. Nothing. I searched the countertops. Nothing.

I stepped back and held my phone close to my chest. In all 22 of the years I'd lived there, Aunt Nina has never made *anything* without leaving a plate for me.

5

The microwave beeped, and I set the book down. I walked over and took the microwave meal out of its cardboard bowl, pouring it onto a plate. I sat there at the counter eating in silence; I didn't dare say a word. Aunt Nina stood at the other end of the white marble island. I hadn't heard her voice since this morning.

I kept my eyes down, only looking up when Aunt Nina's phone slammed next to my plate. Her messages were open; a stream with Josh. He said I wasn't answering my phone and wanted to know if I would want to go to the movies tonight, to help take my mind off of things and relax. The text bubble was open and ready to type.

The clicking of keys split the silence. I slid the phone across the countertop back to Aunt Nina. Her eyes flicked to the right and read the message. She nodded and went back to playing her game of solitaire. I had noticed the glass of red wine that sat next to the cards twenty minutes earlier, but I didn't say anything, "I'm going to go get ready," I said, hoping for an answer; I was failed.

The warmth of the shower wrapped around my body and

the heat was comforting. The water beat on my head and back, red streaking the tiled floors and walls. There was still dirt to be scrubbed from my body; still blood to be washed away. The wash rag that had once been white was red and black when I finished.

I wrapped a towel around my body and plugged in the hairdryer. The blowing air warmed the bathroom, and beads of sweat gathered along my forehead and upper lip. I didn't bother with makeup. I took a deep breath when I looked up. The reflection in the mirror still horrified me every time I saw it. The black stitches ran across my face. The bruising started to yellow. I pulled my eyes away and hurried to my room.

The maroon sweater complemented the dark jeans I pulled from the dryer. I brushed the last few knots from my hair before throwing it up into a clip. I combed the mascara wand through my lashes. Slinging the small over-the-shoulder purse around my body, I opened the door. I looked down, adjusting my shirt as I walked down the main hall. I only looked up when I was knocked backwards.

Aunt Nina didn't look up at me as she passed through the hall. But I could still see her bloodshot eyes. Her long layers laid at chest-length across her back and stuck to her sweaty neck. Her shoulder hit mine as she pushed past me and the smell of alcohol wafted off of her body, "Aunt Ni-" I began to say, but was again cut off by the slamming of the door.

I saw the car lights pour into the driveway as Josh pulled in. I stole one last glance at Aunt Nina's door. But it was no use.

Reaching for the handle of the front door, I called out, "Bye." I waited a second; only silence answered. My shoulders fell and I left the house. After locking the door, I walked to

Josh's car and got in.

The night had already fallen and the sky was black, "You look like you're about to cry," Josh said as I sat down. I buckled my seat belt and looked at him.

"She won't even look at me, Josh," I said, "And she's drinking again." The tears already started falling. I swear, I had cried more in those past three days than I did in my entire life.

"Let's ditch the movie, go to our spot," Josh said. He pulled out of the driveway. As we sped down the highway, I looked out the window. I couldn't stop thinking about Aunt Nina. What if she started drinking again? Like, really drinking? She hadn't touched an alcoholic anything since our cousin's wedding three years ago. And I had sent her out to party on New Year's just so I wouldn't get into trouble. I knew how hard she tried. I knew what that could've done. What it has done. But I still did it anyway...

"Stop," Josh said, "You're spiraling. I can tell by the look on your face. She'll be fine."

"Yeah," I said, "But she's never been this upset, Josh. She's never *not* spoken to me."

"Well, that would be because you do everything in your power to please her," he said. I rolled my eyes, "Think about it, Allison. You didn't go out with that guy in high school just because Nina thought he was rude. Every paper, every homework assignment, you've run by her. You need her approval. You live for it." And after thinking about it, I did, "You've always known how she felt and what she thought. And now that she won't talk to you, you have no idea what's going on in her head, and it's driving you crazy. That's why I want to get you out of the house. So you don't think about it. I mean, you laid some pretty big news on her. But she knows everything now, and she just needs to process it. Besides, Nina never stops talking, nor can she hold a grudge. Just give her time."

The road twisted up the mountain. Gravel crumpled under the wheels of the car. The beam of the headlights disappeared when we pulled over the top of the mountain. The roar of the engine went dead as Josh took the keys out of the ignition. I opened the door and walked to the edge of the lookout.

The city was beautiful at night. The lights sparkled and the wind blew softly. A small shiver ran up my spine as a breeze swept through the trees around me, and the chilled air seeped through my jacket. Josh threw a blanket around my shoulders. I smiled at him as he lowered himself to the soft soil beside me. My eyes flicked back to the city, "You really think she'll be alright?" I asked.

Josh took a deep breath in, "I do."

I nodded and stared out to the distance. We sat still for minutes, admiring the view. I didn't look away until I heard Josh's weight shuffle. When I turned, his arm stretched, holding a bottle. I smiled and took it from his hand. The bottle hissed as I popped the cap off. I took a sip and swallowed, allowing the muscles in my body to relax. The sweetness simmered my nerves. The freedom of June, July, and August flood back with the taste of summer. The root beer was oddly warm, but with the coolness of the night, and the new found peace that laid over me, I didn't mind.

But that state was corrupted when my phone rang and I pounced. I looked down hopefully at the bright screen, but threw my phone into the damp earth in disappointment. Josh looked down at the phone then up at me, "Not Nina, I'm assuming?"

"Nope," I replied, "Just that stupid study group."

"I told you, stop worrying," he said. I heaved a deep breath and laid my head against his shoulder. The wind blew gain and Josh put his arm around me, pulling me close. I nestled myself into the pockets of his shoulder and elbow. He rearranged the blankets with his free hand until we were just a ball of flesh and blanket sitting at the edge of a drop off.

The smell of fresh rain drifted through the air. A smell so fragile, I inhaled deeply to guess its fragrance. It was clean and crisp like mountain air but not strong. It was the smell of childhood memories; searching for a four-leaf clover, cartwheels, and skipping home with Aunt Nina, jumping with her through puddles and following her through the fading chalk hopscotch boards.

Coolness surrounded my shoulders and I closed my eyes to relish the moment and the smell of the rain, but could not capture words. Steel clouds consumed the sky and traveled our way. The moon disappeared behind them, and the overhead turned darker than the night sky had already been.

Lightning cracked the sky into fragments, and the sound pierced our ears. It sliced through the peaceful scene, the brightness prying a flinch out of my eyes. The roar of the night rolled and rumbled through my being, gripping my soul and pulling me in. A light mist showered down from overhead. The patting of the rain against the clay was the only sound to be heard through the silence. It was as if the world was still. I caught glimpses of the beads collecting on my hands and the droplets that ran down my nose through bursts of lightning in the darkness.

The earth was moist against our backs. I could feel the silt hold onto by neck and slink down my shirt, but I remained still. Still nestled in Josh's arms, I curled up even tighter, my cheek resting on his body. My hand fell onto his, which was wrapped around my waist. The rhythmic rising and falling of his chest was soothing. And this is what I loved about Josh, the feeling of finally being safe. The feeling of home.

We lay there, and the softness of the tugging wind drifted through our hair and out to the night. It whispered against branches and rustled through leaves. The whistling of the bottle and the swishing of grass. The patter and the crash. The chill and the icy damp. That night, the outside world was *alive*.

The inches of time slithered by and the night grew heavier and colder. The chill pierced to the bone and crystallized the blood in my veins. Even the heat of the car struggled to melt the cold from our trembling hands and stuttered voices when we got inside. The clock on the radio glowed almost too bright to look at. *1:04.* I felt the haze of sleep push its way closer and closer to the center of my mind, but I still noticed how we traveled opposite of home and Aunt Nina as we were moved down the highway.

The palm trees that lined the rows of parking spaces swayed with the breezes. The two of us rushed to the automatic doors, escaping the freezing wind. Josh grabbed a buggie. The screeching of age old metal filled my ears as the cart rolled into motion.

Walmart in downtown LA at one a.m. made *The Walking Dead* look like *America's Next Top Model.* As we flew down the aisles, the loudness of our presence rose to an almost alarming level. The laughter rang out through the store, traveling the many aisles and to the walls, bouncing off and echoing throughout the dead, night struck building. I pushed Josh into a cooler, snatching the buggie. My left foot gripped firmly onto the bottom bar, and the ball of my right pushed off of the ground until I had a good start. I sped through the aisle. But my heart stopped and I hopped off, slamming both feet into the concrete below.

The old man who had stopped in the middle of the aisle stared at me, horror on his face. He was a short little thing. His white hair was sparse on his head and his banana colored shirt was tucked into khaki pants. Why did they always wear khaki pants? His brown leather shoes spun on the floor, and his blue eyes that sulked behind a pair of circle rimmed glasses took one last look at me before leaving the aisle.

When the last of him was out of sight, Josh and I looked at each other, and the laughter poured out. I gripped the handlebar of the buggie, clasping my other hand over my mouth. My eyes shut and I snorted, which only made us laugh louder. Josh was still hunched over, and I took a quick swipe at his leg with my foot. He looked up at me and grabbed me around the waist, pinning my arms to the sides of my body.

He slung me over his shoulder. He just stood there, and I reached out for the cooler door. Pulling it open, I sifted through the tubs of ice cream, still thrown over Josh's body. I lunged for a tub of cookie dough ice cream. Grasping it with both hands, I picked it up. Josh turned around and I shut the frosted door with my foot. I threw the tub into the buggie, and Josh put me down. We walked past six aisles and turned. Josh made a beeline for the chips. He tossed the red bag of Lay's originals on top of the ice cream, followed by French onion dip.

I pushed on, but jolted as the wheels hopped over

something. I heard the most girlish scream escape Josh's mouth and was sent into another laughing frenzy. Josh gripped his foot and I still laughed, asking if he was okay and apologizing. I didn't know what it was, but we both had the giggles that night.

But that was shown when we went through the self-checkout. Dear God. We restarted four times because Josh scanned things two, three, four times. He scanned the bottles of root beer and threw them into the buggie, and I punched his shoulder, "Don't do that!" I laughed, trying to be serious, "You're going to shake them up!"

As Josh swiped the orange Discovery card, I picked up all of the bags and turned for the parking lot. But I had underestimated the weight of the bags and overestimated my strength. Josh ran to my aid, but I ran ahead. We ran in circles around the parking lot spaces, weaving between cars. But after only a few minutes, I felt my arms growing weaker and I hurried back to the car.

I pranced in place as the biting cold showed my breath and Josh purposely took forever to unlock the car. The blasting music deafened as the ignition kicked on. We did not turn it down, but sped down the highway, the rap beats and Broadway melodies penetrating the night. I rolled down the window and sat in it, holding tightly onto the roof racks for balance. I felt the freedom and adventure Josh hoped I would find.

Turning the dial on the radio as we pulled onto my street, the music was left at almost a whisper. We veered right and slowly climbed the driveway. The car jerked to a halt. I hopped out and picked up the bags from the floor of the car.

Fumbling with the key, I danced as I tried to unlock the door. The rev of an engine cut through the night. A lime green

Veneno flew down the street, the driver ducking, hiding his eyes. Like he was hiding from someone. When I heard the lock click, I turned back and shoved my hip into the door. I pranced through the doorway, about to make my way upstairs when Josh's voice broke my elated aura, "Hey, Allison what's this?"

I spun around, the beat still in my step and the music still in my head. Until I looked down. My blood ran cold and the plastic bags slid from my hands, crashing to the ground. A gold-lined envelope laid there on the ground, stamped with the fresh footprint of my cream and brown Sperry's.

"Allison, what's wrong?" Josh asked as he picked the matte black horror off of the ground. I ripped it from his hands and started for the couch. I fell into the cushions, and Josh's weight dipped next to me.

I looked up at Josh, "It's from them," I said.

"Wait, *them?*"

I nodded my head and looked back down at the envelope. I tore the flap away, pushing it up and back. I pulled the printer paper out first, "Nice place, Allison," I read aloud, "Nice guy you have there too. Tell dear Josh I said hi. And who's your aunt? She looks pretty. And drunk. And alone."

Something pulled at my brain, something distant, but I couldn't put my finger on what. But that was not where my focus was. I was numb, no emotion, no tears, as I revealed the remaining contents of the envelope.

Again, three pictures. But this time, not from the photo center; instead, Polaroids.

The pulling pried harder this time, but I still ignored it.

A picture of me slung over Josh's shoulder in the frozen foods aisle. My heart quickened.

A picture of the house. My heart fluttered.

The third picture drifted from my hand to the ground, and my entire spirit fell. My heart hurt and I thought I was going to die. The Polaroid of Aunt Nina, sitting in her bed and petting our yellow-haired golden retriever, rested on the ground.

The nag that pulled at my mind since I sat down finally won my full attention. Josh grabbed the note and pictures, and I flew up to find out what it was that pulled so hardly at my being. It was a sound, something soft and faint, but out of place. A small pitter-patter seemed to draw me to the kitchen. When I entered the room, I had been right. A puddle of water spread over the tile in front of the open door. I ran to it and slid it shut, and the sound of glass pelted by rain followed.

I peered through the back door, my hands and face resting on the glass. Josh sat the photos on the countertop and walked over to the door. Small, barely noticeable footprints led down over the hill. I ran to the next window. The footprints wrapped around. I ran to the grand window in the living room; they were still visible in the yard from there, too.

Finally, I made my way to the windows in the foyer. The footprints fell with the side of the lawn and ended at the street. Skid marks made a U-turn in the middle of the road.

Fumbling with the key, I danced as I tried to unlock the door. The rev of an engine cut through the night. A lime green Veneno flew down the street, the driver ducking, hiding his eyes. Like he was hiding from someone.

I inhaled sharply, so sharply and dramatically that I choked on the saliva in the back of my throat. I gripped my chest and looked up at Josh, "They were here when we came in," he said. He took me in his arms, expecting me to be crying. I expected myself to be crying too. But nothing came out.

My whole body shook, and a single thought filled my head. *Where is Aunt Nina?* I clenched Josh's arms in my hands and lost the sanity I still had left, "Jo-no-I"

The words struggled to come out. I couldn't organize my thoughts. They were a whirling blur, a maze that could not be escaped, a storm that could not be calmed. We ran back to the kitchen and I fell to the ground, sloshing in the puddle of water beneath me. Josh pulled me up as the footsteps thudded down the stairs. I neither looked up nor budged; I knew who it was. Still, I let out a breath I didn't know I had been holding.

She walked into the kitchen, but froze when she saw my petrified form standing in the puddle of water. Her eyes darted away and she held the empty wine bottle a little closer to her body. I heard the cupboard open and the clank of the glass bottle in the trash. Her veiny hand pulled on the refrigerator door, the other clasping a new bottle of Pinot Noir, "I didn't hear you come in," Aunt Nina said as she poured the red wine into a glass. And I was sure that was the first glass she'd used since I left the house. But I knew that wasn't the first bottle she'd opened.

"Yeah, we tried to be quiet. Didn't want to wake you," Josh said, his muscular frame still supporting my weight.

Aunt Nina's eyes met mine, but quickly darted towards the wall. She went to turn away, but stopped when her glance caught the photos on the counter, "What's this?" She reached for the Polaroids. Josh gasped and shot his hand out, grabbing the photos before she could. I stumbled forward, for all of my weight had leaned on him.

"They are from tonight," Josh said, holding up the stack. The front photo was that of my body slung over Josh's. I released a breath, relieved that another picture didn't sit on top.

"Oh," she said, "Well, good night, Josh. Travel safely," Aunt Nina said, nodding towards the window and the raging storm that continued to worsen outside. She took one last glance at me, but shifted her gaze to the floor. She turned around and grabbed the wine bottle off of the counter, sliding it under the arm that held her already empty glass. I watched as her figure disappeared into the darkness.

After he was sure her door was closed and Aunt Nina could no longer hear us, he turned to me, "Where are the other photos?" he asked.

"What do you mean?"

"The other pictures. The one of the dead guy and the beach and the airport..." Josh replied.

"Oh, oh. Okay, they are still in my suitcase. Why?" I asked. I'd thought about throwing them away, but I didn't think I should've. Something just told me not to.

"Because, we need to keep them together and hidden. That was too close right there. Do you know what would've happened if she would've saw the bottom picture just now?" he asked as he held the picture of my aunt, giving no time to answer, "She would've killed us. So, we have to make sure she doesn't get ahold of them."

I walked over to the sky blue suitcase, which still sat by the front door. Unzipping the front pocket, I reached for the letters and pictures. My hand slid against the smooth gold that lined the flaps and I pulled them out, handing them to Josh. He took them from my hand and ran up the steps. I followed closely behind.

We made a right at the top of the stairs and entered the guest bedroom. Hurrying past the two twin beds, I watched as Josh opened the door to the walk-in closet. I followed him inside, finding him reaching for a shoebox on the top right-hand shelf. His hand wrapped around it and he lifted it from the metal rack. He sat down on the floor next to my feet and I dropped onto the wood floor beside him. Throwing the pair of Valentino Garavani's from the box behind him, he pulled the cardboard closer to him. He shoved the pictures inside, and the letters beside them.

The box fit perfectly behind the many others that lined that top shelf. Snuggled behind a Calvin Klein and an Ugg box, it was nearly invisible. To see it you would have to be looking for it.

"If you get any other pictures, or notes, or anything, put them in there then call me," Josh said. I nodded. We stood from the ground and left the closet. I closed the door silently behind me. I hurried across the room and headed for the stairs. Before we made our descent, I hurried to the laundry room across the hall to grab a few towels. I reached for a stack that had been recently folded in a basket. Grabbing the basket, I turned the light off and went back to where Josh stood at the top of the stairs.

Josh stayed and helped me clean the water up off of the kitchen floor. We kneeled down, throwing towels down to suck up as much water as possible, "I don't want to leave you and Nina here alone tonight," Josh said. He picked up a soaking wet blue towel and moved it to the side, throwing it into the basket, "I mean you saw how easily they got in here without Nina noticing. I don't want anything to happen."

Normally, I would've fought it, told him I didn't want him to stay and that we would be fine without him. But honestly, I didn't want to be alone. Aunt Nina wouldn't be much help locked up in her room, and Josh was strong. His presence would just make me feel safer, and I knew it. That's why I didn't fight him, "Okay. Thank you."

He looked up and smiled. I grabbed a dark green towel and wiped the remaining water from the tile. Josh picked up the rest of the wet towels. He threw them in the basket that sat beside him on the floor. I finished wiping the last bits of water and threw the towels into the basket as well.

Josh picked up the basket. He looked at the microwave clock, "It's three-thirty. We should get to bed," he said. He turned to walk away, motioning for me to follow. And I wanted to. But curiosity got the best of me.

I opened the door of the dark hickory cabinet and pulled out the trash can. Nothing but glass bottles sat inside. Two empty bottles of wine. Several smaller bottles that once held craft beers. They all lay at the bottom of the bin. Josh had walked over and looked into the trash can. My hand rose to my mouth and I turned to face Josh, "Let's just try to get some sleep," he said. But I could pick out a slight fear in his voice.

I reluctantly nodded my head and trudged across the floor and through the living room. We were silent as we climbed the stairs. Once at the top, we looked at each other. Josh's strong arms wrapped around me, holding me in a gentle embrace, "It's going to be okay," he said. He turned, and I was left alone at the top of the grand staircase. I looked over the railing, to the main floor, just staring for a moment before finally leaving. As I walked to my bedroom, I heard the door to the guest bedroom shut.

I walked into my room and closed the door. I slid off my

jeans and pulled off my sweater. I slipped a silk nightgown on. I sat down at the white vanity that sat in the corner next to a large window. I took my hair out of its French twist and laid the clip on the vanity. My worried eyes looked back at me in the mirror, and I picked up my brush and brushed my hair. I brushed and brushed and brushed.

6

"But what if she is?" I asked, stabbing at the whites of an egg with my fork.

"Allison, Nina's not falling off the wagon. Just chill," Josh said. He stuck his fork into a piece of sausage and shoved it into his mouth, "You worry too much."

I looked back down at my plate, rubbing the toast in the spilling yellow yoke that slowly took over my plate. I sat the bread down, "But what about what we saw last night? I mea-"

"What we saw last night was someone who used to drink a lot but then took a twenty-two year break with only one slip up make up for lost time - or something like that," he said, shoving another piece of sausage into his mouth, "You have to understand that she hasn't touched anything since your uncle left. *And* you laid huge news on her. *And* I took her out and got her wasted. She's stressed and doesn't know what to think or how to react, and honestly, I think I would be drinking too."

I ripped off a piece of the bacon strip and laid it on my tongue, pulling it back between my teeth, "I just feel like it's my fault. Like I caused this. Caused her to start again," I said, keeping my eyes down.

"You gotta stop telling yourself that," he said looking up at me, "You told her something that she wasn't ready for. It's not like you brought up the reason she stopped drinking in the first place."

I looked away. *That's exactly what I did,* "You did, didn't you?" Josh asked, "Jesus, Allison." He let out a sigh and buried his face in his hands.

"Well, I didn't *exactly*. I just brought up Mom," I said and Josh shook his head, rubbing his eyes, "I know. Sorry."

"I'm not the one you need to be apologizing to," he replied, "I mean, what did you say? You didn't say anything about the accident, did you?"

"No, never," I said, "I just told her I tried to do what Mom would've done. Something clicked, and then she completely lost it. Backed me into a corner and told me 'her sister' never would've done something so stupid." By now, I felt so dumb for even mentioning my mother.

I knew how badly what happened had hurt her.

Aunt Nina sits next to me on the couch. The shoebox of pictures lays on the coffee table in front of her. In her hands, she holds a photograph of two young women in their twenties; she and my mother, "She was such a wonderful person," escapes my aunt's mouth in almost a whisper.

I reach for the photo in her hand. Looking at it, at the women, I notice the features they shared. They had the same eyes and nose. My mother's smile was brighter than her sister's. Her lips were perfectly symmetrical and her eyes smiled. My aunt's smile lay slightly crooked, where the left side of her lips dips slightly lower than the right, stretching out slightly longer as well. Her eyes are more rounded than my mother's were.

I flip the picture over. The back read: Spring Break '93; Caroline 24, Nina 21. *I flip it back over. Fourteen years ago. My mother and aunt wore matching bathing suits; a blue, high-waisted bikini with a thin strap that wrapped around their necks. The beach waved peacefully in the blurry background.*

I lay the picture down and pick up a locket. The same locket rests around both my aunt's and mother's necks in every photo. The silver heart shines in the light, and I look up at Aunt Nina, "What's this?" I ask.

Aunt Nina looks down at the necklace in my hands. I open the heart, "It was my sister's," Aunt Nina says. The locket's heart holds a picture of the two sisters. Aunt Nina pulls something out of her shirt.

A locket identical to the one in my hands hangs around my aunt's neck, the heart clasped between her fingers. To this day, I have never seen her take the locket off. Aunt Nina takes the locket from my hands, "And now," she says, fastening the silver chain around my neck, "It's yours."

I smile, holding the heart in my hands, "What happened to her?" I ask.

Aunt Nina is looking down at a photo of her and my mother at Aunt Nina's graduation. A tear rolls down her face, and she ever so lightly closes her eyes so that the lashes barely touch, "She died in a car accident," Aunt Nina says, looking at me. The droplets of tears rest on her wet lashes, "I killed her."

I am taken aghast and don't know what to think, "Wait, what?"

Aunt Nina takes a deep breath. She lays the picture back in the shoebox and turns to face me. She sticks her elbows into her lap and her shoulder hunch over, "I was 24, we had gone to a bar in town. You were eight-months-old, and your mother was always stressed. She didn't want to go, but I made her. I told her if she didn't, I would tell Mom about how she wrecked the car when we were in high school."

"Wait," I interrupted, "I thought that was you?"

"It was," Aunt Nina laughed, "Anyway, she came with your uncle and me, and she brought you father with her. Uncle Peter was supposed to be our 'designated driver', so none of us hesitated to let loose. We were all sitting there at the bar, laughing, telling old family stories, and your mother looked up at me and told me she was so glad she came.

"She and your father were completely wasted by ten o'clock, but I moved at a slower pace. Then your uncle got a call in from work, said he had to leave immediately. But we stayed. Your Uncle Peter kissed me, making me promise I would get someone to drive us home. Then he left.

"We stayed for hours after that; it was almost two when we left. But your mother was getting restless about being away from you so long, so since I had the least to drink, I said I'd drive us home. She fought it, but I walked a straight line for her, even did a cartwheel. After a few minutes of begging, she caved and we walked to the car.

"The whole way down the road, we still laughed and told stories. Your mother started telling your father about the time when we fell out of the second story of our parents' house. We all laughed so hard, and I started hitting the wheel and my eyes closed. My eyes closed for a second. And after that...

"I felt the car jolt to the side, and I heard your mother scream," Aunt Nina starts to choke on her words, *"The next thing I remember after that is waking up with my head on the*

wheel. I awoke crying and yelling. Like I had just woken from a nightmare. I was drenched in sweat, and glass lay throughout my hair. My ears rang and cuts and slices from the glass covered my arms and legs. Blood ran down from my stomach. That's when I noticed the large chunk of the shattered windshield in my side." Aunt Nina pulls up her sweater, revealing a long scar that stretched from her belly button all the way to her rib cage.

"I pulled the glass out and covered the gash with my hand, but blood still poured through. I went to move my other arm, and I felt something on it. I looked over, and my sister's hand held onto my arm. I called her name several times, but she didn't move. I turned around and your father's body stretched from the back seat over the center console.

"I could tell from one look he was dead. His body was stretched over the center. The oncoming car hit the passenger side of ours. He died protecting me." Her words are becoming more and choppier with every sentence.

"Aunt Nina, you don't have to-"

"No, I'm okay," she says, rubbing the tears that collected under eyes, "I'm okay." She pauses then continues, "Your mother's hand still gripped my arm. But I knew she didn't stand a chance. The car had hit her straight on and a shard of glass was stuck in her throat. I picked my hands up and took her face in them. I begged and pleaded and prayed. Her eyes were open, but they weren't alive. And I knew. I knew I killed my sister."

My thoughts were interrupted by a slamming upstairs. Footsteps pounded the floor above, echoing through the house. Another door slammed and I jumped up, running out of the kitchen. I held on tightly to the railing as I ran up the left staircase, almost falling to the ground as I swung around.

When I pushed open the bathroom door, Aunt Nina kneeled on the floor, hunched over the white, ceramic toilet. Her face was pale and vomit that reeked with the stench of alcohol floated in the bowl. Her hands, veiny with nails bitten to stubs, gripped the ceramic, and she heaved. I could tell she was going to throw up again and ran to her side.

I pulled her hair back, holding it above her neck. The heat radiated so strongly off of her body and I reached for a rag. Trying to keep her hair back and support her weight with my thigh, I ran the washcloth under cold water. Her body heaved again, and the vomit poured from her mouth, "I'm fine," she choked.

She didn't look up at me, but held herself up with her arms still wrapped around the toilet, "No, you're not," I said, laying the cold, wet washcloth on the nape of her neck, "Josh, can you get me a clip for her hair?"

He stood in the doorway, looking down at us, "I don't know where one would be," he said.

"Just grab the one off of my vanity," I spit back as Aunt Nina hurled again. I shifted my weight and moved so that I sat directly behind her. I wrapped my hand around her waist.

When I heard Josh's thunderous steps come back down the hall, I faced the doorway and he tossed the clip into my hands. I twisted Aunt Nina's hair into its usual French twist and clipped it up and out of the way. I placed my hand back on her waist and rubbed her back with the other, "Seriously, I'm fine," Aunt Nina said, pushing my hand off of her back, "I'm fine. Just leave me alone."

She held her head in her hand, her elbow propped up on the toilet seat, "Aunt Nina, really, you're not well," I said. But she just waved her hand while her eyes were still buried in the other. She pushed my body back lightly so that it didn't touch hers, "Just go away."

I stood up, looking down at my aunt, just a crumpled heap of body lying on the bathroom floor. She looked up at me and her eyes widened, her eyebrows rose, and her head jerked forward. And I knew that was my cue to leave.

I walked down the stairs to find Josh sitting on the couch, "Is she alright?" he asked.

"I don't know; she told me to leave, so I did," I said and sat down next to him.

Hours later, we heard the clack of Aunt Nina's heels coming down the stairs. We turned, leaning our heads around the corner. Aunt Nina stood in the foyer. Black lace tights hugged her legs and peeked through the open toed boots that laced up her calves, past her knees, and to her thighs. She wore a long coat the color of coal over her arms, but left it unbuttoned. A lace dress as colorless as the night ended in frays and hung right above where the velvet boots ended. The whole thing was see-through except the black, padded strip that ran across her breasts and the matching skirt that started at her waist.

Her hair hung straight, shining in the light. The long layers feathered into her face and her bangs were clipped into a bump at the front of her head. A nude gloss tinted her lips and winged eyeliner lifted her hooded eyes. She looked twenty again. And opening the front door, she left without a word.

"Wow," Josh muttered, still staring at the door, "Is she wearing makeup?"

"Yeah," I said, watching with raised brows as she pulled out of the drive.

"Well, Nina wears hung-over really well."

"Always has," I said. I leaned back on the couch, picking up the Xbox remote. Flicking through the titles, I clicked on some random Netflix Original, "What are we going to do about her Josh?" I asked, "If this is anything like when Uncle Peter left, she's not going to stop. Not until something makes her."

Josh didn't answer. We both knew I was right, and that there was nothing we could do about it. We sat there in silence, watching the movie on the flat screen. The warmth of his body was like a blanket.

We were almost halfway through the sequel when the front door opened. The shuffling of a coat and the clicking of Aunt Nina's steps resonated throughout the foyer, "Hey!" I called out.

No words replied, "Just give it up, Allison. She'll talk when she's ready," Josh said.

The clicking continued through the opening below the staircase, and Aunt Nina entered the room. She walked up behind the couch and dropped something in my lap.

Allison was scrawled in shimmering gold ink against the black paper of the envelope. "What's tha - oh my God." Josh could not have been more pronounced with his concern. His mouth hung wide open, and I wanted nothing more than to slap him.

"What?" Aunt Nina asked, setting her bag on the counter and coming back into the living room. Her arms were folded across her chest and she hovered behind me. My fingers traced the gold that lined the edges. I barely opened the top, peering inside. Catching a glimpse of a Polaroid, I squeezed the paper together and held it close to my body.

"Oh, nothing," Josh said. His pitch raised almost an entire

octave, and it took everything I had not to punch him in his face. I turned and glared him in the eyes, "That's a… note. From a guy. At school."

Dear God. And at this time, I honestly think I would've shot him if I had been given the chance.

Aunt Nina raised her brows, "Uhkay," she said. She took a double take before moving towards the foyer and stairs. She went to speak, but stood there mouth open for a moment before finally giving up and walking upstairs.

I grabbed Josh by the ear. Dragging him into the kitchen and farther away from Aunt Nina, I felt my temperature rise. When I made sure Aunt Nina had made her way off of the first floor, I turned around and slapped Josh upside the head, "What were you thinking?"

"Hey! Hey! You weren't saying anything!" he said, "I was just trying to keep her off of your tail!"

I scoffed, "Yes, because saying 'oh my God' like a girl then tripping over your words like a toddler learning to walk is definitely not suspicious."

"Well, I'm sor-ry!" he yelled and his face turned serious, "But is it from them?"

"What do you think?" I asked. I started pacing. Josh grabbed the envelope that sat on the counter. The gold shimmered in the light as his fingers lifted the paper's covering, leaving the contents open to the world.

I ripped the envelope from his hands. Pouring the pictures and paper onto the counter, my heart pounded in my ears.

Again, three Polaroids. I took the first one in my trembling hands. Aunt Nina drove down the highway. The second one lay beneath my hand. Aunt Nina crossed the street, her hands in her pockets and her leg outstretched mid-step. Josh held the third. Aunt Nina sat at a bar, laughing with the guy next to her.

I lifted the white piece of printer paper from the counter.

Wow, Aunt Nina's a gem when she cleans up. Definitely more attractive than last night. I'd invite our boy Josh to stay another night if I were you.

"Godda-"

"Just shut up," I said, cutting Josh off. Infuriation pulsed through my veins. My fists clenched into balls, and for the first time since this whole mess started, I was angry.

I unzipped the old swim jacket that covered my arms and threw it on the counter. I heard the knife block tip over, but I left it as I let out a frustrated scream, "I'll go upstairs and get the shoebox," Josh said as I covered my face with my hands, practically clawing my eyes out in irritation.

"What shoebox?" Aunt Nina said from the cased opening that joined the kitchen and living room. Josh and I turned to face her. My eyes met Josh's. His met Aunt Nina's. Aunt Nina's met mine, then Josh's again. Then she turned and bolted.

I shoved the pictures into my pocket and we chased her up the stairs. But she had the lead and her speed. I lost my footing as I swung around the banister. I winced as my face struck the wooden floor. I held my wrist against the unstitched, bleeding gash on my face and scrambled to my feet, chasing the two into the guest bedroom. Josh had shimmied past her and beat her to the closet. He flung open the door and grabbed the box from the shelf.

Aunt Nina's robe caught wind, opening behind her. She turned the corner and wrapped her arm around the box in Josh's hands. She pulled the other back, and with a loud *'crack',* her finger nail clocked bone and sent Josh to the ground.

"Ow!" he squealed from the floor. He lay on his back, rubbing the red mark in the dead center of his forehead, "Did you just flick me?"

"Yes I did," Aunt Nina replied, barely glancing at him; all of her focus was on opening the box. I lurched forward, but her eyes shot daggers, and I backed away. With her eyes still locked onto mine, she lifted the cardboard top of the box, "Sweet Jesus, Mary, and Joseph."

Her hands shuffled through the pictures, "What the - *oh my God.*" she held up the picture of Leo, his lifeless body sprawled out on the alley floor, "What is - who the *hell* is this?"

The piercing pitch of her voice made me cringe, "Leo," I answered.

"Who is that?" she spit with impatience.

"The guy she met in New York," Josh answered for me after the deafening moments of silence.

"Was I talking to you?" Aunt Nina's asked, her voice almost a screeching pitch. She glared at Josh, her eyes wide with anger. She whipped her head back to face me, "And now he's dead?"

After not answering for moments, Josh opened his mouth to speak, "Don't." Aunt Nina spoke with a biting fierceness. Her finger was in his face. Her eyebrows raised, she looked down at him.

She flicked her gaze back to me. I nodded, my head down. Searching through the other pictures, she let out a short laugh. I tried to stop her before she found the photo I feared she would, "Aunt Nin-." But I was too late. When she froze, my eyes closed and I let out my breath.

"Is this me?" she asked, "And Cooper?" The picture of her and the dog was held up in her hand. She breathed in giving *the look*. The hazel irises looked up at you from the corner of her eyes. The muscles on her face hung without feeling, other than her jaw that clenched. Her lips barely parted in the center, and all of the blood in her body poured into her face. And her manner said *you're going to die*. She picked up the envelopes that lay in the box, "These are the same as the one I gave you earlier."

Knowing what she would ask next, I pulled the envelope out of my back pocket. She snatched it out of my hand, digging through. She pulled out the pictures, and a wave of horror washed over her face.

Flipping through them, she looked up at me with that look again. And all I could do was sit and wait. The blood rushed to my face, burning, and sweat collected around my face and neck.

She unfolded the letter, "*I'd invite Josh to stay another night*, what's that supposed to mean? Did you stay last night?" Her eyes continued scrutinizing the photos in her hand as she waited for an answer. When Josh didn't answer in fear of my aunt's wild temper, Aunt Nina spoke again, "Well? Did you?"

"Yes," he answered, still lying on the ground.

Aunt Nina turned to face me, "And how would they know that?" Her eyes were ice. The tone if her voice cut deeply, but the motionlessness of her body only cut deeper.

"I don't know."

Her fingers folded one by one into two balls of contracted muscle, folded bones, and a pounding pulse. She raised her fist, but pulled back and glared as she marched past us. She turned in the doorway of the closet and looked at Josh, "I want you here tonight," she said. She looked at me, "And you... just go to your room." And with that, she left.

He waited until she was out of range, "Did she just tell you to go to your room?" Josh asked.

"Yes. Yes she did," I replied.

"Are you gonna go?"

And having heard those words many times in my life, I knew better than to not obey, "Yep." And I turned and made my way down the hall and to my room.

<hr />

I sat on the edge of my bed, the sheets balled up in my hands, "I can fix this tomorrow," Josh said as he maneuvered the wash cloth through the bleeding gash on my face, "Here, let's go to the bathroom. I need the peroxide."

We walked across the hall. The bathroom door opened before I could get my hands on the doorknob. Aunt Nina walked out with a snow-white towel wrapped around her body. She rolled her eyes without taking a second look at me.

I opened the medicine cabinet and grabbed the peroxide. Sitting on the toilet seat, I squirmed as Josh poured the dreaded acid onto my face. It burned, but I completely forgot about it when I glanced at the counter.

Aunt Nina's phone still lay charging on the marble top. I reached for it. Laying my finger gently over the home button, I unlocked the phone.

"Allison, I don't think that's a good idea." Josh said from where he kneeled on the floor.

"Oh, hush. I just want to see if she got in contact with her therapist again." I tapped the *Messages* icon. But what opened was not a conversation with Aunt Nina's therapist.

"Josh, who is Aaron? Does that name sound familiar to you?" I asked reading the messages.

"Nope, doesn't ring a bell," he said.

"Didn't think so," I said, "So why are there red hearts by his name?"

"What?" Josh scooched in closer. I flashed him the screen.

I read through the messages. *I'm so worried,* Aunt Nina said.

It'll be okay, Aaron said. I scrolled form the top down to the most recent messages.

I can't, Aaron, I'm sorry, Aunt Nina said.

Nina, we've been together for almost two years now. If anyone knows that you aren't perfect, it's me. But that's what I love about you. The way your smile is slightly off line. The perfectionist inside of you that fixes everything. *The way your laugh cackles and snorts. You don't have to be afraid. I won't leave you. I know you have baggage. I know it's hard for you to trust. But please, don't walk away. I love you,* Aaron said.

I felt my heart ache as if it were being torn piece by piece. Like a snagging shirt, ripping at the seams. *Two years.* Two years, and I didn't have a clue. And he really seemed to love her. Why was she willing to throw it away? A message set typed in the bubble, but was never sent.

Aaron, you don't understand. I love you. I really do. But I don't trust you. It's not that I don't want to. It's that I can't. It hurts me to do this. But I will never be able to leave my heart in someone else's hands again, and that's what I'd have to do for us to go on. And you're so amazing. The way you can make me laugh even on my toughest days. The way you see the best of me on the worst days. You give me more than I deserve, and I can't give it back in return. That is why I have to let you go. Because you deserve so much better than what I am.

"What are you doing?" she shrieked form the doorway. Her voice was shrill and broken. She seized the phone from my hand and held it close to her chest. She looked back at me, terrified. As if her whole heart had been opened and exposed, and now I was picking at it, ravaging and ruining it.

"Aunt Nina, I'm sorry, but why are you leaving him? And two years? Why didn't you tell me?" I asked. I had so many questions running around my mind.

"Because it's none of your business, that's why," she said. She was hurt and furious. I had invaded her privacy and learned something she wished to keep hidden, "Don't ever go through my phone again. What goes on in my life is my business not yours. Understand?"

I nodded my head, but I couldn't leave it at that. "But why are you breaking up with him? I read the messages. He thinks you are a gift sent from God. Why would you want to let go of that?"

"Allison, enough."

"But, just *why*? I don't get i-"

"I said enough! You don't have to get it, it's not your choice; it's not your life," she snapped. She eyed me closely, like she was waiting for me to lunge at her throat, "Why were you going through my phone anyways?" she asked.

"I wanted to see if you were talking to Dr. Hart or not," I said.

"Again, something that is none if your business. So just do everyone a favor and butt out. You've already ruined enough," she said. And with those bitter words hovering heavily in the air, she turned and left the room.

I stood there. My breathing was heavy and my teeth grinded together. Sweat gathered in my palms, and my chest tightened. I wanted to chase after her. To tell her she needed to stop being such a-

"Well," Josh said awkwardly and let out a gust of air, "At least she's talking to you."

I rolled my eyes and jammed my elbow deep into his gut, up and under his ribcage.

7

A wail resonated throughout the second floor. *Aunt Nina*. I flew out of my room and down the hall. The coolness of the air was unsettling and a shiver shook my body. Josh met me in front of Aunt Nina's door, and we pushed past the frame and inside.

Aunt Nina lay on the floor, her chest heaving. I ran to her side. Holding her arm, blood leaked onto my other hand from her abdomen. I rolled up her black t-shirt. The scar on her stomach had been ripped open.

Blood dripped from where a blade had torn her skin. She pushed me away, sitting up and leaning against her bed. She winced with pain, and I noticed the shattered glass on the floor around her.

Fractures of glass laid on the floor and on the vanity. The broken mirror shined in sprinkled pieces across the room. Her arms were littered with slices and pricks. A long trickle of blood slowly slid down her leg.

Josh, who stood next to the wall, closed the window, taming the wild curtains and angry winds. Water dribbled down the hanging fabric and fell in droplets to the floor. He looked at me, "We need to get her to a hospital," he said. I looked up, holding my hands over the wound in an attempt to slow the bleeding.

But the warm blood continued pouring through my fingers, running freely from jagged ridges in thick scarlet rivers across her waist, and I knew he was right. Josh brought me a towel from the basket freshly folded, clean towels, and Aunt Nina fought as I tried to hold it over the tear, "I can do it myself," was all she said as she ripped the towel from my hands, her head tilted towards the sky in agony.

Before she could lay it over her gaping incision, I noticed something, "Wait," I said. I pushed her hand away. Something bright lay within the torn muscle, "Hold still."

I dug my hands through the flesh and blood. Aunt Nina yelped and pulled away. She held the towel over her middle. Glaring at me, she began to stand up. I had had enough of her over the past few days, and gripped her by the arm and pulled her back to the ground. I shot my hand back into her stomach.

I felt the crispness of what I had seen and wrapped my fingers around it. Aunt Nina's eyes widened, and her mouth hung open. She lowered the towel to her wound, "What the…"

I held a piece of red-stained paper between my thumb and index finger. Scrambling to unfold it, I heard Josh shuffle closer. He peered over my shoulder as I read the familiar scribble of writing.

Let's reopen this later, shall we?

"Aunt Nina, what happened?" I asked, but she did not answer. She clasped the towel in her hand, the other was gripping the bed and she tried to stand up. Josh ran to her side. I wanted so badly to help her, to hold her hand and never let go. But I knew she wouldn't let me. If she'd let Josh, then I would have to live with it; at least she was getting help. I hung back as he talked to her.

"Nina, how did this happen?" he asked, holding his hand over hers as she pressed the towel against her stomach.

Her right hand reached out and held onto Josh's arm, "I don't know how he got in," she hissed. Her words came out quick, in a sputter, "All I know is I felt something sharp, a knife, and I woke up. A man in all dark clothing hovered above me on the bed, and I pushed him off. But he took me down with him," she stammered. Her sentences were choppy and the words escaped in forced whispers through gritted teeth, "I stood up, but he grabbed me by the throat and threw me into the mirror. Then the pain where he had cut me was back. I figured he was trying to finish the job or something. Then you came in."

Her face went pale and she clenched tighter onto the towel and Josh's arm. The towel grew redder as a surge of blood seeped through. The bright red leaked in pools from her lap, to the bed, to the floor.

"Okay," Josh said, pulling Aunt Nina close, holding onto her by the shoulder as her face rested against his body, "Allison, we really need to get her to a hospital, now."

Josh lifted her arm and draped it around his neck, and I hurried to do the same. We carried her across the room, her weight fully supported by ours. She had no strength left for herself. Her eyes hung heavy with the midnight and her breathing was staggered.

The blood had completely consumed the towel that had lain over the wound. Josh wrapped his arms around her and lifted her from the ground. He held her in his arms, "Get another towel," he demanded, "And grab my keys. They're on the nightstand in the guest room."

I grabbed another towel from the laundry basket. Laying the thick, white cloth in the pocket where her body caved in Josh's embrace, I gripped her hand. I looked into Aunt Nina's eyes, but she turned curled in closer to Josh.

I ran to the guest room. My whole body was numb, along with my mind. I couldn't think. I couldn't speak. When I returned to the head of the stairs, Josh was already waiting by the front door. I rushed down the stairs.

Opening the car door, I lowered myself into the backseat. Josh followed behind. He laid Aunt Nina's tight and unmoving body next to mine.

I tried again to hold her hand, and this time she didn't pull away. A wave of delight rolled through my body until I noticed why she hadn't pulled away. The car lurched forward and flew down the streets. Josh looked up into the rear-view mirror, "Don't let her close her eyes," he said. I turned to face her. Her eyes were closed, and I shook her.

They opened, and she rolled her head to the side-away from me. I just wanted to pull her in close, to hold her and make sure she was alright, "Listen, Aunt Nina, I know you're upset. But I need you to look at me," I said.

She didn't turn, but let out a short and irritated laugh. And I acted, "Hey," I spit grabbing her arm, "Look at me. You can be mad all you want, but you're going to look here so I can make sure you're alright. Because I'm going to let anything happen to you. This was all my fault, and I know it. But do you know how hard it is to sit here and watch you be in so much pain and not be able to help?"

She was too weak to react. Her body fell limp, and she collapsed in my arms. I held her up. Her eyelids just hovered above one another and I went cold. I honestly feared I was going to lose her.

Josh and I jumped from our seats as the doctor walked into the waiting room. He approached me, "Allison Schwartz?" he asked. I nodded, shaking his hand, "Dr. Greene. I'm glad to tell you your aunt is going to be alright," he said, and all of the pain and fear I had harbored inside of me spilled out. I cried there in Josh's arms.

Once composed, I looked back at the doctor and he spoke, Josh's arm still around me, "Now, she did lose a lot of blood, but she's a fighter. We would like to keep her here, though, to monitor her vitals. She should be safe to go home in a couple of days," Dr. Greene said.

I smiled, "Thank you so much," I said.

"You're welcome," Dr. Greene replied, "You can go see her if you'd like."

I knew he had good intentions, but I couldn't help but let my face fall at his words. I knew I was the last person she would've wanted to see, and Josh did too, "I don't think that's a good idea right now," he said then turned to me, "But we need to get you taken care of."

I looked back to Dr. Greene, "Thank you, again," I said shaking his hand once more before following Josh down a hall.

I winced as Josh re-stitched the gash. I fought to stay awake. My eyes weighed a thousand pounds and my head spun with exhaustion, "You need to go home. Get some rest," Josh said, finishing the last of the stitches.

I peeled my eyes open, shaking my head, "No," I said through a yawn, "I need to stay here with Aunt Nina. You go."

Josh cleaned up what he had gotten out to fix me up, "Okay," he said fighting sleep himself, "I know there's no point in trying to change your mind. Call me if you need anything."

I sat alone in the waiting room. Fear, hunger, and exhaustion ate away at my being. After what seemed like hours, I finally mustered up the courage to go see Aunt Nina.

I trudged down the hall. When I reached her door, I took a deep breath before opening it. The door slid open and I crept inside. Aunt Nina's eyes were closed and her chest moved rhythmically; she was asleep. I walked to the side of the bed and cradled her hand in my own.

The saltiness of the tears slipped into my mouth and tightened my face. I just wanted her look at me, hold me and tell me everything was going to be alright. Her hand was soft against my cheek, and I held it there, "I'm so scared, Aunt Nina," I said through choking tears.

I thought of what she would've said, would've done if there wasn't such a huge mess between us.

Her thumb would rub the tears from my eyes, "It's okay, pumpkin," she'd say, taking my face in her hands, "Everything's going to be okay. I love you so much, no matter what. Always remember that."

I missed her so much. The sweetness of her voice. The tenderness of her touch. The love of her words. I would've given anything in that moment for her forgiveness. Resting my forehead against her limp hand on the bed, I lost control once again. Sobs escaped my mouth and the tears fell in puddles.

My chest heaved and my heart throbbed. It ached. It ached for Sunday game nights and movies on the couch and walks on the beach. It ached for gentle hands, soft embraces, and words of warmth.

But the time came when I couldn't fight the cloudiness of slumber any longer. I leaned in close, kissing Aunt Nina on the forehead, "I love you."

I sat in a chair in the waiting room and let the haze of sleep take me away...

I was thrown out of sorts when a hand shook my arm. The muscles in my body clenched, and I almost tipped the chair in a panic, "Are you Allison?"

A man hovered over me – *the man from the photo of Aunt Nina in a bar.* His hair was short, brown, sparsely flecked with gray. His eyes were brown also, but not as dark as his hair. More like a milk chocolate drizzled with caramel. They were big and bright, and the largeness of his pupils gave him a bubbly, friendly air.

I stood up and he towered almost a foot over me. My words caught in my throat, "Uh, yes. Yes I am," I said through a stutter, "And who are you?"

"Aaron," he said, shaking my hand, "Aaron Harris."
Aaron. Aunt Nina's boyfriend.

"Is she alright?" Aaron asked. His words snapped me back, "Allison, is she okay?"

I looked up at him, "Yes, she'll be alright. She was asleep when I was in there last, but you can go check if you'd like." I was staring at him, scrutinizing and judging, and he knew it. He stood there for a moment before turning to run down the hall. But a new question crossed my mind, "Aaron, wait!"

He slowed his jog and waited for me to catch up, "Yes?"

"How did you know Aunt Nina was here?" I asked as we walked down the hall.

Aaron nodded his head, "A kid, Josh I think it was, called from Nina's phone. Said she was hurt and thought he'd let me know."

We turned the corner of Aunt Nina's doorway. I could see

her eyes from where I stood outside the door. And Aaron could, too. He ran to her side, collapsing next to the bed. He grabbed her hand, and he looked up at her as if she was an angel sent from heaven. I had never seen my uncle look at her the way Aaron looked at her now. Aunt Nina pushed herself up, and a beaming smile broke through, shining from her face.

Aunt Nina rested a hand on Aaron's face, and bringing up the other, she kissed him. When she pulled away, her eyes were flood gates about to let loose, "I'm so sorry," she said through tears, "I love you, I do. Please, don't go. I, you-"

Aaron's eyebrows rose sympathetically, "Nina, I told you, I'm not going anywhere," he said, "I'll never leave you." His fingers rubbed the tears from her face, and he pulled her close into his embrace, kissing the top of her head.

Aunt Nina wrapped an arm around his back and looked up at him. Her smile widened, and I had never seen her so happy. Aunt Nina planted a soft, gentle kiss on her boyfriend's lips, and she rested her face against his chest, closing her eyes.

"So, what happened?" Aaron finally asked. He looked down at her with concern.

Aunt Nina's eyes opened, "Um, I was…uh, trying to fix the window in my bedroom. You know how it sticks. And, um, my hands, they broke the glass and went through. When I stumbled forward, I accidentally cut myself on the sharp edge."

"I told you to stop trying to do these things on your own," Aaron said, "You should've called. I would've helped."

"Yeah, you're right," Aunt Nina said. She forced out a laugh. Aaron crawled in bed next to her, and Aunt Nina scooched over to make room. Aaron pulled out a plastic bag that I hadn't noticed when he came in. By the looks of it, Aunt Nina didn't see it either, "What's that?" she asked, smiling again.

"I saw this at work yesterday, and I knew I had to get it," Aaron replied, pulling out a book. Aunt Nina took the pastel pink novel out of her boyfriend's hands, "I figured since you'd be in here awhile, I'd bring it."

Aunt Nina's mouth hung open slightly, and she smiled, "You didn't have to," she said.

"I know." Aaron beamed at his girlfriend's joy.

Aunt Nina looked back at him, "You're the best," she said, curling in close to Aaron as he laid his arm around her shoulders.

Aaron looked around the room, and then back at Aunt Nina like he remembered something, "We're up six percent," he said.

My aunt looked back at him, "That's great!"

"Yeah," Aaron said, "The store looks great; so much better since the last time you saw it." I looked at Aaron's shirt. It was navy blue with *Walmart* embroidered in white across the left shoulder. His name tag was still clipped to his shirt. Below his name was printed *manager*. Aunt Nina's hand and cheek rested on Aaron's chest, and the conversation continued.

I knew it was time for me to leave, and I stole one last glance their way. Aunt Nina's eyes met mine, and she smiled. It was a small, almost unnoticeable grin, but it was there. I smiled back and made my way down the hall.

When I entered the waiting room, a new feeling of peace flooded over me. Aunt Nina had smiled at me, which was definitely a step in the right direction. I was about to head for the food court when someone called my name.

Patricia stood behind me. I jumped back, my hand over my chest. But once I realized it was her, I took a breath and spoke, "Patricia, hi. I'm sorry, you startled me."

"I'm sorry, Allison," she said with a soft smile, "But while you were with Nina, someone told me to give this to you."

The unmistakable gold shimmered in the light. My eyes widened and I took the black envelope from her hand. Patricia's eyes were large and confused. I forced grin, "Thank you," I said sweetly.

I hurried out the automatic doors and across the dark parking lot. The seemed miles away. Slamming the door shut behind me, I stared down at the black and gold envelope in my lap. The paper was crisp in my hands and tore through the silence as I opened it. As always, three pictures and a note hid inside.

The first picture showed doctors rushing Aunt Nina down a hall on a gurney.

The second showed Aaron and me in the waiting room.

I closed my eyes in frustration; this was getting old. But a shiver ran up my spine at the sight of the last photo.

Aunt Nina and Aaron lay in the hospital bed, Aunt Nina curled up in Aaron's arms. But the image of the couple was blurry. The focus was on the side of a neck and a soft blonde curl that hung inches from the lense.

My heart beated out of my chest. *Inches. They were inches from me, and I never would've known.* I opened the note that was now dotted with fallen tears.

Aaron seems like a nice guy. I would hate for him to get hurt.

I threw my head against the headrest. And in that moment all I wanted to do was die. I just wanted to give up and end all of this, because I couldn't let him get hurt. Aunt Nina was finally opening up after thirteen years of hiding from men and love. I couldn't let this end badly; this had to work out, for her sake.

I threw my hands against the steering wheel, and did so again, and again, and again until they throbbed. My chest was so tight and I couldn't breathe. Folded my arms over the wheel and dropped my head onto the wheel's leather covering.

I lifted my head and sucked in a breath, trying to push everything away. Still, hunger tugged and pulled at my stomach. I unlocked the car and went back into the hospital.

The food court was buzzing with people. Screens hung on the walls and displayed menus. The lines were short, and I moved through quickly. I sat down at a small table in the corner. My fork picked through my food, eventually stabbing a piece of chicken. Looking around the space, there were many people sitting, standing, talking to each other. Some were having the best day of their lives, while others were having the worst.

I started stabbing through the food again, but my eyes flicked up against lowered brows when a chair screeched in front of me. Aaron sat across the two-person table, "Looks like we had the same idea, huh?" he said. I laid the fork down on the tray and looked up at him, "Oh, no, don't stop eating on my account."

"No, I'm not even that hungry," I said, "How is she? I saw you got her that book. She's been meaning to pick it up for a while now."

Aaron smiled, "Yeah, I remembered she mentioned it, so when I saw it, I instantly thought of her and had to buy it," he said. He folded his hands on the table, "She insisted that I come and get something to eat, and she'll start on the book." His energy was so bright for so early, and I almost asked him how he did it. It was like he was a teenager crushing on a girl at school.

"Yeah, she likes to be left alone while she reads," I said, sipping on the vitamin water from the vending machine, "When I was younger, she would sit on the back patio, and I'd come out to sit with her. I remember plain as day, before I could even close the back door, she'd always say to me, *'Either sit still in a chair and be quiet or go inside.'* She wouldn't even look up from the book. It was like it was a prerecorded message ready to be played as soon as the door opened." I giggled shyly, but Aaron looked at me intensely, listening closely to every word.

"Yeah," he said, biting into a granola bar, "That sounds like something she'd do." His eyes were smiling, and they were happy and giddy.

"You really love her, don't you?" I asked.

He looked back at me, "More than anything," he said. And you could tell, he really did. He started shaking his head, "And when I heard something happened to her…" His voice trailed off as he searched for words, "I don't even know. I freaked. Hurried here as soon as I could."

The corner of my mouth turned up, "Well, I can honestly say, I think she feels the same way," I said as I twisted the battle cap back on.

"Really?" Aaron asked.

"Yeah, I do," I said nodding, looking into his eyes, "I haven't seen her as happy as I saw her back in that room in a long time."

Aaron's hands started fidgeting, "Well, that's great, because I really love her, and when I thought I was going to lose her - if I lost her, I don't know what I'd do."

And, even with the upbeat of his voice, my heart fell. I thought about the notes. They were coming back for her. When was this going to end? That's when I understood: it wouldn't.

Not unless I did something about it.

An idea so crazy crossed my mind, I pushed it away. But it kept coming back. Mick wasn't going to stop. Not until he got what he wanted, and I realized what I needed to do - to protect her. The only way he would stop was if he thought I was dead.

8

"You want to do *what*?" Josh asked. I shuddered with the bitter January winds. The phone was like a block of ice held up against my ear.

"Think about it," I pressed, "It would solve everything."

"Allison, you're not faking your death. That's just ridiculous," Josh replied, "We will figure out what they want and a way to get it."

I could hear the irritation in his voiced, but still pushed, "Please, I've thought it through. Everything I would need I can get, but I need your help-"

"Allison, the little red phone," he said, and I knew what he meant. He'd always used it as a threat, even when we were kids, "I'll hang up, you know I will."

"Yeah, whatever," I said, kicking the loose gravel across the pavement.

"So, how is she?" Josh asked, "You said she smiled at you? Was it a *smile* smile or a *can you please go away* smile? Because we all know she's mastered that one."

"No, it was a genuine grin," I said, "Nothing too crazy. I

don't think she's mad anymore, just worried."

Josh scoffed at the other end of the line, "Well, Allison, I can imagine why. She was only cut open and threatened. I'd be worried too." I heard a faint beeping in the background, "That would be the coffee. I'll see you later. Tell Nina hi for me."

"Alright, love you, bye," I said.

"Adios. Love you."

I walked back through the hospital doors. The warmth defrosted my fingers, and I wiggled them as the feeling came back. As I made my way down the hall, the rising sun glinted through the window.

Aunt Nina was asleep when I entered the room. Aaron had already left, and the book he had gotten her rested open on her chest. I lifted it from under her hands. Grabbing the top right-hand corner, I was going to fold down the corner of the page so she didn't lose her spot. But then I remembered how she hated when her books didn't look perfect, especially the new ones.

I tore a piece of paper out of the notepad on the nightstand and tucked it within the book's pages. I laid the book down on the stand and sat in a seat next to the bed.

There is a grace which comes with sleep. Aunt Nina's features were much softer without consciousness. The lines that usually creased her face harshly were almost invisible, and the tenseness and constant worry that always filled her was no longer there, but instead replaced with gentle muscles and tranquility.

The days stretched to weeks as no notes or pictures came.

Aunt Nina had come home on the eighth, but was told to stay in bed and take it easy for a week afterwards. Josh was in and out of her room, and Aaron came to visit, but I kept my distance. She had just forgiven me, and I didn't want to push it.

Three days after she had come home, I was sitting on the couch when I heard a crash from upstairs. I ran to Aunt Nina's room.

Aunt Nina knelt on the ground, "I'm alright," she said and looked up at me, "I was just going to open the window and stepped on the lamp cord." I crouched by her side. I reached for the lamp and returned it to the night stand.

Holding her hand, I helped Aunt Nina back into bed. After making sure she was alright, I walked over to the window and cracked it open slightly, "Thank you," Aunt Nina said as she shifted in the bed. She sat up, leaving the side closest to me empty. As I turned away from the window, she glanced down at the empty spot then up at me.

I looked at the empty spot, raising my eyebrows shyly. Aunt Nina nodded and patted the mattress beside her. I shuffled to the bedside. Lifting the cover, I slid my legs against the soft sheets. My eyes flicked around the room nervously.

But Aunt Nina's hand grabbed the side of my face that was farthest from her reach, turning my head. She looked into my eyes with a gentle smile. Then she pulled me in close.

I could feel the tears as they slid down my face. I lay there in her warm embrace, one I had missed so much. My arms, thrown around her neck, ended in clenching fists. One hand clutched her robe, while the other held softly onto the feathery hair that was clipped in a twist.

She pulled away, and I saw the tears that gathered in and around her eyes. Her hands held my face and she let out a short breath and hugged me again.

"I love you so much." The words left both of our mouths at the exact same time. A short laugh escaped from us, but it lasted only a brief moment. My arms tightened around my aunt's body, and hers tightened around mine. She sighed, "I've missed you," she said.

"I've missed you too," I said. My voice was so high, the words sounded like they belonged to a three-year-old. A pressure pushed against the walls of my nose, and I sobbed into her chest, hands grasping at her robe. She held me in silence, rocking slowly as my tears soaked her chest. Her fingers lifted my chin lightly, "I'll always love you," she said, "No matter what."

Her lips were soft as she gently kissed my forehead. A tender hand touched my face again, and her thumb swept across my skin. Her head turned slowly, and she looked at the wall in front of her. I rested my head on her shoulder. Barely a second later, I lifted my head to kiss her cheek then left it to fall back to her shoulder.

Her head lay against the top of mine, and her hand lifted from the comforter. She dropped it over mine, squeezing.

I squeezed back tighter, "Do you think it's over?" I asked, still looking at the gray wall.

"I don't know," Aunt Nina replied, "We can only hope."

A silence stretched as the two of us lay there, each other's company enough. For a short while. With her inability to keep quiet, Aunt Nina's words broke through the silence, "So. What have you been up to?" she asked as the top half of her body turned towards me.

"Nothing much," I said, "How about you?"

"Oh, you know, just recovering from being violently cut

open in my sleep. Nothing much," she said.

I couldn't help but smile, "Yeah, I'm sorry about that."

"It's okay." Aunt Nina's gaze shifted towards the window. Mine followed. A light mist hung low, and the tips of the mountains peeked from the clouds. It was a dark day, the sun hidden within the gray sky. But there was still a beauty to it.

The blanket rustled beside me as Aunt Nina got up. She drifted across the room. I opened my mouth to speak, but Aunt Nina stopped in front of the large bay window on the wall right of the bed. She sat, pulling her knees up to her chest. I figured sitting in front of a window wouldn't hurt her.

I stood from the bed and sat in the window, facing her, knees pulled against my chest as well. Aunt Nina smiled at me then returned her gaze to the mountains. I watched her as she stared out the window. As clumsy and klutzy as she could be, my aunt still had a grace to her. When she wasn't over thinking or worrying, she could be poised and elegant.

She was truly something to be held in high esteem, as her manner and tone did not demand respect, but commanded it. She was a sophisticated, refined woman who, despite what all life had thrown at her, never lost her dignity or class.

But most of all, she was inspiring. She was a beautiful, graceful, compassionate, and loving girl. And I would've been completely content if I had become half of the woman she was.

"You're staring at me," she said, never looking away from the view.

"I am," I said.

"I guess my question is why," she said.

I smiled, "I don't know, maybe it's just how poised you are. How refined," I said.

Now it was her turn to smile, and she looked back at me,

"Oh really? You think I am poised and refined?"

"I do." Aunt Nina nodded, looking back outside. I allowed my gaze to wander around the room. A dresser sat against the wall behind me. In a heavy glass frame was a photo of Aunt Nina and my mother. It was the most recent one I had seen. I took the frame in my hands and looked at the women.

Aunt Nina was younger. The lines on her face were only starting to form and her skin was more firm. Besides that she looked exactly the same. My aunt had always prided herself on looking younger than she really was.

My mother was stunning. Her brown hair was highlighted and cut into layers. In all of the other pictures I had seen of my mother, her hair was blow dried into natural curls. But in this picture, her hair was straightened. She had bangs similar to her sister's except they rested on the opposite side of her face. But still the layers feathered into her face. She had more than Aunt Nina did, starting around the middle of her neck; Aunt Nina's didn't start until right above her breasts.

My mother's eyes were enchanting, just so bright and friendly. She wore more makeup than Aunt Nina did, and from what I understand, it had always been that way. I dragged my hand along the frosted glass. My fingers slid over clear words: *You are the wind beneath my wings.* A smile spread across my lips. I would've given anything to get to meet her, "Aunt Nina?"

"Yes, pumpkin?"

Not looking up, I asked, "What was she like?"

"What was who like, babydoll?"

"Mom," I said. Aunt Nina's gaze ripped from the window and landed on me, then fell to the picture frame in my hand.

"Oh," she said, "Let's see." She turned so her back leaned against the window, and I did the same, "Well, in high school, she was certainly the more popular one," Aunt Nina started, "I may be an outgoing 'social butterfly' that never shuts up, but I mainly hung out in the music suite with the band geeks and the choir. She wasn't as into music as I was, more of the Homecoming Queen type. She was definitely the prettier one, too."

"Really?" I said.

"Yeah," Aunt Nina said, "And, I was a little heavier back then. Your mother was thin; always had been."

"Huh," I said, "What else?"

"Um, she swam; we both did. I was better than she was, though. And…I was definitely the goofy younger sister, where she was the young lady. She was very polite. I talked a lot, which hasn't changed. And usually it was out of turn," she said. She turned and looked at me, "I actually got kicked out of National Honors Society because in my art class, part of our grade was conduct, and I ran my mouth constantly and ended up with a C in art. So they kicked me out."

"Are you serious?" I asked. I couldn't believe it.

"Yep," Aunt Nina said laughing, "Your mother never let me live that one down."

I giggled, "Was she in NHS?" I asked.

"Yeah, she was very bright. Had to be to go to medical school at Harvard," Aunt Nina smiled, but it was distant.

So I changed the subject, "If you were so into it in high school, why didn't you pursue a career in music?" I asked.

"I wanted to," Aunt Nina said, "All through high school." She looked up like something had hit her. She rushed to the closet. I saw the light click on and started to get up, but she had already returned. She sat next to me on the window sill.

In her hands, she clutched an old yearbook. It was red,

white, and blue with the number '86 on it. Aunt Nina flipped through the pages until she reached the senior directory. She turned the pages, stopping when she got to the S's, "Sanchez, Santore, aha! Schwartz!" She scooted closer to me, "They asked us what our ambitions were for after high school," she said.

"What was yours?"

She smiled brightly as she looked down at the fading pages, "To play in a symphonic orchestra."

I looked down at all of the activities listed. I had never been a big music person, so all I knew was I saw marching band and a whole ton of choirs, "Jeez…"

"What?" Aunt Nina asked.

"That's a lot of choirs." She laughed and started turning the pages again. She stopped on the marching band page. I scanned through the students until I found Aunt Nina. And when I did, I couldn't help but laugh.

She stood there, straighter than a board, and you would've thought she wanted to be anywhere but there. She looked absolutely miserable, "Not one of my best pictures, huh?" Aunt Nina said, nudging me with her elbow. She turned the page.

A better, but still not that attractive, picture showed her up close. Below it was printed *Drum Major*. Another girl stood beside her, "Who's that?" I asked.

Aunt Nina looked down at the picture, "That's Melody," she said, "She was the other Drum Major."

We turned the page. Now we were getting into the choirs. And Aunt Nina littered the next four pages. You name it, she was in it. Madrigal Choir. Regional Choir representatives. Everything.

A picture in the top right corner of a page showed Aunt Nina singing into a microphone, the rest of the choir behind her.

Her mouth was mid-word and her left hand gripped the microphone while her right was opened beside her. She wore a dark, short-sleeved top and a white skirt that ended just below her knees. It was captioned: *Nina Schwartz entertains with her dramatic solo 'My Man'.*

On the next page were more photos. In one, Aunt Nina stood with a group wearing a collared white shirt with a bow tied with a thin cord where the men wore bowties. She was so young and innocent looking; a young girl go did not know tragedy or heart break.

I almost turned the page again, but froze when my glance caught a familiar pair of hands. I didn't even need to look up at the face or over at the caption. I knew to whom they belonged.

I sat there for a moment, just looking at Aunt Nina's hands. They were folded over a floral patterned skirt; her right hand was on top, the pointer finger sticking out. All of the others were folded in with the other hand.

Aunt Nina's soft laugh snapped me back to reality, "What?" I asked.

"Your mother did the exact same thing the first time she flipped through that book," she said. Tears welled up in my eyes, and I looked up at Aunt Nina. She smiled back.

"So why did you become a lawyer?" I asked.

She looked out the window again, "Well, at first my mom tried to ship me off to pre-med with my sister. But at the first sight of blood, I was out," she said, glancing back at me, "So, I left, and word got back to my mom that I wasn't in school, so she sent my dad up after me."

"Where were you? I mean if you weren't in school?" I asked.

"Oh, with a friend who was in college near a beach," she

replied and we both laughed, "So I broke the news to her that I wasn't going to be a doctor, but the friend I was staying with was planning to go to law school, which seemed interesting."

I shook my head, but then my brows furrowed, "But if your mom knew you dream was to play in an orchestra, why did she send you to pre-med?" I asked.

Aunt Nina looked down at me, "Because that's just what it was. A dream; and my mom knew it. Dreams don't pay the bills."

Aunt Nina looked down at the ground, "That's where your mother was better than me. Do you think she dreamed of being a doctor? *No.* But she knew it would pay the bills, so she stuck with it. I, on the other hand, was - *am* - much more dramatic, and of course had to make such a big deal about it," she said.

"What was her dream?" I asked.

Aunt Nina smiled, but her expression fell, "She never really knew. It always changed. She was so smart, and she knew it. She could've done anything," Aunt Nina said, "So she never really decided on one thing. Then the day came when she graduated and our mom shipped her off to college for pre-med. And she didn't fight it."

"How do you know that wasn't her dream? Maybe that's why she didn't fight it," I said.

"No," Aunt Nina said, "Your mother was a people-pleaser." She looked down at me, then back to the mountains, "I remember there were days when she hated it so much and all she wanted to do was quit. She would come home for break and when Mom and Dad weren't in the room, she'd tell me about how much she hated it." Aunt Nina paused, "Or really, I pried it out of her. She knew from the start I would be a good lawyer. Said I had an eye for lies."

"Wow," was all I could say. I was learning so much about my mother I hadn't known. Usually by now, Aunt Nina would be a crying mess. But she sat tall, her eyes dry and her thoughts composed.

After a brief silence, Aunt Nina spoke, "But one thing she was sure she wanted to do was be a good mom to beautiful little girl," she said, closing her eyes and whispering, "And I took that away from her."

A single teardrop slid down her face, but she quickly wiped it away, "We always had this dream of having daughters around the same age, raising them together. Something we always talked about since we were really young."

"Ha, that's cool," I said. There were times when I had wished for a sibling, just so we could joke around and make goofy plans with each other.

"Yeah, and it almost happened," Aunt Nina said quietly. Her gaze looked down at the ground and her fingers picked at her nails furiously. There were so many tears in her eyes, it was a miracle they weren't streaming down her face.

"What do you mean?" I asked.

Aunt Nina tucked her hand within the sleeve of her robe and soaked up the tears from her eyes, "Um, there were parts of the overall story I didn't tell you because you were so young," she said, wiping the last of the tears from her face, "Well, I didn't know anything for sure, but I suspected, that maybe, I might've been pregnant."

The words hit me like a truck, and I looked up, wide-eyed and stunned, "Wait, what?" were the only words I could get out, "Then, why were you drinking?"

"Like I said, I didn't know anything for sure," Aunt Nina said, "And when I say I was drinking, I mean like one or two spiked lemonades. They had almost no alcohol to them whatsoever. I barely felt anything. Like I've told you in the past, I walked a straight line and even did cartwheels. And I had read somewhere that one drink early on wouldn't do anything. So, I thought I was perfectly fine, safe to drive home. But I wasn't."

I didn't know what to say. I didn't even know what to think. Looking up at her, her grace was gone. It was replaced with disappointment, regret, and shame. I reached out for her hand. When I grabbed it, she looked at me, "So, what happened?" I asked.

She took a deep breath, "Well, you know, the accident," she said, and I nodded, "And it turned out I was pregnant." My heart fell. It ached for her, "When the windshield broke, the glass...they said that's what caused..." She paused, taking deep breaths and staring out to the mountains yet again. She didn't even try to stop the tears anymore and they rolled down her face.

"I knew," she started, "I knew if I was pregnant, then if the accident itself didn't kill the baby, then the glass did. But I didn't care. In that moment, all I wanted was to save my sister." I could tell by the look on her face as spoke she was going to collapse, and caught her in my arms. I held her as she bawled into my chest, and it took everything I had not to fall apart.

Her body heaved and shook, and there was nothing I could do. So I sat there, rubbing her back and supporting her weight, "Aunt Nina, it's alright," I said, "It's alright."

The moments inched by as the shaking became less and more controlled. Once she was able to, she sat up on her own, leaning against the window. I grabbed the box of tissues from the dresser and held them out to her. She took one, rubbing her red nose, "That's why my ex-husband and I never had kids," she said looking over at me then towards the wall.

"What?"

"I couldn't after that," she said, "We had had troubles before. But the windshield…all hope was lost," she sniffled and wiped her nose with the tissue, "I honestly believe that, me losing the baby, is part of the reason he cheated."

Her eyes were in a blank stare, and though they faced the wall, she looked at nothing in particular, "But hey," she said and turned to me, "Everything happens for a reason. And I still think, sometimes, maybe I wasn't cut out to be mother. Maybe it wasn't meant to be."

Now I was the one with the blank stare. She couldn't be more wrong, and I had to tell her that. I looked up at her, "Hey," I said, grabbing her hand. She looked at me with those bright hazel eyes, "You're a great mom."

Her bottom lip quivered, and an involuntary whimper escaped from her. I hugged her as more tears trickled down her face, dampening my shirt.

I had a new found respect for my aunt after that. Why? Because I learned that not only was she so compassionate, loving, and understanding, she was all of this after being given such a tragic life.

And I'd always known there was something different about my aunt. Because something happens to a person when they lose their brother-in-law, sister, and unborn child all in one day.

9

"Wow," Josh said, setting his mug back on the counter. His eyes, sunken with compassion, hung below raised brows and a creased forehead.

"I know," I said, "I had no idea." It amazed me that so much could hide behind such a strong and light hearted person.

"Me either," Josh said, lifting the mug from the counter again. As he raised it to his lips and gulped, a small drop of light coffee, filled with a little too much creamer, slipped down his chin.

I perked up when I heard a car door close outside. Spinning around on the barstool, I faced the front door just as it opened. Aunt Nina's legs stretched across the floors with her long and unpoised strides. She bent down briefly to kiss me on the cheek as she passed me at the counter, but something was different about her.

When she looked at me from across the counter, her eyes smiled and her teeth glinted in the light. I looked up at her with a confused stare as a grin crept onto my face. She never smiled with her teeth. *Ever.* I never knew why, she just didn't.

Then I heard a voice pass through the front door and it all made sense. I turned around to see Aaron struggle through the door, bags dangling from his wrists. Aunt Nina set the single bag she carried along with her purse and phone on the counter and hurried to help her boyfriend.

She took the bags from his right hand and kissed him before walking away. They both walked through the cased opening and to the counter where Josh and I still sat.

Aunt Nina began unpacking the bags and Aaron came up behind her, wrapping his hands around her waist. He grabbed the wine from a bag and opened the door of the cabinet to which it belonged, setting the bottle gently inside. And I wondered how many times he's been here to know where the wine cabinet was.

But when I looked over at Josh with his constant swallowing and involuntary spazzes of muscles, not to mention the emotionless, concrete face, I could tell he was holding back the urge to laugh as much as I was. So I decided I'd have a little fun.

I looked at Josh, raising my eyebrows with a quick flick and nodding towards Aunt Nina and Aaron. His face tightened, and he shook his head. And I knew I could crack him. I smiled with the intention of holding it back, but I couldn't help but let it take over my face.

A quick laugh escaped through Josh's nose, and Aunt Nina looked up at him. He looked down, picking up his coffee mug and taking a sip. When she looked away, he almost choked on the coffee, and I had to hold onto his arm and mug to keep him from falling to the ground.

"So what's all this?" I asked, trying to change the subject and keep the attention off of Josh, who was going to crumple to a laughing heap on the floor any second.

"I don't know. We were out and decided to stop," Aaron said still unpacking the bags and putting everything in the right place with no help, "And we thought we'd just spend the day here since Nina's not even supposed to leave the house," he said, giving a heavy dose of guilt with his look towards his girlfriend.

"I know, I know," Aunt Nina said, "I just couldn't lay in a bed any longer." Her smile was so wide, and she looked down shyly when Aaron placed his arms back around her waist.

"Aw, well that's sweet," I said. Josh snorted again and Aunt Nina looked up and glared at him.

"Hey, why don't you go upstairs and pick out something to watch?" Aunt Nina said, looking up at Aaron. He smiled and kissed her before turning towards the foyer. She smiled until he was out of sight, "Stop it! Both of you!" she whipped around and hissed, "Seriously, you need to learn to control yourselves!"

She turned and left the kitchen. And Josh and I almost fell to the ground, bursting with laughter, "I've never - seen her - act that way!" Josh barely got out through desperate gulps of air.

I howled and could barely organize my thoughts, "I told you how they were at the hospital," I said, "It's like watching two ninth graders!" My voice trailed off into more hiccupping laughter.

"Yeah, but I didn't think you were serious!" Josh wheezed, "I just thought you were being dramatic!" We sat there, leaning up against the island until we collected ourselves.

The day was still young, only ten-thirty. Sunlight poured into the kitchen, casting golden rays across the white, marble floors, "Hey," I said, looking at Josh, "Wanna go for a swim?" I asked and Josh smiled.

The warmth of the hot tub was refreshing. I could feel the soft music and the rhythmic splashes from Josh's hands as they echoed through the room. The beeping that ended the timer rang out over the speaker, "Stop," I called out. The sloshing of water ceased. I looked over and Josh rubbed the water from his face, "How many?" I asked.

"Thirty-two," he said.

I turned down the music with the remote that set next to me, "Thirty-two laps in ten minutes, not bad," I said. Josh pulled himself out of the water. His feet slapped the floor as they carried him across the tile floors.

He lowered himself into the hot tub. I let the softness of the music take me away and my eyelids fell. But I jumped when a large puddle of water was thrown into my face. I stared at Josh, trying to be serious. But a smile crept onto my face and Josh splashed me again. I threw water at him and before I knew it, we were engaged in a full-on brawl.

I had Josh's arm twisted behind his back when he elbowed me in the gut. I bent down, gripping the spot where he hit and gasped for air. He took advantage of this moment of weakness and grabbed ahold of me. I pushed his arms from my waist and reached for the stairs. Right as I was about to get out, a hand grabbed my foot and pulled me under the water.

Josh's hands were around my neck, and I wrapped my legs around his head. Pulling him under, I ran out of the hot tub and to the tile of the poolroom's floor. I heard footsteps behind me and hopped out of the way last second. A thud followed by splashing told me that Josh had fallen into the pool, and I jumped in after him.

My body shivered in the coolness of the pool water. Josh grabbed me by the waist, and I was pulled underwater once more.

But we both stopped when we heard Aunt Nina's voice echo throughout the room, "Hey!" All motion stopped, and we faced Aunt Nina. She stood in the doorway, arms folded, "What did I tell you about horsing around in the pool? I thought you two were adults. Stop before someone gets hurt!" Her voice was sharp and we both let go of each other immediately, "Thank you," she said and turned, leaving the room.

We watched her as she walked across the marble floors. She glanced our way through the glass that separated the pool from the hall before disappearing behind the solid wall, "*I thought you two were adults,*" I mocked, starting towards the latter.

"I can still hear you!" Aunt Nina called out as she climbed the stairs to the main floor.

Josh and I laughed and crawled out of the pool. Dropping into a lounge chair, I looked at Josh, "What time is it?"

"Around 6:30," he said, "Wanna eat?"

The sound of our feet against the marble floors was the only sound to be heard as we walked up the stairs. I walked down the hall first. Neither Aunt Nina nor Aaron was in the living room, and from where I stood, they didn't seem to be in the kitchen either.

With only a towel wrapped around my body, the cool air that poured from the fridge froze my body, and I shook. I hunted for something that would be good, but ended up just grabbing the bag of chicken nuggets from the freezer. Dumping them onto a plate, I divided the remaining nuggets evenly between my plate and Josh's and put mine into the microwave.

I took my mother's locket out of the swim jacket that was slung over my shoulder. I put the jacket on as another shiver ran up my spine, "Wait, why'd you take your locket off? You never take it off," Josh said from the counter.

"I didn't," I said, "The clasp broke the other day. I need to get it fixed." I took the plate out of the microwave and put Josh's in. Waiting for the timer to go off, I leaned up against the counter. The day was beautiful but cold. My wet, braided hair dripped down my back. I stood when the microwave beeped and brought Josh's plate to where he sat at the counter

We sat there in stools at the island, eating chicken nuggets, dipping them in ketchup like little kids. Hours later, around 8:30, I heard the water kick on upstairs. A text from Aunt Nina immediately followed.

I looked at the bright screen next to my plate on the counter. A frantic message from Aunt Nina read, *'Come upstairs RIGHT NOW.'* I looked at Josh, but he just shrugged. Confused, I shoved the phone into my pocket and hurried up the steps.

When I reached the top of the stairs, Aunt Nina stood in the hallway, glancing nervously at the bathroom door. She saw me in the corner of her gaze and grabbed me by the arm, pulling me into her room and shutting the door, "Alright listen," she started, "I already told him he could stay. I mean, he has in the past so that's not a big deal."

"Wait, what?" I asked.

"Yeah, he's stayed. Anyway, I need you to be my scapegoat," she said.

"Aunt Nina, what's wrong?" I asked.

"Aaron and I were talking, and somehow got on the subject of marriage," Aunt Nina moaned. She was totally freaking out.

I mean pacing back and forth, breathing heavily, full on panic.

"So, hold on," I said, "When you say you were talking about marriage, do you mean he was like 'Will you marry me?' or was it a 'Hey, do you see marriage in our future?'" I was so confused.

Aunt Nina's face was pale and she still paced. "He was all like, 'What do think about us ever getting married? Like, could it happen?' And after he asked me to marry him a few months ago-"

"What?" I asked, "He asked you to marry him?" She nodded, "And you said no?" She nodded again, "Why?"

And for the first time since I had come upstairs, Aunt Nina stopped pacing. She sat on the bed. Her breathing calmed, and she looked up at me, "I couldn't say yes."

I sat down beside her, "Why not?"

Her shoulders fell, "I just couldn't. Not after..."

I looked at her. She looked scared and worried, like she was going to pass out, "Hey," I said, grabbing her arm, "It's okay."

Her eyes met mine and she smiled, "Yeah. So I panicked."

I laughed, "Yeah, a little. But it's alright. What did you need me to do?" I asked.

Her face pinched, "I need to crawl in bed with me and fall asleep so Aaron has to sleep in the guest bedroom." The words came out so quickly, I almost didn't catch them.

"Aunt Nina-"

She folded her hands in front of her chest, "Please," she begged.

"Why can't you just talk to him?" I asked.

"Because," Aunt Nina whined, "It got all weird after that. So he got up and said he'd take a shower and that we'd talk about it when he gets back. And I don't wanna talk about it. So please?"

I rolled my eyes but agreed, "So, wait. He actually asked you to marry him?" I asked.

"Yeah," Aunt Nina said and nodded, "Yeah, he did."

I shook my head, "Wow."

We both froze when we heard the water shut off down the hall. Aunt Nina scrambled under the covers, and I laughed as I made my way to the bed next to her. Memories of the sleepless nights of my childhood rushed back as I wrapped my arms around her chest and threw my left leg on top of hers. I laid my head on her chest and shut my eyes just as the door opened.

Aunt Nina's hand stroked my hair lightly, "Hey," she whispered.

"Hey," Aaron said from the doorway, his voice hushed, "Is she alright?"

I felt Aunt Nina's hair move as she nodded her head, "Yeah, I just think she's sick." Aunt Nina's hand still stroked my hair as another felt my forehead, "She's fevered."

"Aw, that sucks," Aaron said, "I'll take the guest bedroom, then?"

"Yeah, that's fine," Aunt Nina said, and she smiled. When the door closed, I opened my eyes. But I until I had lain down, I hadn't noticed how the sleep pulled down on my eyes and

tugged at my mind. I let my eyes fall shut, and I drift away...

A slam pulled me out of sleep. I looked to my right, but the bed was empty and Aunt Nina was gone. The ground was cold beneath my feet as I crawled out of the bed. I hurried towards the bedroom door.

When I entered the hall, I found Aunt Nina standing at the top of the steps. The sour stench of smoke surrounded me like a gray, suffocating pillow. The door to the guest bedroom flung open and Josh and Aaron rushed out, "You smell it too?" Aunt Nina asked. Then the fire alarm went off.

The loud screeching cut through the dark and silent night. We all flew down the stairs. Josh called 911 as Aunt Nina ran to the kitchen. The blinding flames wrapped themselves around the wooden cabinets. Yellows and oranges danced across the room's edges, their heat smothering.

I stood there, numb to the horror happening before my eyes. Aunt Nina called my name, pulling on my arm, "Allison, we have to go!" I turned my body to leave, but my eyes were still glued to the blues and oranges of the growing flames. Then I froze. *My mother's locket.*

I ran back towards the flaming countertops, "Allison, no!" Aunt Nina yelled from where she stood. The heat radiated off of the surfaces. I set my hand on the metal handle of the stove, but pulled it back.

I lost my footing and fell to the ground. The searing skin on my hand throbbed, and the fires enclosed around me. In every direction I looked, glowing flames grew closer and left light-sensitive blotches in my vision.

The heat broiled at my flesh as the small area I had left compressed. There was shrieking, barely audible in my ringing ears over the crackling of the flames. But there was no mistake whose it was - *Aunt Nina.* There were cries pushing through the roars.

My heart quickened. Looking around the kitchen, I finally understood the severity of what I had done. The skin on the bottom of my right foot bubbled and boiled, and I pulled it in even closer. The smoke was filling my lungs and a dizziness pulled me down. I hugged my knees closer to my chest, feeling the heat against the ends of my toes.

I felt a hand on my arm and looked up.

Aaron pulled me out of the flames. His fingers were gentle against my burns, and he was careful not to worsen the pain radiating through my arm. A short blast of scolding heat flashed over my skin as Aaron yanked me from my little hole on the floor.

When I rose from the flames, I was met by Aunt Nina's hands. Tears flooded her eyes, though they were irately bitter. The four of us hurried across the room towards the living room, but the fire had spread, blocking our exit.

"This way!" Josh shouted, pulling me towards the back door. Aunt Nina and Aaron followed. I looked back at the kitchen before finally leaving, and a memory of Aunt Nina flashed before my eyes.

I stand on my tiptoes next to Aunt Nina at the stove. She glances down at me and smiles. Lifting me from the ground, she sits me on the kitchen counter between her and the fridge, and I look at the frying pan on the stovetop. The searing of skin is followed by a heavenly scent that makes my mouth water.

I swing my legs back and forth, letting them bounce off of the cabinets below me, "Did my mom like to cook?" I ask.

"She loved it," Aunt Nina says, giving me a quick smile, "Said the kitchen was her favorite part of the house."

The outside air was cold and crisp. I gasped for breaths, choking on the smoke that still filled my lungs. Sirens came from the road.

All around me was mayhem. People ran past me while others asked questions. A man asked us to back away from the house, pushing me further down the lawn. Then I felt a sharp grip dig into my arm, "What were you thinking?" Aunt Nina yelled, "What on earth possessed you to run into the fire like that? Do you know what could've happened? What would you have done if Aaron didn't get you? Ugh, you're such an idiot!"

She glared at me with drilling eyes, "I'm sorry," I said, my head down, "I left Mom's locket on the counter. I was going back for it."

Aunt Nina's face relaxed, "Listen," she started, "It's just a locket. You're more important than a necklace. I can replace the locket. I can't replace you." Her words her soft and she pulled me into a close embrace.

We all waited until a man dressed in heat-resistant clothing came up to us, "How the fire started is a mystery," the man started, "The oven was off, and nothing was plugged into the outlets in or around the kitchen," he said. He lifted his hand, "We found this inside. I thought I'd bring it to you."

The silver was still warm in my hands. I opened the heart. The picture of my mother and Aunt Nina was still safe inside. The bottom half of the heart was darkened, but the black was wiped away with a few strokes of my thumb, "Thank you," I whispered through a throat choked with tears.

Aunt Nina wrapped her arm around me then looked back at the firefighter, "If everything was off and unplugged in the kitchen then how, and where, did the fire start?" she asked.

"Well, the fire started in the garage and spread to the kitchen by the looks of it," he answered. A man walked up to the firefighter. After a moment, the firefighter turned back to us,

"This was found in a pool of gasoline in the garage."

The neon-orange flare was blackened, but something seemed familiar about the casing. I struggled to put my finger on it. Where would I have seen this before? Then it hit me.

As I run out of the room, stuffing the money in a bag, I notice something on the door. A symbol, spray painted in black, covered most of the metal. I look at it for a second and continue running into the street. But I am picked up and thrown against a wall, hands tightening around my throat...

The black symbol was unmistakable. Looking at Aunt Nina, she stood as still as a cement statue. Her eyes were wide and her mouth barely opened, her hand covering it. She knew what this meant. This meant it wasn't over yet after all.

But why would Mick start the fire in the garage? It was nowhere near where Aunt Nina and I slept, "Wait, Aunt Nina?"

Her head turned, but it was slow and empty, her eyes lifeless. Josh, standing next to her, turned to face me. I looked from Aunt Nina to him, "The garage, it's right below where you and Aaron were sleeping."

Aunt Nina brought her hand up to her head, the other on her hip, the words, "Dear God," barely escaping her mouth. She bent over and crouched to the ground.

Josh didn't respond, but stared at the flare in the firefighter's hand. His gaze still on the blackened casing, he took a breath and whispered into my ear, "Do you want to tell me about that idea you had at the hospital now?"

10

"Lost at sea?"

"No," I said, "She'll never really let it go, spend the rest of her life looking for me."

"So then what *can* we tell her?" Josh asked. His legs were thrown over the side of the white armchair in the corner, and he fiddled with a Rubik's cube, but had no real intentions of solving it.

"I don't know." It broke my heart to think about this. What could he tell my aunt? *How* could he tell my aunt? The thoughts, a whirlwind in my head, were too much, too confusing to sort through. Lying on my back, the sill of the bay window below me, I dropped my hands over my face.

"The easiest way to do it would have to be suicide," Josh said after a moment of silence.

"No," I said, sitting up, "I can't do that to her. She would always think it was her fault, and that's not something I can live with." And it wasn't. I was already going to hurt her so much, I couldn't leave her with that burden as well.

"Well, if you don't make up your mind, you're not going to have to live with anything, because you won't be living at all," Josh said, tossing the Rubik's cube onto the vanity. I glared at him and he shrugged, "It's true," he said.

"Jesus, and I have to go back to school next week," I said, dropping to my back again. I looked out the window. The morning was dying, fading to noon. I heard the sounds of power tools downstairs. Men were replacing our cabinets, and Aunt Nina had told us not to get in the way, banishing us to my room.

"Really?" Josh asked.

"Yeah," I said and rolled onto my stomach, "Dorms open Saturday." I folded my arms and rested my head in them. How was I going to do this at school? I barely had time to breathe, let alone plan and fake my own death.

"How are you gonna do this, then?" Josh asked as if he read my mind. Then he looked up as if something hit him, "What if you ditch?" he asked. I rolled my eyes, "No, really. You can stay with me so Nina doesn't find out," he said, "And wouldn't a fake ID be something you're gonna need? I have a buddy in Mountain View who could help us. We could go, and you get your stuff, and I'll get the ID."

"Okay," I said. I still wasn't completely sure about this. Something could easily go wrong. What would happen if I failed? I tried to clear my head and spoke, "Back to the original question: how will I 'die'?" I asked, using my fingers to put quotes around the word.

Josh and I sat in silence, thinking. Neither of us spoke for minutes, until Josh sat up with an idea, but caught himself before speaking, "No, what were you going to say?" I asked.

He shook his head, "After suicide or lost at sea, a car

accident would probably be the easiest thing," he said. And I knew why he hesitated before speaking. He could read on my face how I felt about this, "See. Suicide is easiest," he said.

But I still couldn't do that to Aunt Nina, even if it meant - to her - her niece would die the same way her sister did, "No, we'll go with an accident," I said. I rubbed my face with my hands, feeling a slight sting where my fingers touched the stitched skin. Dear God, I hoped she wouldn't start drinking again.

I froze for a moment, a memory from middle school making me shudder.

The halls feel different. I feel different. Everything *feels different. I just couldn't understand why - or how. How you can do that to your wife, someone you supposedly love? If he really loved us, he never would've done that.* This.

I am embarrassed, honestly. How horrible of a man do you have to be to even consider it? He claims he was drinking, and that's the reason why he did it. But that's not true. If you cheat when you're drunk, you'd considered it sober; alcohol affects your actions, not your morals.

No one will know, I've decided. Unless Aunt Nina tells them, no one will know what went down at my house last night.

"Hey, Allison," Ethan says, stepping out in front of me, "I heard about what happened last night."

Great.

"How?" I ask. My hands start trembling, and I wonder if he knows, who else does?

"My mom's friends with your Aunt Nina, I guess," he says, not even looking at me, "I was listening to my mom talk to her on the phone last night." He stares over my shoulder, "Don't

worry, I won't tell." He looks back at me, "My dad left not that long ago."

I nod, "Oh," I said. I turn. This conversation is awkward, and I just want to go to class.

"But," he says, grabbing my arm before I push past him, "don't expect your aunt to be the same."

I am taken back by this, "What do you mean?" I ask. My heart starts pounding. What is he talking about?

"When my dad left, my mom was changed. Has been ever since," he replies, "Some of the things we loved to do we don't even do anymore. And, from what I've gathered from my... sources...your aunt had a drinking problem, didn't she?"

I stare back at him wide-eyed, "Yeah," he continues, "you'll have to watch out for her from now on."

I want to hit him. Who does he think he is, telling me what's going to happen to my aunt? He doesn't know her. She wouldn't do that to me, "You're wrong," I shoot back.

"Excuse me?"

"You're wrong. My Aunt Nina is smarter than that. She wouldn't do that. She won't!" I turned and stormed down the hall. But for the rest of the day one question buzzed around my mind: Will Aunt Nina actually change?

I spoke through my hands, which covered my face, "God, I just hope Aaron takes care of her."

"And you're sure you're not forgetting anything?" Aunt Nina asked as I loaded my bags into the car. She stood there with her arms crossed in the darkness that comes with the early morning. She rubbed her eyes with one hand, the pale wash of sleep still over her face. Her black robe blew lightly in the wind and she shivered.

"Yes, now go inside before you get pneumonia," I said and slammed the trunk shut, "I love you." I wrapped my arms around her tightly, and her hands flattened against the small of my back. I stayed there for minutes. I wanted to stay forever and never let go. Stay in her arms and let the world around me slip away, along with the fears and worries, and never return to reality.

But, eventually, I had to, "Bye," I finally said, pulling away. She took my face in her hands. I rested my palm against the top of hers, and I could feel the veins that ran under her skin. With a smile, I turned and got into the car.

Josh sat in the passenger seat as I started the engine, "You're very brave," he said and fastened his seat belt.

"Oh, no. Not yet," I said. I wasn't. The day I would call myself brave would be the day I walked away knowing that was the last time I'd see her. Until then, I was just a coward, running from all of her problems and fears.

I put the car in reverse and trailed down the driveway. Looking through the windshield, I stole one last glance up the drive. Aunt Nina stood in front of the door, arms folded and body caved inwards. She blew a kiss and waved. I smiled and lifted my hand briefly from the wheel before finally pulling out, speeding down the road.

"Dear God. You're not going to cry, are you?" I whipped my head around to face Josh and coughed, clearing the tears that blocked my throat, "Because I love you Allison, but dear God, I cannot take one more meltdown."

I looked at him, wide-eyed, "I'm not going to cry," I said, trying to convince myself more than him. His brow arched, "I'm not," I repeated and turned back to the road, beginning the six hour car ride.

The air chilled me as I stepped out of the car. It was colder there at Stanford, and the light jacket I barely got away with at home was not cutting it, "So, you know what you're going to do?" Josh asked.

I nodded, "Go inside, 'get settled in', meet you out here when everyone goes to sleep." Josh nodded, getting back into the car, "Josh?" He looked up just before shutting the door, "What if they're watching us?"

Josh's face rose almost unnoticeably, and then fell back into place, "Then they're going to see a guy drop off his best friend then go meet up with a buddy from college," he said, "And that's it."

I looked into his eyes, fighting to push back tears, and I tried to believe everything he was saying. *What if something went wrong?* The question ran circles around head, even minutes after Josh left.

Walking silently to my dorm, I breathed in the crisp northern California air. It was different from the busy, heavy air of Los Angeles. Somehow, out there, the air seemed cleaner, and unbroken. The silence of the morning wrapped itself around me, giving me a peace and moment of relaxation.

The only sounds came from the birds and the rhythmic tapping of feet from other students travelling in, still dead to the world with sleep. I almost couldn't wait to get to my dorm just so I could fall back asleep. The hall of my building was completely silent, so I nearly jumped out of my skin when I heard a voice over my shoulder as I unlocked my door, "Hey, Allison!"

I flinched, almost falling into the door. Fidgeting with the keys, I unlocked the door and turned to face whoever was talking to me "Jillian, hi. Sorry, didn't see you come up the stairs."

When I turned, around her eyes tripled in size, "OMG, what happened? Did you, like, get into an accident?" She asked.

"Um," I stammered, "Yeah, Josh and I went out for a drink. I'm fine, though." I really did not feel like talking to her. I just wanted to sleep.

"Ohmigod, so like is everyone alright? Like was it just you two?" She asked. I tried to speak when I thought she was done, but she kept pressing, "Where were your parents? Ooohhh, what happened when they found out?"

Oh, yes. The hidden secret. No one at college knew what had happened. At home, everyone knew, and I was the just little girl who lost her parents – it was a constant pity party. And it got old.

I wanted a new life for me at college, so I never told anyone about what happened to my parents. I guess they just assumed I had them, even if I never mentioned them. Some days, we would all be out, and someone would say something like, "...then my parents said no. Parents, you know how they are." Everyone would smile and agree, and I would just nod along. I'd always believed there was no point in revealing what didn't need to be known.

"Um, it's fine, no one got really hurt," I replied to Jillian's hundreds of questions, "I got it worse, Josh is basically unscathed." I let out a little laugh, trying to make the lie believable.

Jillian eyed me. Then she shook her head, losing interest completely, "Hey, the girls and I are going out later. Last night before hell starts back up. Wanna come?" she asked. She tugged on her black Calvin Klein top and leaned against my door frame, her arm raised above her head.

"Nope," I answered a little too quickly. Her brows furrowed and she looked hurt. "I'm good," I said a little slower this time, "I think I'm just gonna sleep, relax and rest up before the hundreds of lectures I'm still not ready to endure." I laughed again, but I could tell Jillian wasn't going to leave it at that.

"Why don't you ever come?" she asked bluntly, "I mean, out to drink and let loose? You're always 'sleeping' or 'resting' or 'doing homework'," she said. Her arms were folded across her chest now, and she was waiting for an answer.

"What do you mean?" I asked, "I just went out..." I trailed off and tried to think of the last time I actually went out. *Shit.*

"See, exactly. You avoid it like the plague, like you're scared of it."

And she was right on target.

The sunlight feels so good on my face. I couldn't take that stuffy school much longer. Today was so different, and I just can't wait to get home. I start scanning the line of cars, looking for Aunt Nina's. But I can't seem to find it. I shrug and work my way down the line. Maybe she's parked at the end.

As I walk down the hill, my phone buzzes. I look down, and I see a message from Aunt Nina. Just a simple message saying, Ride the bus home.

Why? *I ask.*

But she simply replies, Just do it.

I get onto the bus. The bus driver doesn't even know who I am; I've never ridden the bus. Aunt Nina has always come to get me, "Excuse me?"

The bus driver looks up at me just before she pulls out of the school parking lot, "Yes, dear?"

"May I sit up front?" I ask, "I don't normally ride, and the principle said this would be my bus if I did."

My hands are fidgeting. I am nervous and the bus driver can tell, "Sure, where do you live?"

I sit down in the seat diagonal to the bus driver, "903 Alpine Dr., in Beverly Park." The bus driver's eyes grow large, and the kids behind me cease to speak. I know I live in a rich neighborhood, but I swear, every time? Like it's a shock to them. My best friend, Josh, who's in the eighth grade, says it's the sweat pants and t-shirts that throws everyone off.

"Okay," the bus driver says and pulls out of the school. I was one of the last kids left on the bus. I pointed to my street and the bus driver opened the doors, "Have a nice day now, dear," she says and closes the doors. I wave, then turn to walk up the drive.

I open the front door and drop my bag, "I'm home!" I call out. But as soon as I walked into the house, I knew something was wrong. Walking through the opening under the staircase, I call out again, "Aunt Nina?"

The living room is empty, and it's weird. Every day, ever since I was in preschool, Uncle Peter sat on the couch, waiting for me to come home. I would walk through the door, run and hug him, and tell him about my day. Aunt Nina would come, sitting down on the other side of him, and kiss her husband. With him missing, and the spot on the couch empty, I feel as though a piece of me, of my childhood, is gone and empty too.

I hear a shuffle in the kitchen and hurry there. The question I had asked myself when Ethan spoke to me earlier returns. Will Aunt Nina actually change?

I gasp when I walk into the kitchen. In all of the time I have lived with my aunt and uncle, I have never, ever, *seen my aunt drink. Ever. But when I walk into the kitchen, Aunt Nina is sitting there at the counter, an open bottle of whiskey next to her at the counter, "Aunt Nina?"*

My words startle her, and my heart is pounding so loudly in my ears, I'm amazed the thumping hadn't given away my presence earlier.

Something is in her hands - a picture. I slide ever so slightly to the left, just enough to see what the photo is of. Aunt Nina and Uncle Peter on their wedding day. *My heart breaks. This is hurting me so badly, and I can only imagine how it's killing her.*

Her big, hazel eyes look at me, but they don't look the same. Not the eyes I have seen every day for the past eleven years. They seem scared and hurt. They seem broken.

I walk over to the counter and wrap my arms around Aunt Nina, "Wanna go sit outside? The mountains are beautiful toda-"

But mid-sentence, Aunt Nina throws my arms off of her body and pushes me back, "No," she says, not even looking up at me, "Just go to your room."

The weeks stretched, and the communication between us grew less and less until it was almost nothing. Aunt Nina, already model thin, lost tons of weight, and I realized Ethan was right. My aunt had a drinking problem. And what was happening to her, I knew I never wanted that to happen to me. Because she's changed.

And she had never been the same.

"Hello. Earth to Allison," Jillian said, waving a hand in front of my face.

I was getting annoyed and pushed my things through the door, "Not tonight Jillian. See you in class." And with that, I closed the door and got my peace and quiet. And man was it amazing. No crazy murderers. No alcoholic aunts. No suffocating worries. Just peace and quiet.

The day went by too quickly, though. Before I knew it, a strong buzzing pulled me out of my nap. It was Josh.

"Are you coming?" he said when I answered the phone. I pulled the glass away from my ear. It was already 12:30 a.m.

"Crap, yeah. Just let me get everything together and I'll be out." The words were a whisper with sleep as I literally fell out of the bed, intentionally.

The car was warm when I finally got into it. The short walk from the dorms and across the parking lot was ridiculously cold. I grabbed a blanket from the backseat of my car - wait, why was I sitting the passenger seat of *my* car? - and wrapped it around my shoulders, "It's fucking freezing," I mumbled.

"Yeah, yeah," Josh said and cranked up the heat.

The car ride was silent as I shivered in the cold. I had never been a morning person. Ever, "Shit," I said about three hours into the drive back to Josh's place.

"What?"

"I forgot to call Aunt Nina and tell her I made it safely," I said. I reached for my phone in my pocket. But it wasn't there. I looked down, digging through a second time to make sure. But all I found was a twenty and three pennies, "Josh, I had my phone when I got in the car, right?"

"I have no idea, but I am *not* turning around and driving another three hours."

"I had it," I started, sorting through the trash on the floor of the passenger side, "before I got in. I sat it on the hood when I was putting my stuff in the car. Did I pick it back up?" My actions were more frantic now, hands sifting and objects flying.

"I don't know, but I'll tell you what. I'm starving and this gas station has a McDonald's. We'll stop to get gas, and while I get the food, you'll stay to pump gas and look for your phone. It has to be here somewhere." He flicked on the turn signal, veering right.

I shifted my weight back and forth between my two feet, waiting for the gas to finish pumping. The blood inside of me was at a skyrocket temperature. How could I not find my phone? Josh had been inside for fifteen minutes already, and I searched the whole car. Nothing.

I just couldn't understand how a phone could just get up and walk away. Finally, I heard the *click* of the pump and pulled it out of the car. A sharp stench wafted from the station and my whole body twitched. I never could stand the smell of gasoline.

The cold metal of the car sent a chill to bleed through the blanket and my clothes as I leaned against it. I could see Josh through the glass, paying for our meals. Then he froze.

His head nodded and I realized the idiot was talking to the cashier. I thought he was starving. I cursed under my breath and slammed the car door shut after sitting inside. The warmth slowly slipped out of the vehicle, and without Josh, I had no keys to start the car.

So, I sat there, rubbing my arms, but as I did, my eyes caught glimpse of something on the hood of the car. Something shined under the light. *Glass.*

I pulled on the cold, metal handle of the door and pushed it open. I walked towards the hood of the car slowly, one foot after the other. I tried to steady my hands as I brought both to my mouth. But they, as well as the rest of me, trembled, and my heart stopped beating.

Right there, glinting under the lights overhead, laid a shimmering black glass along with the rest of my phone.

11

But how?

The question drove me mad. There was something pink, a sticky note, gripping the screen. I stood aghast, staring at the cell on the white Ferrari's hood. Almost cowering away, I pulled away from the phone. I was hesitant to pick it up it, scared, as if even touching it would end my life on the spot.

That's just ridiculous. I ripped the note from the glass, feeling the crisp, new paper between my fingers. The blue writing bled through to the back of the paper, and when I pulled the note off of the screen, my fingers smudged the still drying ink.

How's college life? Must not be too great if you're running off so quickly. Is it me, or do you have a problem with following the rules? And oh, I almost forgot! Don't forget to call Aunt Nina - she's worried about you.

The air may have been frigid, but I was not cold. The blood that pumped through my veins could have made a fresh, whistling pot of tea. I turned around, kicking a garbage can. The note still crumpled within, I threw my fist at the concrete pillar behind me.

But it was soft. *Wait, soft?* I opened my eyes to find that my fist hadn't hit the concrete, but, in fact, was stopped by a hand inches before slamming into the pillar. My gaze trailed across the skin, up the arm, until it landed on the familiar tattoo of the ram, "That will not end well. For you or your hand," Josh said. He threw my hand back down to my side, "What was that all about?"

"They had my phone the whole time!" I screeched, "They had it, and they know I left!" My hands balled into fists, and I almost went for the pillar again, "What are we gonna do now?"

Josh grabbed me by the shoulders, steadying my pacing body, "I don't know, but you need to chill. And an anger management class. Here," he said, handing me something from a bag, "Have a snickers. You're not you when you're hungry."

I sent my open hand into his shoulder and reluctantly opened the candy bar. I really was hungry, "But seriously, what are we gonna do?"

"Nothing at four in the morning," he said, "We're both exhausted. Just wait 'till we get home, then we'll figure it out," he paused, "Only a few more weeks and it will all be over." There was a pain in his words, a small sliver of weakness that showed through his voice. He dropped himself into the car and I followed.

The phone's icy glass fogged up in my fingers. I held it in front of the blowing heater, trying to zap the life back into it. The screen brightened, glowing blindingly white and illuminating the entire car. Eight percent. *Assholes. It was on 76 before I left.*

My phone, as if it were trying to run away, buzzed in my hand uncontrollably. Messages from Aunt Nina poured in one after another.

Hey, just checking, did you make it?

Are you there?

Allison?

1 missed call from Aunt Nina.

Are you alright?

1 missed call from Aunt Nina.

After all that's happened, I'd like to know you're okay.

3 missed calls from Aunt Nina.

ANSWER ME, PLEASE.

Josh isn't answering either. Are you two together?

1 missed call from Aunt Nina.

Fine, I'm going to bed, if you don't call me in the morning, I'm coming up there.

I scrambled for the lime green phone icon on the screen. Aunt Nina woke up at five every morning, and the last thing I needed was for her to drive to school and find out I'm not there.

"Aunt Nina, hi," I said when the line picked up at the other end.

"I'm severely pissed."

"I know, I'm so sorry," I said, "Really. My phone's been...dead. And I fell asleep. I'm really sorry again." I held my breath; this could go one of two ways.

She let out a breath, "Don't let it happen again," she said, "I was just about to get into the car. With all of the things that have been happening, I need you to answer me and let me know you're okay, understand?" Her tone was firm, but there was an underlying tenderness in her words.

"Yes, yes. I understand," I said, "It won't happen again. Really sorry."

"Yeah, yeah," she said. There was a shuffling in the background, followed by a noise. Aaron? "I'll see you Saturday?"

"Saturday," I said, "Love you, bye."

"Bye. Love you."

The line went dead and I let out a gust of breath, "Thank God," I said to Josh. I laid my phone in the center console, plugging the charger into the bottom.

Lying back in the seat, I pulled the blanket over my whole body and locked my arms within its warmth. I kicked off my Uggs and closed my eyes, slowly letting every muscle in my body relax.

I fought to peel my eyes open under the bright lights of the lobby. Raising my arm above my head, I was able to shield some of the light, but it barely made a difference. My feet slid across the floor, lethargically; I just wanted to go back to sleep.

We walked to the elevators, the only people in sight. I looked up, about to hit a button, when Josh hit my hand away. I glared at him, but he pointed at a sloppy piece of paper taped to the elevator doors.

Out of Order. Please take stairs.

I dropped my bags on the floor rolling my head to look at Josh. He shifted his finger towards the stairs. Josh's apartment was on the sixth floor. *Sixth.* I was *not* walking up six flights of stairs.

"Let's go," Josh complained, as if reading my mind, "There's no other way." I whined and pounded my foot against the concrete floor before following Josh up the stairs, stomping the whole way up, "Nina's right," he said, turning to face me, "You act like a three-year-old."

Josh's apartment was absolutely *frigid*. Like, liquid nitrogen frigid, "What the actual hell, Josh?" My voice chattered with my teeth, and I curled up under a blanket thicker than mine. But the comforter only made me colder.

Throwing it off, I stared Josh down, "It's my apartment," he said, "If you don't like it, then you can go home with your aunt and explain to her why you're not in school. Now, get out of my bed."

I knew he was right, and I hated it. I stared him down, pulling my purple fleece blanket back over me and walking to the black futon under the window. I dropped into the soft fabric and fell asleep as soon as my head hit the pillow.

Josh killed the engine, and we got out of the car. The old funeral home looked as run-down as ever. When we walked inside, the smell of 'old people' greeted us, "Who is it?" someone called out from a room.

A short little man with feathery, snowy hair came down the hall, a slight limp from his disabled right leg, "Allison! So nice to see you, dear," the man said.

"Hi, Richard," I said, hugging the little man, "Listen, I need a favor."

"I assume you do," Richard laughed, "No other reason for you two youngins to be coming around a funeral home. Whatever you need, I'm at your service." He gave a small bow.

"Thanks, Richard," I said with a smile.

"Anything for Caroline and Ben's little girl," he replied, "What is it you need?"

I looked uneasily at Josh, "I need you to hold a funeral. My funeral."

At first, Richard laughed. But once he realized I was serious, he stopped instantly, "Wait, you're joking, right?"

"No, I'm not," I said. His face changed and I could tell he was confused. I looked again at Josh, and he nodded, "Well, you see..."

I gave Richard the quick, basic version of the story, "And now she wants to fake her death," Josh cut in at the end.

"You want to do *what*?" Richard asked.

Josh slapped my arm, still looking at Richard, "I said the exact same thing."

"Allison, you know it's against federal law to fake your own death, right?" Richard asked. His face was deeply concerned, and he looked at me as if I had gone mad.

"Yeah, I know," I said, "But Richard, they'll kill me if I don't. And Aunt Nina."

At the mention of my aunt, Richard's face changed again. He'd been close with my family for as long as I could remember, "Well, like I said, anything for you, darling," he said and kissed my hand.

"Thanks, Richard, you're the best," I said with a smile.

"Okay, great, now can we get out of here?" Josh spit from behind me. He drove his hands into pockets, looking around impatiently.

"Okay, then," I said and turned, "Thanks again, Richard." I gave him another hug, and then turned for the door. Right before exiting, I looked back at Richard, "We'll keep in touch?"

"Yep," the little man said, "Just give me the details and you'll have the most beautiful fake funeral the world has ever seen." I smiled and waved, "Bye bye, now," Richard said as I closed the wooden door behind me.

On the safety of the empty steps, I pushed Josh into a metal banister, "What the hell was that about? He's doing us a favor!"

"*You*," he said, "He's doing *you* a favor." His words were harsh and biting. He started down the steps, towards the car.

"What is your problem?" I asked trailing behind him, "Did I do something to piss you off?"

"No."

"That's what I thought," I said. I opened the car door as Josh started the engine, "So again, what is your problem?"

"I just needed to get out of there! Sorry for not wanting to hang around the last place I ever saw my sister."

The words hung in the air, their heaviness weighing down on the both of us. I couldn't believe I had been so insensitive, "Josh, I am so sorry," I said, resting a hand on his arm, "I completely forgot."

Josh looked over at me, "It's alright," he finally said, "Just was unsettling, you know?"

"Yeah, I wasn't thinking," I said, "An-"

"Listen," Josh said, pulling onto the road, "I told you it was fine. I don't want to talk about it."

"Yeah, ok." There was a tenseness in the car, and I looked out the window, trying to escape it. As we drove down the road, I caught glimpses of the mountains through the buildings. If I tried hard enough, I could almost imagine the windows to disappear, and it was just me and the mountains. No one in my ears, no cities. Just me and the mountains.

The silence was first broken by Josh, "Hey. What do you wanna eat?"

"Whatever you want is fine," I said, "Oh, but not Arby's. I hate that place."

Josh laughed, "Yes ma'am." We eventually decided on a McDonald's drive through. Balancing the cup holder with two green milkshakes in my lap, I opened the bag and handed Josh his food, "Okay now that you're done being a crabass," he started. I looked at him in protest, "Don't even try to deny it. You cussed me out, like, thirty times last night. Anyway, I have your ID at home. Don't let me forget to give it to you. It's in my bedside table under all of the books."

I took a sip of my Shamrock Shake, "Okay."

When I walked into Josh's apartment, I headed straight for the shower. The tiles under my feet sent a chill through my socks and up my spine. I turned the handle, pulling it a little over half way, and waited for the water to warm.

The mirror that hung above the sink showed my reflection. The white, scarring skin ran across my face. A smaller wound lay over my jaw. I ran my fingers over the scars, remembering the fear from when I got them.

I closed my eyes and looked back at the shower. Steam fogged the glass. I opened the door and climbed inside. The water was so warm, so comforting. I had always found peace in the shower. I was alone, no one to bother me.

I grabbed a brown rag, covering it in soap. As it ran over my body, I felt the tug on the skin that still healed from the burns, and avoided those areas. I washed my hair, the back of my head still tender to the touch, but bearable. My fingers massaged my scalp, rubbing away the stress and worry I harbored inside. Then the water went cold.

I screamed a loud, angry scream. Laughing followed. I grabbed a towel from the closet, tracking water all over the floors. Wrapping the towel around my body, I stormed to the kitchen. I threw the wet rag I still had in my hand at Josh, and he ducked. The rag hit him square in the face, "You jerk!" I hissed.

The sound of the running dishwasher and the steam that rose from its vents made me furious. I marched over to the dishwasher and held down the cancel button. The whole thing jerked as the water kicked off and drained. I hit Josh, who was still laughing, and hurried back to my shower.

The water had warmed by the time it took me to get back and wipe the water from the floor. Ever since I was a little girl, Aunt Nina had always scolded me for tracking water on the floor, and now, I couldn't help but clean it up out of habit.

Rinsing the conditioner from my hair, I finished my shower then turned the water off. I dried down with a towel and pulled on a Stanford hoodie and gray leggings. When I walked past the kitchen, the dishwasher was running again, and Josh was cooking something at the stove. I looked at the time on the microwave, "How long had I been in there?" I asked.

"Almost an hour," Josh said, "I'll let it slide this time, but don't expect to take an hour shower every day."

"Yeah, ok," I said, biting into an apple from the bowl on the island, "What are you making?"

"Marinated chicken," Josh replied, "It's gonna have to sit for a while, though, that's why I'm starting it now."

I nodded, "Wanna watch a movie?" I asked, sitting on the

couch. I picked up the PlayStation remote and flicked through the titles. Then I remembered, "Oh, Josh! The ID," I said and looked back at him.

"Oh, yeah. You go get it; I'll finish up here and find something to watch."

While Josh remained at the stove, I walked to the bedroom. Looking around the room, I let my eyes flick around until they laid on the nightstand. I walked over to it and dropped to my knees.

I opened the drawer and lifted the books, looking for my ID. But I only saw the wooden bottom of the drawer. I sifted through the drawer's contents, lifting each individual book. But there was nothing there.

I tried the bottom drawer, but as I had suspected, it was nothing but Josh's underwear. I knew him well enough to know that when he hid things, that's where he would put them - in his top drawer of the nightstand.

And now it seemed someone else did too.

12

"What do you mean *it's not there?*" Josh called from the living room. His thunderous steps pounded the wooden floors of the hallway. In the doorway he stood, a shock over his face, "Are you sure?"

"It's not here, Josh," I said, lifting the books one by one from the drawer, "I've looked twelve times. *It's not here.*" My voice was quiet and sharp, and I pushed away Josh as he hovered over me, pushed past me, "I'm not stupid. If I say it's not here, *it's not.* Will you stop?" I yelled as he ripped the drawer from its track and dumped its contents onto the floor.

"It *has to be,* Allison. *This is where I left it.*" We were both immensely irritated at that point, each other's presence enough to push the other over the edge, "Will you move?" Josh pushed me against the bed, still sifting through the contents of the drawer.

"Agh!" I screeched and left the room, throwing the white

wooden door into the wall.

"Well, sorry," Josh yelled as I crossed the length of the hall, "that I don't want to get caught with a fake ID! It's not exactly legal you know!"

The wooden floors, like ice, were freezing beneath my feet.

Even rooms away, Josh knew what I was thinking, "Don't you *dare* touch the thermostat!" I heard him call, still shuffling through the mess he had dumped from the drawer. I heard two thuds, almost in sync, but just milliseconds apart, as Josh threw his fist into the floor. The whole flat vibrated.

Rounding the corner into the kitchen, my eyes fell to the counter, and I froze, "Josh!" My heart-quickened, "Josh! Come here!" My head spun in circles, and my vision shifted between clear and cloudy, "Josh!"

"What now?" he yelled, finally standing next to me. My arm shook, and I raised a trembling hand, pointing at the matte black envelope on the counter, "Son of a bitch."

I held tightly onto Josh as he walked over to the island. Moving my hands to the countertop for balance, I gave room for Josh to pick up the gold-lined envelope. I winced at the tearing that came when he opened the flap. He reached inside.

In his hand, he held up my ID. On it, a headshot I had taken not too long ago that I was going to use for a project in school - figured I wouldn't need it anymore. Below the photo I saw the name we agreed on a few days earlier: Tiffany Waterborough.

I took the envelope from his hands. There was still something else inside. I pulled out the white piece of paper.

Looking for this? You are truly terrible at hiding things, Tiffany.

"Wait," I said, almost a whisper, "Wait, this means they

know." I looked up at Josh, "They know I'm planning to run. Dammit, Josh, what am I going to do? What if-" My body went numb, and I couldn't hear the words I was saying. Still, they poured from my mouth in a blurb of voice and screeching. Everything sounded as if it were miles away, every noise echoing.

I reached for Josh's arms and stumbled, "Hey," he said, and I felt his arms around my shoulders, "Hey!" His voice sounded closer now, and his hands gripped my face, "Allison, look at me!"

I took deep, filling breaths, each one calmer than the last. *In - one, two, three, four.* My vision began to clear. *Out - five, six, seven, eight.* My heartbeat began to slow.

In - one, two, three, four.

Out - five, six, seven, eight.

Something I'd done for as long as I could remember.

In - one, two, three, four.

Out - five, six, seven, eight.

"Are you back?" I heard Josh ask through my breaths. I nodded, "Ok. Listen, my friend - he can get us another ID. We'll go this weekend. You'll come, and it will go straight into your wallet. We won't leave it anywhere this time. Okay?" I took a deep breath in. I nodded. I let my breath out.

The drive back to Mountain View didn't go nearly as quickly as it had last time. Not for me at least. But that would probably be because I had slept the whole way, though, a my boredom grew with the list of cities we passed through.

When we arrived in front of the dilapidated building, my stomach did a little turn inside, and I swallowed the lump in my throat, "Don't worry," Josh said, noticing the fear on my face, "It's not as bad as it looks."

Josh walked ahead of me. He opened the door, and the thick stench of smoke and whiskey drifted through the doorway. I suppressed a cough, covering my nose and mouth with my sleeve. Then there was a loud crash upstairs.

I jumped back into Josh. A door slammed, followed by thudding down flights of stairs. A man whipped around the banister, flying down the stairs. Another man followed him, but stopped at the top of the last set of steps. Josh watched the man run out the building, and his friend looked down at him. "Nice," Josh said.

"Sup, bro?" The man took his time walking down the stairs, each foot hovering over a step for a second. He was fairly tall, with big hair and dark eyes. His skin resembled a rich, milk chocolate, "You need another favor already?"

"A continuation of the last, actually," Josh answered, clasping the man's hand in his own, leaning in and slapping his back, "The people she's running from," Josh nodded towards me, "found her ID and know the name."

"So she just needs a new one?" the man asked, sizing me up. He folded his arms across his chest and looked up and down, scrutinizing every inch of my being. He smiled, "I think I can do that."

"So, Dame, how's the girl?" Josh asked as we climbed the stairs. The stench that met me at the door only worsened as we got higher.

"Who, Meriam? Oh, I dumped her," Dame said, barely looking back at Josh.

"You dumped her? Metaphorically or in a ditch?" Josh

asked. I laughed, and looked back at Josh. But he looked serious with only a slight smile one his lips.

"Is there an option C?" Dame said, looking directly into my eyes, "A 'both', perhaps?" He smiled, sickly, twistedly, and continued climbing the stairs. But when Josh started climbing, I turned and stopped him.

"Wait," I said, placing a hand on his chest, "I don't want to do this if he's like that," I said. I was already getting caught up in illegal business; I didn't need to be involved with a sketchy man that dumps women in ditches, too.

"We'll be fine," Josh said, pushing through my hand, past me, "I've been friends with him since I was a freshman in college. He was probably just trying to scare you. He likes to do that."

"Probably?" I said to myself quietly. I followed Josh up the stairs. We climbed all the way to the top. On the last floor, there was only one door, and it hung wide open. Dame and Josh walked inside, and I followed.

It was drab little room, with a kitchenette, a bed, a couch, and a TV. And that's it. In the corner, a large white background hung up against the wall. A camera, perched on a stand, stood in front of it.

Josh sat in a barstool at the cheap counter that was falling apart. Dame walked around to the other side. He leaned against the counter, folding his hands. He said something to Josh, but I wasn't listening. My eyes were focused on the piles and piles of toppling mail on the counter behind him.

Damien Mullens, 240 Vista Ave., Mountain View, CA.

There were dozens of letters, bills, and various random pieces of junk mail. There were pictures, facing the envelope so that only the back faced outwards, stapled to every 'junk' envelope. But that wasn't what bothered me.

There were red fingerprints covering every envelope.

"Allison?" My head snapped at the sound of Josh's voice.

"Jeez," Dame said, looking back at Josh, but his eyes still flicking back to me, "You're girlfriend's hard at hearing."

"Again. She's not my girlfriend," Josh said, "Just a close friend. When my parents died, her aunt was kind and there for me, helped me pay through college."

"Ah, yes," Dame said, focusing his full attention on Josh now and handing him a beer, "How is the dear mother-in-law to be, Nina?"

"She's alright," Josh said, opening the beer, "Drinking's under control."

"Good, good," Dame said, standing straight and walking towards the couch, "Follow me," he said.

I followed, infuriated. Why on earth had he told Dame about Aunt Nina? How was that any of his business? "Josh, you have to drive," I said.

"Chill," he said, looking back at me, "I'm not a lightweight like you."

Dame laughed and fired up his computer. I had to give it to him, for such a crappy place, he had a nice set up. Three screens sat on top of different monitors. He had two laptops, Macbooks, one at each end of the line of monitors.

Dame sat, legs crossed, in front of the computers, and Josh and I sat behind on the couch behind him. I watched as Dame's hand dragged the cursor to a blank-white file on the middle, largest screen. He double-clicked on the white, and a program opened, covering the screen.

A small, gray box popped up in the middle of the screen. Dame typed something furiously, then quickly, as if on a timer, clicked on a letter in the second line of text in the box. Another box, blue this time, opened with two white buttons. The buttons were not labeled; no words told what either would do.

Dame clicked on the left one, and he typed in another password. And I wondered what the other did. A list of states under the heading *United States* lined the side of the screen, followed by other headings, all different countries around the world.

The cursor hovered in the middle of the page, and Dame turned back to face me, "Still wanna go with New Jersey?" he asked, "Or wanna go with another state?"

My eyes were glued to the screen, and tons of thoughts went through my head, most regarding my safety after doing this. Finally, I pulled them away and looked down at Dame, "Um, yes."

"I don't know about that," Josh said from the floor. I hadn't even noticed that he moved, "I would change the state. Michigan, maybe?"

"Oh! What about North Dakota?" Dame asked clicking on the state on the screen, "No one goes to North Dakota. And, that way she's close to the border if she needs to run."

"Oh, yeah," Josh said, a smile creeping onto his face, "Can you get her a passport too?"

"Of course."

Josh spoke, eyes still on the screen, "When do you think?"

"Monday," Dame answered, "I'll bring it down; would love to see what you've done with the place."

Josh looked at Dame, "I'll be at work, so she'll be there,"

he said and looked at me.

I shifted in my seat, "Um, yeah, okay."

After a few minutes of clicking and dragging and typing, Dame hit my leg, "Alright, how's this?"

I dropped to the floor next to Josh and looked down at the screen. It looked great - like a real ID, "Looks good," I said.

"Alrighty," Dame said, clicking a few last buttons, "I'll get this for you, then your free to go." He unplugged the Macbook on his left and stood up with it in his hands.

The air outside air had never seemed so fresh. Dame had followed us to the door of the building, and Josh gave one last nod before getting into the car. Dame flicked his chin upwards and turned, going back into the building and closing the door behind him.

When I was sure the door was completely shut, and Dame was no longer watching, I smacked Josh, "You told him about Aunt Nina?" I yelled, "What else did you tell him about?"

"Oh, nothing. Chill," Josh said. He looked back at me. I glared, "Chill! He can be trusted." I scoffed, "Fine, think whatever you want. But he's doing us a favor. Now, we need to get you a bank account under your new name."

"Fine," I said, "But we need to be back by six. It's Aunt Nina and Aaron's anniversary, and I told her I'd be there for dinner."

"Okay," he said, pulling from the curb onto the small street, "Why does she want you there? I mean, no offense, but wouldn't they want to spend their anniversary together, just the two of them?"

"That's what I thought," I started, "But she said she wanted us all to have dinner, the three of us. Said she wanted me to properly meet Aaron and really get to know him." As I thought about it, it sounded strange. No man Aunt Nina had ever gone out with since my uncle was properly introduced to me - she knew he wouldn't be there long. But now she wants me to have dinner with Aaron. *Maybe she'll keep this one,* I couldn't help but think.

"I'll get you around eight?" Josh asked as I got out of the car

"Yeah, sounds about right," I said, my folded arms sitting in the rolled-down window, "Wish me luck."

"Good luck."

I rang the doorbell, the familiar chime echoing through the thousands of feet of house. I heard the quick patter of bare feet on marble, followed by a quick *'click'* and more pattering.

When I opened the door, Aunt Nina had already made her way through the foyer, living room, and back to the kitchen. God, she was like The Flash, "Hey! We're in the kitchen!" she called.

"Okay," I replied. I pulled my phone out of my pocket, scrolling through Instagram as I walked through the house.

Aunt Nina looked over her shoulder when she heard me walk in, and her face lit up when she saw me. I walked over to her, and she made a poor attempt to kiss me on the cheek and stir the contents of a sizzling pan, "Honey, can you hand me the butter?" she asked, glancing over at Aaron, who was diagonal to her at the island.

"Yep," he said, handing her the white-wrapped stick seconds later.

"Thanks, babe," she said, "Can you take over here while I set the table?"

"Of course!" Aaron kissed her and took the handle of the pan and the large oven spoon from her hands.

She opened the cupboard that hung on the wall, pulling out plates, and I helped. Grabbing the smaller plates and glasses, I looked over at Aunt Nina. She nodded towards the dining room then turned. We walked the short leg of the L-shaped kitchen and entered the dining room through the cased opening.

I had barely set the stack of glass on the table when Aunt Nina grabbed my arms. She checked over my shoulder, biting her lip. Then she looked back at me and smiled, "Oh, isn't he great?"

I could see it in her eyes. She was in love, "He really is," I said, and we turned to look at the poor man juggling three different dishes while mixing a salad and trying to get a bottle of wine from the cabinet, "Now, go help him." She smiled and kissed my head. I watched as she hurried into the kitchen, grabbing the wine bottle just as it fell from Aaron's hand.

A flood of warmth washed over me. Even when my uncle was around, I had never seen her so happy. My aunt had to try to find a time to catch my uncle in between his constant coming and going. But Aaron, he made time to spend with her. He took days he didn't have off of work to be with her when she was in the hospital and when she came home. He bought her flowers and books and anything she even looked at. He spoiled her. But after all she had been through, she deserved someone like him, someone to truly be there for and love her.

We all sat at the same end of the twelve-person table. Aunt Nina sat at the head, with Aaron to her right, and me across from him, "So Aaron, when Aunt Nina was in the hospital, I saw that you're a manager at Walmart. How's that going?" I asked, taking a bite of my salad.

"Well," Aaron started, finishing the food in his mouth and swallowing, "It's going pretty well, actually. I started eleven months, so almost a year, ago. And there is such a difference. When I came, it was terrible. There were lines and lines of empty shelves and so many palettes in the back room. Now there are no palettes in the backroom, except for the first hour after they are unloaded of course, and the shelves are always stocked. Even the head of my region said it looks so much better than before." He smiled, trying to be modest about his proudness.

"Yeah, Josh, the other day, just said he didn't know why, but for some reason, Walmart looked like an actual store and not a complete dump," I said, taking another bite of my salad.

Aaron let out a laugh, "Well," Aunt Nina said, grabbing his hand, "That's because they got the best man - the one who will get the job done." She took a bite of her salad and shifted her chair closer to Aaron as he put his arm around her.

"So," Aaron started, looking at me and catching me mid-bite, "Nina tells me you're in Law School. Do you like it?"

"Um." *Um*, "It's great. It's a little hectic right now, coming back from winter break and all, but before we left, we did a mock-trial, and I had the highest grade. A 98."

"Wow, that's awesome!" Aaron said.

"Nah," I said shyly, picking at my food, "It was only because I had Aunt Nina's help."

"So?" he said, reaching across the table to pat my shoulder, "That doesn't matter. Yeah, our genius may have helped you, but that's how it works. Several people work together to make a case work. And she wasn't there when you presented the case was she?" I shook my head, "See? You had to have presented it well to get that great of a grade! Give yourself credit! And if it means anything, I'm proud of you."

My head snapped up at these words. He looked at me with loving eyes, "So am I," Aunt Nina said, grabbing my hand.

I smiled, "Thank you, Aaron," I said, "That *does* mean a lot."

And it did. I tried to think of one time when my uncle had told me he was proud of something I did. But I couldn't. Not even a good job, nothing. The only thing I can remember was a 'cool' when I showed him I had won a poetry contest at school. Then he ran out the door.

"So, I've always wondered something," Aaron said, snapping me back to the moment, "What do lawyers major in? Like, for their Undergrad? Because, I remember wanting to be a lawyer for a short time, and I specifically remember having no idea what to major in." He looked at us both.

Aunt Nina spoke first, "Well, I majored in *Sociology*," she said, bringing her hand to her chest, and then gesturing towards me, "But she dual-majored in *Psychology* and *English*, with a minor in *History and Literature*."

Aaron looked at me, "Wow, I'm impressed," he said, "And I remember Nina mentioning that you graduated with highest honors. That's amazing!"

"Oh, it's not that grea-"

"Allison, listen," Aaron cut in, "You need to stop putting yourself down! Dual-majoring with a minor is extremely challenging, and you did it *and* managed to graduate with highest honors!" He grabbed my hand, so that one arm stretched around Aunt Nina, and the other held my hand, "I would be proud to have you as a daughter," he said. He looked at Aunt

Nina then back at me, "I know she is. She talks about it enough." He laughed, and Aunt Nina did too.

I smiled, gripping Aaron's hand tighter, "Thank you so much," I said, "I guess I never thought of it like that. Just always as 'What do I have to do now?' and 'This is what I have to do next', you know?"

"Oh my God, yes," he said, "I used to be like that, never slowing down. Then one day, I realized my wife and I were strangers." He poked at a piece of chicken, lifting his fork, but speaking before putting it into his mouth, "Then she left with a man, and I realized: If I don't slow down, don't love what's in front of me, I'll lose it without even knowing."

"Wow," Aunt Nina said. Her mouth hung slightly opened, and her face looked as if she were deeply listening to and analyzing his words, "You're amazing you know that?" Aaron just laughed, and Aunt Nina rested her head on Aaron's shoulder.

Aaron kissed her on the forehead and raised his glass, "A toast," he said, "to a beautiful woman. One I am lucky enough to call mine."

Aunt Nina's eyes teared at the corners. And I knew. Forty-five minutes, and I knew that this was the man that she was meant to be with. He made her feel special, and loved, and all of the things my uncle took away from her.

I jumped when my phone rang in my pocket. I pulled it out. It was Josh, "I'm so sorry," I said and looked at Aunt Nina, "It's Josh. May I be excused?"

"Oh, yes, definitely," she said, "Tell him I said hi."

"Will do," I said, passing through the cased opening and into the kitchen. I answered the call and held the phone to my

ear, "What's up? But, wait listen. Dinner's going so well. Aaron,
I think he might be-"

"Allison?"

My muscles stiffened, "Wait, Patricia?"

13

The thin glass slid from between my fingers and fell to the ground. The hushed conversation between Aaron and Aunt Nina ceased at the crash of shattering glass on the marble floors, "What's wrong, babydoll?"

How could this happen? We have never been together, *but after Aunt Nina, he meant everything to me.*

But I knew how; I just couldn't understand. They knew where he lived. They found the ID. Hell, they knew he was helping me escape. They knew ending him would end me, end this. They knew.

How could I have been so naive? After what they did to Aunt Nina, how could I, a soon to be lawyer, not know this would happen?

Only one thought was going through my mind: *Will he live? He has to. I mean, he* has *to, right? I couldn't bear losing him. I couldn't bear losing my best friend.*

Aunt Nina's eyes looked up at me through furrowed brows. But I couldn't seem to focus on them. Her voice barely registered in my brain, almost inaudible under my quickening breaths, "Allison, are you alright?"

I looked down at her, and with a motherly instinct, she stood from her chair and caught me just as I collapsed. Aaron's eyes widened and he gasped, "Oh God."

He stood from his chair as Aunt Nina dropped to her knees, unable to support both of our weights with her lanky frame. We sat up against the wall, my uncontrollable breathing and trembling shaking both of us violently, "It's alright. She's just having a panic attack," Aunt Nina said, looking to Aaron. Her voice was firm, and she held my face with one hand and my arm with the other, "Has had them since she was a child. Get a paper bag from the drawer next to the dishwasher."

Aaron scrambled out of the room, stealing a concerned glance before disappearing behind the door frame. I tried to speak through fleeting moments of sanity, "Aunt Nin-no-Josh-he-"

"Allison, you need to pull it together," she said, her voice even more firm than before. I nodded, "In - one, two, three, four. Out - five, six, seven, eight."

In - one, two, three, four.

Out - five, six, seven, eight.

Aaron came, whipping around the corner and laying the paper bag in Aunt Nina's hands. She mouthed a quick 'thanks' and turned back to me, handing me the bag. Her hands rested over mine to keep them from shaking, holding them still enough for me to breathe.

In - one, two, three, four.

Out - five, six, seven, eight.

In - one, two, three, four.

Out - five, six, seven, eight.

"Are you good?" Aunt Nina asked when I pulled the bag away from my lips and took a deep breath, laying my head against the wall. Her hand still rested on mine, while the other rose to my shoulder.

"Yeah, I'm good." I felt ridiculously light-headed and thought I might pass out.

Aunt Nina knew this, and did not rush me to stand, "What happened?" she asked. She held the back of her hand against my forehead. When I had a panic attack, all of my blood rushed to my head and it almost felt like I had a fever. Once I cooled down, I could stand.

But Aunt Nina's hand was ice against my sweaty skin, "It's Josh," I said, "Aunt Nina, they got to Josh. They shot him. He's going into surgery now, but it was his chest. What if-" The words came in a whine, and I couldn't breathe.

Aunt Nina looked away for a moment, placing her hand on her chest. When she turned back her eyes had reddened slightly, the smallest ring of tears hugging close to her lower lash-line, and there was a slight choke to her breath. Her cold hand pulled my face into her chest, and I felt her racing heart against my cheek.

The muscles in my face, pinched in with the pain of crying, were tightened into an ugly twist, an equally distressed noise escaping with every intake of breath. As Aunt Nina's hand softly stroked my hair, running through every piece gently, I could feel her chest catch with her breaths.

Thhh, th, th, thhh.

Thhh, th, th, thhh.

Aaron crouched down next to us on the ground, sitting in front of me, "Josh," he said, looking to Aunt Nina. I felt her chin lift from the top of my head, "Is that the boy that's always hanging around here?" he asked, his words filled with unease.

"Mhm," Aunt Nina barely squeaked out. She lifted one of the arms that held me within the warmth of her embrace, and she swiped at a single tear that escaped from her flooding eyes. The sweater dress that covered her arms and body held in the heat as my body began feeling cold, and I took one last deep breath, holding back a new wave of tears.

"Here," Aaron said, grabbing my arm as I stood.

"Thank you," I said with a smile. Aunt Nina and Aaron followed as I walked into the kitchen and grabbed my purse, Aunt Nina picking up her light brown Michael Kors bag next to mine and slinging it over her shoulder.

The brightness tore through the darkness when Aunt Nina unlocked the black Range Rover in the drive. I opened the heavy door behind the passenger seat, leaving the front seat open for Aaron. The car's doors slammed shut, one right after the other, and Aunt Nina's hand gripped the gear shift, throwing the car into reverse and pulling down the driveway.

I walk through the front door and every light is off, "Aunt Nina?" Has she already gone to bed? I look at my watch; 6:30. There's no way.

I hit the switch in the foyer with my fist and walk through the stairs towards the living room and kitchen. Punching at the switch on the wall of the living room, I passed through swiftly. The kitchen was completely dark, but something was off.

My eyes grazed over the room, everything in order. It was warmer than usual, and there was a heavy scent of chocolate in the air. Wait, chocolate?

The lights flick on and a squeal escapes my mouth. Josh and

Aunt Nina rise from behind the island, "Happy birthday!"

"Aw, you guys," I start to say. A tray of fresh, warm, gooey brownies sits in the middle of the counter, along with red and white wines, "You didn't have to. I told you-"

"Yes, yes. We know," Josh said walking over and hugging me, "We know you said you didn't want anything, but you're 21! How could we not do something? We made brownies, your mom's old recipe. Nina said she used to make them for you when you were younger. So I said we should try it, since you hate cake."

We walked to the island where Aunt Nina waited, "Yes, the only person I know who hates birthday cake," she said, hugging me and kissing me on the cheek, "Happy birthday, pumpkin." She made side glance at Josh, "This was all his idea."

I smiled.

The car had barely even stopped when I jumped out, running for the building. I hardly noticed the stingy, sterile smell of the hospital when I burst through the doors. I saw Patricia standing, looking around the room, waiting for someone, "Patricia!"

"Allison!" I ran to her, "He's in surgery. But I heard the bullet missed his heart, so that's good." I felt Aunt Nina's hands rest on my shoulders. Lifting one of my own, dropping one cold hand on top of another, I held onto her hand over my shoulder.

I tried to force a smile and nod, but it was a painfully horrible attempt, and the words were not coming, "Thanks, Patricia," Aunt Nina said, rubbing my arm with the hand that was free, "Let us know if anything changes."

Aunt Nina's grasp pulled me towards the rows of chairs,

and the three of us sat in a circle around a coffee table. Aaron spoke first, "You know," he said, and Aunt Nina and I looked up at him, "This is where you were sitting, Allison, when we first met."

I looked around the room, my hands wrapped in Aunt Nina's, and smiled, "Yes, it is," I said, remembering it plain as day. I was asleep. A hand grabbed my shoulder. I almost tipped the chair over. We both raced for Aunt Nina's room.

I looked up at Aunt Nina and smiled. She smiled too, knowing what I was thinking about. Aaron's hands joined the ball of flesh, "Jesus, Nina, your hands are freezing. Here," he said, starting to pull of his jacket.

"No," Aunt Nina said, holding up a hand, "It's a family thing. Schwartz women have cold hands. We're fine, it's completely normal," she said.

"Oh." Aaron nodded and shrugged his shoulders back into his jacket. He started looking around the room.

"Thank you, though," I added. Aaron looked at me and smiled, bringing his hands back to ours. I felt like I was really getting to know him, bond with him, over these past few weeks. He was a truly kind and generous man who treated my aunt like a queen. And after learning these things about him, I wished Aunt Nina had found him sooner; it would've saved her so many years of heartbreak, thinking that she was useless and unlovable.

"You are not useless and unlovable." Josh's voice was slightly patchy over the phone, "Listen only a few more months. Just wait 'till you get to Harvard. Everyone is so different here. Tell you what, why don't you come up here for a little while in the summer. I was going to come home, but we can spend a few weeks here, and I'll show you around. You won't even think

about him after everything I have to show you."

"I don't know, Josh," I said through tears, "I ju-"

"You just need to get out of there," he said, "I know how that school can be. It's suffocating. Your graduating this year, and you can leave him, along with everyone else behind to deal with their own petty lives. So James is a douche. So what? You're so much smarter than this, wasting and crying over guys. You're a 17-year-old that is graduating high school and got accepted into Harvard when she was 16. You don't need him!"

"Yeah, you're right," I said, "Is it really different there?"

"So different. Listen, there's this amazing thing that happens here. When someone asks you how you're doing, they actually care to know!" I let out a small chuckle, "See, you're alright. I'm no genius, graduating early like you, but I do know this: you're going to do something great one day Allison Schwartz. Remember that, and don't let anyone take that from you."

All three of us stood up when Patricia walked back into the room, "He just got out of surgery. But only close family is allowed in there, and Allison, since your his emergency contact, that's you."

I looked back at Aunt Nina, and she nodded and placed a hand on my arm. I looked at Aaron. He took a step towards me, and his massive, built arms wrapped around me. I was truly shocked, standing frozen stiff. My chin stuck out over his shoulder, and there was a strong scent of cologne filling my nose. My arms, held like sticks, were straight and unmoving. But after a moment, I relaxed, laying my hands in the small of his back, realizing how much I missed having a fatherly embrace to comfort me. Something I hadn't had for a long time.

When he pulled away, and I took a step back, Aunt Nina shuffled to his side, sliding into the nook where her slender body fit perfectly, and Aaron stretched his arm around her. I turned to follow Patricia down the hall.

I picked and peeled at my nails furiously. The taupe hall lasted for miles. I could feel my heartbeat quicken until it was almost a flutter. When Patricia stopped in front of a door, everything in me stopped completely. I laid my hand on the cold handle and pushed the door open.

Josh laid there, his eyes closed. My arm instinctively shot up to cover my mouth as I bent down and turned away. Patricia had already left, the door closed behind me. I turned back around and walked towards the bed.

I grabbed a chair. Sliding it across the floor with a screech, I pulled it as close to the bed as I could get it. Taking his hand in my own, I felt a tear run from each of my eyes. I lifted his hand to my face, kissing the cold, motionless flesh, "You're going to be okay," I said, his hand still at my lips, "You're going to be okay."

"You're going to be okay," I say to Josh. His face is in his hands, and for the very first time, I'm seeing my best friend cry, "You're going to be okay," I keep repeating, rubbing his back, "You're going to be okay."

The minutes tick by slowly as I watch the clock. When I feel Josh's body shuffle, my head snaps down. His hands are folded in front of his face now, "I just can't even begin to fathom..."

"I know," I say, "me either." I had lost my parents at a young age but not by their own hand. My father never would've done that to my mother, nor would he have done that to himself afterwards. Though I may be two years younger, I must be the

adult here, I keep telling myself, because Josh needs me.

Aunt Nina walks into the room, and we both look up. She sets three glasses of water down on the coffee table in front of us and sits on the other side of Josh, "Hey," she says lightly, laying her hand on his back, "It's going to be okay. I promise. And you can stay as long as you need to," she says, holding his chin in her hand.

He looks up at her and nods, his face pinching in with a cry, and she takes him in her arms. He falls, crying into her embrace. I had never seen Josh shed even a tear, but when he was fifteen, he cried a river.

When I walked back into the waiting room, I was met by Aunt Nina and Aaron, "How is he?" Aunt Nina asked.

"He's alive," I said, "He's not awake yet, though." I looked at a digital clock on the wall.

12:27. "You guys should go home, really. I'll be fine," I said.

"No," Aunt Nina said immediately, "I'm not leaving you or him. No way."

"If she's not leaving, neither am I," Aaron said, "But I am starving, and we never got to finish dinner."

"I can't believe you just said that!" Aunt Nina said, holding back a smile. Aaron was in stitches, a curled, laughing ball of mess.

"It's so true, though!" I said, "And Josh agrees."

"Wait, Josh said that too?" she said, pulling her fork out of her mouth just as she was about to take a bite.

"Yeah, don't you remember? *Stop it! Both of you!*" I laughed so hard, and Aaron pounded the table, his face red as a tomato.

"Oh my gosh, yes! I was going to hit both of you," Aunt Nina said, chewing a piece lettuce and laughing, "I was so mad." She let out a sigh, and Aaron wiped his watering eyes, "I still can't believe you said we act like middle-schoolers!"

At the mention of the word, Aaron laughed again, almost spitting coke everywhere, but catching it last second. He meshed in so well with the two of us, and conversation came easily, unforced.

I laughed as the conversation went on so fluently, so unforced, "And then," Aunt Nina continued, "She snorted and spit Root Beer all over the guy!" Josh and Aunt Nina fell apart, and Josh pounded the table with a clenched, white fist.

It seems that even though we've been friends for four years now, Aunt Nina still hasn't run out of embarrassing stories to tell Josh, "The sad thing is," Josh says, "Is that I have absolutely no doubt that's true and no troubles picturing it. Do you know how many times I've been victimized by her laughing with something in her mouth?"

God, please let him be okay. That was the only thing running through my mind.

I clicked the home button on my phone. *4:42.* The hours dragged by slowly, but we did our best to keep them moving as quickly as possible, "So, I've been meaning to ask, how did you two meet?" I asked.

"Ahh, well," Aunt Nina started with that stretched out smile that turned downwards at the ends, "One night, well I guess three years and a day ago, you had really pissed me off. I can't remember why, I just remember being pissed. I think you said something about your uncle. Anyway, I went to the bar in town and asked the bartender for the strongest vodka they had at the moment, and he poured me some Pincer. That stuff's like, what, 89 percent or something?"

"Yeah, around 89," Aaron chimed in, "I walked in and said that was really strong for a little lady like you. And you rolled your eyes."

"I rolled my eyes," Aunt Nina said as Aaron said the words, "Yup, then-"

"Then, you tried to chug the thing just to prove me wrong. You made it barely over half way, and you slammed the glass down on the counter and choked, holding the back of you other hand up to your mouth." Aaron mocked her, pinching his eyes shut and holding his hand against his face.

"Yeah, I remember thinking, 'Way to go, Nina, that's how to show him'. Then you sat down next to me, and I just looked at you..."

"...and you rolled your eyes again." Aaron looked at me, "Stubborn as a mule, your aunt," he said, and Aunt Nina let out a short laugh, almost like a cough, and slapped his arm, "Listen, I love you to death, but you are *so* stubborn."

"You really are," I said, laughing and taking a sip of my Vitamin Water.

Footsteps rolled around the corner, and we all looked up to see Patricia coming towards our table. We stood, "He's awake," Patricia said, looking between Aunt Nina and me.

We both hurried down the hall, Aunt Nina and I. When I finally reached his room, I whipped around the corner. I fell to my knees with a thud at the bedside, leaving Aunt Nina in the doorway.

I laid my forehead on the bed beside him, holding his hands in mine, shaking with sobs, "Whoa, slow down tiger," Josh said.

His voice was weak, but he was still the same, joking man I knew and loved, "Hey, lil sis."

I smiled and heard a sniffle from behind me, and we both looked up to see Aunt Nina walking towards us. I slid to the side, and Aunt Nina took Josh's hand. She smiled, and tears ran down her cheeks and fell to the bed, "Why are you crying?" Josh asked, "I expected it from this one, but you? Come on, I thought we were the tough ones."

Aunt Nina let a breath out through her nose, and her hands encased Josh's, "You're like my son, you know that? I love you like I love her, and the thought that something happened to you…" Her voice trailed off and she shook her head, "I couldn't imagine."

Josh smiled and raised his fist, and Aunt Nina rolled her eyes, fist bumping like they always had for as long as I could remember.

I crawled in closer, cuddling up against Aunt Nina and laying my hand on top of theirs. Aunt Nina looked down at me and back at Josh. Leaving one hand on his and wrapping the other arm around my waist, she said, "You two are the closest things I will ever have to kids. You *are* my kids. And I love you both *so much*, more than anything in this world." She pushed the hair out of my face and laid a hand on Josh's, "I couldn't live without you two."

I felt a small pang of guilt at her words. Because, soon…

"So, wait, before I keep going and forget, what time is it?" Josh asked. He took most of the line of cards, starting at the eight and going the whole way down. Now only seven cards lay next to the rest of the deck on the tray. He shuffled through his hand, adding and taking cards before finally laying down four Jacks, three eights, and the four, five, and six of clubs. He laid a six of diamonds along the line.

"Rummy," Aunt Nina said, picking up the card and adding to her line of diamonds. She tapped her Apple watch, "Almost eight a.m."

"Please tell me you guys got some sleep," Josh said. Aunt Nina and I looked at each other, "You didn't, did you?" We shook our heads.

Aaron left around 5:30 when Aunt Nina assured him Josh would be alright. She had gone out to get some cards, and we had completely forgotten he was out there. So she kissed him and told him he didn't have to stay. He had to get ready for work, anyway.

"So, anyway, where was I? Oh, yeah. Well, I got out of the car and someone yelled, 'Hey!' from behind me and I turned around. But when I did, some guy punched me square in the face. But I got back up.

"We started fighting. I threw him up against the car, but this guy was massive. I honestly think the only reason I could was he didn't think I'd be up so quickly. Then the next thing I knew, a shot rang out and I was on the ground," he said. It hurt so badly to know that they could've killed him. All because he was helping me, "When I looked up, the guy with the gun looked just like the other I was just trying to beat up. I thought I was going crazy for a moment, but then I remembered what you said about them."

"Wait, what?" Aunt Nina said looking at me, "You've been

involved with these men?"

I nodded and drew a card from the deck, an ace, "In New York. They were the ones that did this." I pointed to the scars that ran across my face, though it was barely visible through the makeup, "One threw me into a brick wall and strangled me, while the other one had the knife." I looked straight ahead at the wall, remembering the two men in the darkness of the alley, "They're Mick's sidekicks, or something," I added.

"And Mick's the one behind all of this?" Aunt Nina asked, "The one who you lied to, you told you were engaged, caught you kissing another guy, and handed you money that, seconds later, you ran with?"

I nodded.

"God, you're such and *idiot*," she spit.

In silence, I rearranged a few cards and laid the rest of my hand, hearing Josh curse under his breath, on my section of the tray over the hospital bed, "I'm out. Aunt Nina, count them up? I need to use the bathroom."

I left the room as Aunt Nina and Josh counted up their cards. It was cooler in the hall, and I breathed in the crisp air. My hands in my pockets, I cruised towards the bathroom with no sense of time or rush. Just a relaxing walk. Until I heard a loud, blood-curdling scream echo down the hall.

14

My head snapped towards the source of the cry. A girl around my age ducked out of a room down the hall. Her hand covered her mouth, and a man - her father? - came to her side. The girl sobbed in her father's arms.

She caught a glimpse of me watching her over her father's shoulder. Our gaze locked, and I flicked my eyes away, walking around the corner at the opposite end of the hall.

I pushed on the metal double doors that led to the lobby. A patter, like water running from a shower, grew louder when someone walked through the front doors tapped at the shuffling silence - like a child's finger on an already cracking window.

I slid through the automatic doors just before they closed. The outside met me with the soft dripping of waves of rain across the concrete of the parking lot and sidewalks. I stood there, lifting my chin towards the sky, and let the beat of each drop that hit my face keep me hostage, stuck in the moment.

The tiny droplets gathered in the sockets of my eyes, crept down my face. The heaviness of my clothes steadily grew with every minute I spent soaking in the tears of nature. My black sweatshirt hung in slumping bags from my frame; I'd lost almost 20 pounds since New York.

I stood there, and let the people walk past me, the time slip away from me. The quiet slap of feet on a concrete walk that grew louder then faded. Dozens of trails came and went.

But one opened my eyes, not fading into the rows and rows of cars sitting and glimmering under the sparkling of rain met by an early morning sun, but ending at its loudest point.

"Josh is asleep."

Aunt Nina stood there, next to me with her arms folded over her chest as they always were, looking out at the morning rising, "I knew," she started, eyes locked with the sun's, "the moment you were born, the first time I held you, you and I were gonna get along." A smile pushed through the pain in her eyes, "I looked into your big blue eyes, and I saw a connection with the world outside of cities, and industries, and money, with the natural part, untouched by man. Just nature in its most beautiful, peaceful state."

I looked up at her. Her features were harsh in the beams of light, which casted shadows on the left side of her face. I saw the lines that creased the skin around her mouth. The dark dress, a classy pattern of maroon on black, hugged her torso and arms, accentuating every curve of her body.

The golden caramel highlights shimmered with the water covering every visible surface. She stood tall, her legs stood straight and together. But her upper-body leaned backwards, her lower back supporting all of the weight above it, "You're mother told me I was crazy," she said looking at me, "But I told her, I said, 'No, there's something special about this one'."

She paused, and I thought she was going to say something,

but she let the breath out. Her body turned towards me, and she took my face in one hand and rested the other on my shoulder, "I know I can be bitchy sometimes," she said, "And I'll say things that I don't mean. But just know, I will never stop loving you. Ever."

I felt her words. Actually *felt* each one, "I know, Aunt Nina," I said and threw my arms around her neck.

She pulled me in and kissed my hair, "And, those few days I spent not talking to you, those were some of the most painful days of my life. I never want to lose you, and I never want you to think I don't love you. Because I do, more than anything on this earth. And nothing can change that. Nothing."

Josh's apartment was no longer frigid. On bed rest, there was nothing his weak, heavy limbs could do as he watched me turn the thermostat. He tried to move, leave the bed, but he moved too slowly and frailly to do anything.

I stayed with him, took care of him, only leaving his side to take showers, make dinner, or get groceries - which I usually did when Aunt Nina came.

As far as she knew, I was at school, only coming home to take care of Josh after class on Saturdays, and leaving Sunday after lunch. And I wanted to keep it that way. But, since he was 'all alone', Aunt Nina dropped by for an hour every day of the week, checking up on him after work.

I sat in the car, waiting in the Walmart parking lot for the message. The warmth of the car's heat restored life to my fingers, chilled by the late January cold. Staring at my phone, at the picture of Aunt Nina and me on my lock screen, I waited. *Wednesday, January 31.* The massage came in at 6:12 p.m. *She's gone. But, we don't have to make dinner tonight; she brought back Chinese and it smells AMAZING.*

I smiled, and threw the car into gear. The drive to Josh's apartment was shorter than that to my house. He lived closer to the city, where I lived in the mountains. *Used to* live in the mountains. It broke my heart, leaving my home, my life, my Aunt Nina. Would this destroy her?

I shake the thoughts from my head and pull into a parking slot in front of Josh's building. The air, cold and damp, bit at my nerves as I crawled out of the car, the weight of the straining bags pulling down on my wrists.

"Ugh!" I squealed as soon as I walked through the apartment door, "Josh, I swear to God!"

"It was Nina," was all he said from the bedroom. I dropped the bags on the counter and walked to the bedroom, "She agreed with me. Said she was roasting and turned it down. I swear."

He stood by the thermostat, blocking it from my touch. The goose bumps ran across my arms and legs, and I grunted as I walked to the closet, digging a sweatshirt and pair of sweatpants from the hidden suitcase. How could I fight through a guy who was shot I little over two weeks ago? I couldn't.

I glared at Josh, staring him down as I yanked on the sweatshirt and walked across the room. I didn't understand why it had to be so cold.

The Chinese warmed my body, and I felt the heat as it trailed down my throat. Josh sat next to me on the couch. He's been slowly moving about the apartment more and more, "Listen," he said out of the blue.

I lifted the remote and paused the TV, "What?"

"We're gonna need to start getting things in order," he said. He could see the conflicted and pained look on my face, "I know, but we've been putting it off."

And he was right, "Yeah, I know." I set the box of white rice down on the glass coffee table in front of me, "So what's next? What do we need to do? What do *I* need to do?"

Josh shifted, and he looked down at the ground, "Well," he said, "We have the ID and bank account. You bought the plane ticket with my card on Monday, right?" I nodded my head, "Next, I'd say, is start transferring money. Make sure Richard knows when this is going down. And we're gonna need someone who can do stunt makeup."

I looked at him, clearly confused, "Well, unless you plan on actually driving your car off of the ridge with you in it, then we're gonna need someone who can make it look like you did, so when Nina and everyone else at the hospital sees you, they think you really were in an accident." He raised his brows.

Yeah, I wasn't planning on actually killing myself, so, "I know a girl from school. She's really good, and we're kinda close, I guess. I mean, she wouldn't tell anybody." I thought of her, the first time I saw her work. She'd done someone up like they had been in a serious accident for a movie seen, and it looked *amazing.*

"Oh, that Rebecca chick?" Josh asked, and I nodded, "I remember reading that she did work for movies. She would be great." He paused, going through a checklist only he could see, "I talked to a handful of people at the hospital - a handful, only the necessary; I can't do this all on my own, Allison," he said.

Still, I couldn't help but worry. The more people that knew, the more chances of something slipping through there were. This couldn't get out, they couldn't know. Not again.

"Other than that, all I can think of practicing," he said.

"Practicing? For what?"

"Well, you're going to have to lie there in a hospital bed while your aunt cries over your body. I could probably talk her into a closed casket funeral, if Rebecca does the makeup well enough." His words, each one a dagger, lodged itself into my heart. It was as if someone stabbed and cut through my flesh, pulling the serrated edge in and out with each syllable. How could I just lie there while my aunt lost the most important thing in her life?

I looked back at Josh. He knew what I was thinking, but he also knew I had to; I didn't have a choice. I grabbed my phone from the coffee table and messaged Rebecca.

"So let me get this straight," Rebecca said, clutching the coffee mug between her fingers, "You want me to do you up like you were killed in a car crash so you can flee the state?"

"Yeah," I said. *Jesus, what am I doing?*

"I love it," she said with a smile. Her teeth were impeccably white. The black curls that fell over her shoulders looked soft, with streaks of a teal, almost sky-blue running through, perfectly blended, like misting waterfalls. The dark brown center of her eyes, a color like freshly brewed coffee, stood out among the light layer of hazel that wrapped around them, "You mentioned that I get paid, how much?"

I lifted my purse from the floor, dropping it in my lap, "Well," I said, digging for my wallet, "I don't have it all right now, but I should be able to get the rest to you before I leave. If not, Josh definitely will. Anyways, I was thinking two?"

"Hundred?"

"Thousand," I said. I handed her nearly a thousand dollars in crisp bills, "Listen, I know you're doing me a huge favor, and really, I'm trying to buy your silence as well. And like I said, I don't have much now, but I can get the rest later - and more if needed..."

"No," Rebecca said, shifting the money through her fingers with a twisted smile, "This is great."

The outside air, warmer today than most, still had the remnants of a relentless winter, "Hey, do you need a ride?" I asked Rebecca. She stood on the curb, not really going anywhere. Her ripped, black t-shirt and matching snagged leggings looked like they provided no warmth at all.

"Nah," she said and held up a pack of cigarettes and a lighter, "Just hanging back for a smoke. Got the mother's car, a '*no smoking zone*'." She mocked her mother, thickening her Mexican accent and drawing quotes around the words as she said them.

When I got into my car, I called Josh, "Dammit, lost again. I absolutely suck at Solitaire," he said when he answered. A deck of cards shuffled in the background, "So, you got her?"

"Yep," I said, "I'll be home in twenty."

"Alright," Josh said, "It says here to think of something that calms you. Well, no shit, I could've told you that - I did," Josh said, slamming the laptop shut and throwing it across the couch, "Just think of the ocean, and what's that one song?"

"*Wind Beneath My Wings*?"

"Yeah," he said. Then he paused, "Wait, scratch that.

You're an emotional mess, you'll start crying. I swear, if I didn't know *you*, and who you are, I would think you're pregnant with all of the crying and emotional breakdowns. Anyway, I digress. Just think of a song that you listen to in the car. But not with it a beat that you will start nodding or tapping to."

I just stared back at him.

"Well, go," he said.

I took a deep breath in and let my back fall until it lay parallel on the couch. *Steady breathing.* I let some song I heard earlier on the radio push through my subconscious. *Still as a statue.* Every muscle in my body clenched. *Wait, no. Not like that.* I slowly relaxed the muscles in my body, one muscle at a time. *No flinching.* I let my mind drift away, almost in a day dream.

Aunt Nina's crying voice. Wait, what? Aunt Nina's crying voice? I sat up, almost too quickly, and a rush ran over my head, "What the hell was that?"

But I knew what it was. I guess my real question was *why*? Josh held my phone in his hand, the voicemail paused.

"She's gonna be there, Allison," he said, "And 99 percent of the time, the families *talk* to their loved ones," he said sarcastically. And until that moment, I didn't think to worry about that part; I didn't even think about that part.

I looked again at the phone in Josh's hand. I remembered the day I got that voicemail. It was the day after my uncle had left. The voicemail had been for him. I had noticed that the second I opened it.

Aunt Nina's shaky voice spoke at the other end. I never told her I got the voicemail, though. And for some reason, I never deleted it.

"So we'll use this to condition you," Josh said, breaking the on-stretching silence, "Just listen to the parts, and use what you can to pretend she's talking to you."

I lay back against the soft cushions again and closed my eyes. The voicemail rolled, "Hi, listen..."

And I did. I waited for her to get through the part about the cheating, the lying, the heartbreaking. And while I did, I ran through the other steps.

Steady breathing.

Still as a statue.

No flinching.

Deep breath in, deep breath out, and now the hardest part.

Aunt Nina's crying voice, "And, I loved you. Always had, and always will." The words struck something inside of me, and I had to fight not to choke, "And losing you, it's something I don't think I can bear."

And though I tried to stop it, it was too late. A tear slipped from the corner of my eye, escaping down my cheek, and my nostrils flinched, "Dammit."

I sat up, and Josh paused the voicemail, "Well, that was a fail," he said. But I barely heard him. The tears flowed more heavily now. *What if this, what I'm going to do to her, is something she can't bear?* I needed to stop thinking like that. *What if this really is something she can't live with?* No. *What if I destroy her?*

"Oh, God, come here," Josh said, scooching over, closer to me, on the couch. I hugged up against him, grabbing his shirt. I took stifled breaths, calming the madness within me.

"Remember what's at stake," he said. And he was right. I needed to remember why I had to do this; what would happen if

I didn't. But damn, how it hurt so much. I glanced at my phone; I knew how badly this would hurt her. And yet, here I am, still willing to do it. But if I didn't, I would be putting her life at risk. This is what's best. And whether I want it or not, this is my truth; this is what I have to do.

So I sat up straight, quickly flicked the last tear from my cheek, and went again. I dropped to the couch and let my lids fall.

The warmth of the evening air encases my body as soon as I open the back door. She's sitting there, reading a book on the lawn chair, facing the mountains, as usual, "Either sit still in a chair and be quiet, or go inside," she says.

So I tiptoe lightly to a chair next to her, and lower myself gently onto the soft surface. I am sure to make no sound. I look around. It's been almost three weeks since my uncle left, and everything still feels so different. It all looks *the same. It just doesn't* feel *the same.*

The mountains, green and textured, like little balls of fuzz from a wool sweater, sit peacefully in the distance. They are so beautiful. I've always loved the mountains, loved nature. There's something so innocent, so pure about it. But after so long, I'll want to go inside. Aunt Nina will stay out here for hours, not coming inside until the setting sun and rising moon force her to. And even then, she'll steal away to the night, to the stars.

I look at my aunt. Her nose is still a little red. I wish there was something I could do to comfort her. I've been keeping up on my chores lately, trying not to let them slip like before, and doing extra work. She's just so hurt, so torn apart, so broken. It's like a piece of her is missing.

But her eyes are sparkling. I've always loved her eyes. The color of the outside world. The color of the bark of a tree. But not a normal tree; they were cooler than that. Usually they had a warmer tone to them, but in anger, they turned an icy brown - a color didn't even know existed until I was about 6-years-old. But no matter what time of the day, what mood, where she was, or what she wore, her eyes always sparkled - like they do now. Her veins run visibly up her hands, wrapped around the book's cover. A warm glow from the summer sun has kissed her skin. And she's so beautiful; how could anyone not love her? The way her hair falls naturally over her shoulders, and the way her eyes glow, "You're staring," *she says not looking up,* "It's not polite to stare."

Her eyes are drilling into me now. Beautiful, yes. Petrifying, even more, "I'm sorry," *I say, flicking my eyes back towards the yard. Aunt Nina's eyes fall back down to her book,* "Aunt Nina?"

"What?" *There was a slight irritation in her voice, but it only just laid on the surface of her words, not going deeper than that.*

"Why do you stay out here so long?" *I ask.*

She shows no signs of even hearing me except for a few words, "Because it's peaceful. And quiet." *She side glances me, and I squirm in my seat. But why? I want to ask so badly. What makes it so peaceful? What makes it so captivating that it holds your attention for hours and hours?*

"But how?" *She rolls her eyes, checking her page number before shutting the book and chucking it onto the chair on her other side.*

"Because, it's so simple and complicated. It's just, I don't* *know, incredible." She looks at me, clearly seeing me try to understand her words, "Come here."*

I crawl next to her in the chair that's feet from the pool. My body fits perfectly in her arms, so small against hers, "Look," she says, lifting her hand, "The mountains. They roll and fold into the earth; they change colors with the seasons. They see it all. And the rivers and streams that run through them," she says, shifting her finger, "You will never see the same one twice. And the stars," she looks up at the sky, and my eyes follow, "They are secrets, wishes, lives. They've heard it all."

I look around the landscape again. Before, that's all that I saw – a landscape. But now, I see this new light. I see the last rays of liquid gold saying goodbye to the earth. I see the soft wings of birds, fluttering against the breezes. I see the life that the mountains see and hear the voices of the stars.

I look up at my aunt, into her eyes. And I see it there, too. There is something so much more than just us, than just money, to this world. You just need to have the right eyes to see it, "I see it," I say, looking out at the breathtaking beauty of nature "It's all...alive."

I feel Aunt Nina's arm pull me in closer, and I let my head fall to her chest. We sit here for hours. And after today, I understand why.

"Hey," Josh said, and my eyes snap open, "Hate to break your mojo, but it's been 27 minutes, you can take a break now."

15

"Wait, seriously?" I asked sitting up. No way was that 27 minutes.

But Josh responded, "Yep. I thought you were dead for a minute." I rolled my eyes and he laughed, "Jk, jk. Dinner's ready if you want some."

"Yeah, hand me a plate," I said, sitting at the counter. Josh opened the cupboard he was just about to close and pulled out a plate, handing it to me. Maybe I could actually do this.

I knew this was a long shot, but still I asked, "So how long do you think it would be until I could see Aunt Nina again?"

"Allison, we talked about this-"

"I know, I know." And we had, "I just don't understand why I can see you and not her."

He sighed, "Because it's too risky. We've been through this a dozen times already."

"Well, wouldn't it be risky for us then, too?"

"Yeah, I guess, but-"

"So then why can't I see her too? If we're already risking it with us? Or, if it's so risky, why would you want to take the chance of them finding out about us?" My voice was harsh, strong, "It's not fair that I can see my friend but not the woman who has been raising me for the past 22 years," I said.

I wasn't finished, but Josh cut in, "Yes, but-"

"No, I don't care if it's too risky. And like I said before, if it is why are you-"

"Because I can't lose you!"

The words came out in a quick outburst. His eyes trailed the counter's top, and he rocked against the island.

"What?"

He looked up at me, straight as a board, "I can't lose you. Or Nina for that matter. You two are all that I have left."

Now I looked down, "Josh, I'm so-"

"No, it's fine," he said, "I can hold things down here. Nina is the closest thing I have to family after you. I couldn't - and wouldn't - ever let anything happen to her. She'll still be here - I can keep an eye on her, keep her on her feet. But when you're gone, if I don't get to see you, don't get to know you're okay, I'll go insane."

"Josh…" I started, but I was at a loss for words.

"Do you know what was going through my mind when I became close with you? Like, *really* close?" he asked, "I was walking down the hall, and saw that jerk - who was it? Nathan Ramey? - push you into a locker. I hated when guys picked on girls, especially ones younger than them. I walked over to where you two were, you on the ground and him hovering over you.

"But when I got there, I took one look at you, and something clicked. My sister had died four years ago, and you looked *exactly* like her." His eyes looked at the counter, avoided mine.

"Wait, what?" I asked.

"You reminded me of her so much, and maybe it was the fact that you were the same age as she was when she ended it, or that it was bullying from people like him that caused her to do it, but whatever it was, something snapped." His eyes met mine. I had never known any of this, "I really reminded you of your sister?" I asked. Josh nodded. Then I remembered a picture Josh had shown me of his sister, taken only days before she died. She *had* looked like me. I noticed that. I just didn't know for sure if he did too.

I could only imagine how hard it was to see that happening all over again, especially when I had looked just like her, "When you told me about what people were doing to you," he started, "What you were thinking of, something inside told me I couldn't let this happen again. And as I got to know you, got to know Nina, I don't know, it started to feel like it was my job to protect you. Both of you.

"And that's why I agreed to let you do this. Because, even if it meant only seeing you once in a blue moon, you living as someone new is better than you not living at all." His words were quiet, almost nothing under the rattle of the dishwasher.

"Wow," I said, "I had no idea." I took his hand in mine, "And I'm sorry. You're right. I won't be able to see Aunt Nina; it would be too risky. Plus, if she found out, she'd try to find me and bring me home, which wouldn't end well for any of us." I let my head fall, "But it's just gonna hurt, you know?"

"Yeah, I know," said Josh. He rubbed my hand in his, "But, I promise to keep you in the know. Every time anything happens, I'll make sure to tell you. If Nina gets a paper cut, you'll know." I let out a short laugh and looked up at my best friend.

"Thank you."

We both jumped when a knock pounded the door, "And that would be Dame."

Josh walked over to the door of the apartment and opened the latch, twisting and pulling on the door handle, "How're my two favorite star-crossed lovers?"

"We're fine, Dame. How are you?" I asked. We, Josh and I, have officially given up all hope of Dame not referring to us as a couple.

"I'm doing mighty well, Miss Juliet. I see Romeo is up and running again?" Dame walked over to the counter and dropped into the seat next to me. He pulled the navy blue passport out of his inner-coat pocket.

"Thanks for bringing this over, dude," Josh said, handing his friend a beer, "And I'm sorry I couldn't get it earlier, but, well…you know."

Dame nodded, taking the beer from Josh's hand, "Yep, and it's no problem." He looked at me as he twisted the cap from the bottle, "I just don't know how you're gonna let her go. Look how pretty. Speaking of which, how does mommy-dearest, Nina, feel about this?"

My eyes widened and Josh's gaze flicked to the floor, "She doesn't know, does she?" Dame asked. Josh shook his head, "Oh, wow."

"Yeah," Josh said, "We figured it would be best not to tell her. She's too nuts, would lose her shit if she found out."

"Yeah, but," Dame started, shaking his head, "You're really alright with this? From what I hear, your aunt is like a fucking goddess to you. Do really think you could do it?"

I tried to keep my thoughts straight. *Yes, I can do this. No, it won't be easy. Will you shut the hell up?* "We've talked about it; I can do this, Josh'll keep me in the loop."

"Okay," Dame said, but he didn't sound too convinced. He leaned in closer to Josh, "Fifty bucks she's back by Easter," he whispered.

"I can hear you, you know," I said as the two men started laughing.

Josh shook his head and took a sip of his drink, "I don't know, this was her wack-job idea," he said, "Maybe summer?"

The men started laughing again, "Oh," Dame said, holding his hand up, "Joshy, boy, you better watch out, or Allison might find herself a new man. Have little rats and everything."

"That's not even funny," I said, trying to hold back a slight smile and talk over the never-ending pool of laughter.

"I thought it was," Josh said, taking another sip of his drink.

"Shut up, you don't count. You started laughing in the middle of Mr. Madioski's funeral because you thought of a meme you saw on Facebook."

The laughter grew, but when it finally died down, Dame stood from his place at the island, "Well I gotta split. You know, the works."

"Yeah, dude. Thanks again," Josh said, slapping his back and walking him to the door. There was a loud *whoop* as Dame trailed obnoxiously down the hall. Josh just laughed, shaking his head, and shut the door.

When he turned to look at me, I sat at the counter, the remains of a smile on my face, but something bothered me, "Oh God, what now?" Josh asked.

I looked up at him, "What if I really can't do this?" I asked, "What if I really do come running back here?"

Josh sat in the stool next to me, where Dame sat only

seconds ago, "You won't," he said.

"But how do you know?" I asked, "I'm the weakest link, emotionally, always have been and always will be. How do you know I won't come crawling back-"

"I know you won't," he said. I rolled my eyes, "You wanna know how I know? Because as emotionally all-over-the-place you may be, you love your aunt more than anything in this world. And coming back here could get her killed, and you would never do anything to jeopardize her life, would you?"

"No."

"See," he said, rubbing my arm, "You can do this. I believe in you." I just looked at him. I still worried, worried I'd mess things up, say or do something I shouldn't, "Do you know what Dame said when we were leaving his place a few weeks ago?" I shook my head, "As you were hurrying down the stairs, he said to me, 'She's a strong and intelligent girl, Josh. If anyone can pull this off, it's her. Don't ever let her go'."

I was shocked, "Wait, really?"

"Yes," Josh said, "So, you can do this, trust me. I believe in you, Dame believes in you. Now, you just need to believe in yourself."

I paced back and forth. I paced and paced *and paced.* Rebecca would be there any second. I looked at the money on the dresser next to the bed, sitting there. The only sound in the room was that of my footsteps. *The pacing.*

I hadn't slept at all the night before. There was a constant rushing in my head. All of the voices and tapping and fears. I couldn't lie still. So I had done the laundry, for the last time. I had washed the dishes, for the last time. I had stopped in to check on Aunt Nina, as I often did when I was afraid for her, for the last time.

The metal of the door clicked, and I turned. Josh closed the door silently behind him. I didn't stop pacing. I bit and tore at my nails and the skin around them. And I had this twist in the pit of my stomach. Like something was going to go wrong. I mean, it could. *In so many places.*

"Are you alright?" he asked, walking towards me. I didn't answer. I just paced. But I felt his hands, firm on my arms, grip and stop me, locking me in place, and I couldn't move, "Listen, it's going to be fine. Everything will be fine." I nodded, but I know Josh noticed the blank expression on my face. There was too much going on in my head to feel one thing, to let one thing show.

A scrape and then a loud thud shattered the silence, and both Josh and I jumped, "So, are we ready to do this?"

Rebecca moved quickly across the room, setting her stuff down on the bed. She spread a collection of powders and shadows and foundations over the length of the bed, only leaving a small space at the foot. "Sit," she said and tapped the empty spot. Her eyes fell on the nightstand, "Thank you," she said perkily, stuffing the money into her coat pocket, "Let's begin, shall we?"

I sat still as she worked her magic. She started on my leg. Using scar wax, foundation, eye shadow, and some fake blood, she created a gash that was horrifyingly believable in minutes.

She bent over, coming back up with a blow dryer in her hands and drying the blood until it crisped and scabbed. Around the torn wax and down the rest of my leg, she added little flecks of blood and dabbed yellow and purple bruises over my shins and thighs.

After fifteen minutes, my arms became a strategically-placed array of nicks and scratches, woven between scrapes and lacerations, all lying over colorful bruising. She didn't bother with my torso - no one would see it anyway.

She moved up to my neck. She started with a small incision below my jawline. After, she added more bruising and bloody cuts around the sides. I felt a little prick on my skin near my throat and instinctively pulled away, bringing my hand to my neck. A little spot of blood dotted my finger, "Oh well, nothing that won't help us right?" Rebecca said.

Finally, she began working my face. This was the hardest part because I had to remain still, something I had struggled with. She worked on the bruising around my eyes, "Look up," she said.

The blood was surprisingly cool against my skin. It ran along my forehead and nose, speckling my jaw and cheek bones. She added wax to the places where the cuts needed to appear deeper and along my nose so that it appeared broken. She tapped at the wax with her finger, like a painter lightly smudging paint on a canvas. Then she pulled away, "All done."

She pulled a mirror out of her bag and handed it to me. It was *amazing*. I gasped when I first saw it, and Rebecca laughed. I brought my hand to my face, "Dude. Don't touch it," Rebecca said, "Is it good. I wanna make sure it's what you want before I set it."

I was about to say yes when the door opened and Josh, who had left not too long ago, came in, "Whoa," he said slowly, "Yes, yes, yes! This is amazing! Rebecca, you are truly a wonder."

Rebecca bowed, "So it's good? I can set it?"

"It's great," Josh said with a nod. Rebecca pulled a setting spray from her bag and spritzed every inch of makeup. After she was sure it was dry and added another layer of the mist, she stood up and grabbed her bag from the ground, "Alrighty. Let me know how it goes."

"We will," I said. She smiled and left the room with a single wave. In his hand, Josh held a neck brace, "That does *not* look comfortable."

"Well, it will only be for a half an hour until I kick Nina out," Josh said. I sat up and he crouched down in front of me, fastening the brace around my neck, "How does it feel?"

"Stiff." I couldn't move my head in any direction whatsoever. I pulled at the plastic, trying to adjust it, "Do I have to?"

"Yes, so stop whining and leave it alone."

I sat there on the hospital bed. Josh had taken a step back and I knew what he was going to do next, "Wait."

"What?" he said, holding his phone in his hand. Then his face changed, "Allison, don't you dare do this 20 minutes before you we go through with it."

"But what if we made the wrong choice?" I asked, "What if you were right the first time? It's not too late to turn back."

"Turn back? To where?" he shouted, "To a place where there are 'evil henchmen' or whatever after you? To a place where you and your aunt are both murdered?" His voice had risen, and he spoke firmly, "We're doing this for a reason, remember why."

"But-"

"No."

"I just-"

"Allison."

I let out an aggravated breath and shifted in my seat, "Fine," I said, looking at the floor, "You're right."

"Now, remember," Josh said, "You're a human vegetable. You *cannot* move. Got it?"

"Got it." This was killing me. *But you're doing it to save her.* So, I sat up straight and took a deep breath in, "Call her."

Josh sucked in a breath of courage and glanced at me one more time before unlocking his phone. My stomach twisted in the silence. Would she even believe it? *The phone starts to ring.*

I can hear my heart thumping in my ears. *There is a click at the other end of the line and Josh speaks,* "Nina - shit, take her through here! - oh my God! Nina, can you hear me?"

His voice was so frantic, so scared, "Josh, yeah. What's up?" Her voice was next to normal, only borderline fearful. She had no idea what was going to be laid on her next, "Is everything alright?"

"No, Allison was in an accident," Josh said. He shuffled and moved around the room. His voice was strained, like he had been out of breath.

"Wait, *what?*"

"Allison, she was driving up to the lookout. She went off road and over the bend. The one you and I almost went over the first time we went up." Josh breathed heavily, his chest rising and falling, huffing over the phone.

"Oh my God." She spoke quickly, like she was trying to

think, trying to do 20 things at once, "Um, okay. Jesus, I'll be there in ten minutes. Oh my God." She paused for a moment, and I heard her keys lift from the counter, "Josh?"

"Yes?"

Aunt Nina tried to suppress a cry, "Please take care of her."

"I will." Then the line went dead. A small tear started to pull at the corner of my eye, but I wiped it away.

"You good?" Josh asked.

I nodded, rubbing the sweat from my palms onto the nightgown, "Yep."

"Good," Josh said, "Because we have about ten minutes 'till show time."

16

The sheets of the bed were cold against my skin, and the hairs on my exposed back stood on end. Still, beads of sweat trailed down the sides of my face and neck. Sickness bubbled in my stomach and throat as the minutes crept by so slowly. She told Josh she'd message when she arrived. Until then, we had nothing to do but wait.

A light rush of air blew from a vent overhead. Outside, the sun fell over the mountains, strips of golden light ducking, hiding, peeking from behind buildings that lined the city's streets.

Josh stood near the door. His arms crossed over the gray long-sleeve shirt that covered his arms. His hair, gelled back like it always was, stood stiff, like soft spikes pointing to the ceiling. There was something about the way he stood, staring at his watch, occasionally glancing around the bright room. He seemed…flighty, skittish.

My hands shook like they had been for the past three hours. I hadn't gotten out of bed until two in the afternoon, and by the time I was able to collect my bearings, I had to leave for the hospital. There was something in my mind, a constant worry that couldn't leave me to lay in piece.

The room was dead still - until an ear-splitting tone shattered the silence like a shattering glass pane, it and pierced my heart, "That's her," Josh said. His eyes had been on the phone, and he shifted them to catch my gaze. I nodded, making one last shift to my position on the bed, "Good luck," he said. He turned and the left the room.

I lay there, staring at the ceiling. The white of the panels, so bland and boring, somehow held my attention. Then I closed my eyes.

Steady breathing. I took low, controlled breaths, letting each one grow smaller and lighter than the last.

There were footsteps coming down the hall. *Still as a statue.* I focused on letting every muscle in my body fall numb, as if moving them was a task my nerves could no longer manage.

But the footsteps left as quickly as they came. *No flinching.* I let my mind drift, not thinking of the constant twitching and rolling of my eyes behind my lids. The more I thought about it, the worse it would become. So better to not think of it at all. A new pair of footsteps came down the hall, thick and heavy. But they were not alone.

Heels, those of a lawyer that had just came home from court, clacked, running behind, eventually passing the other. *Aunt Nina's crying voice.*

"Nina, it's not good. She's-" Hands slapped the door frame as she whipped around the corner and into the room. A gasp, followed by the clapping of her hand over her mouth, echoed in the empty space. I heard each heavy step as Aunt Nina grew closer. The sound of agonizing breaths was the only one to break the quiet of the hushed room. I could only imagine what she looked like; a red nose and puffy eyes that sparkled. *Because they always sparkled.*

There was a small whimper as she fell to her knees. Then she was at my side, "Oh, God," she said through a developing sob, taking my hand in one of hers, "Please don't take her." Her forehead pressed tightly against our hands, and the bed and her body shook with the inhales and staggered exhales of weeping breath.

Though I was not looking at her, I could see her face, crouched there against the side of the bed. I could imagine the lines on her forehead, all bunched together and the tight spread of her lips in anguish.

I could feel the breaking of my heart in my chest, like a flower knowing it's losing its petals one by one, watching them fall helplessly below. There was a long draw of breath and I felt her head lift heavily. A slight shuffle behind Aunt Nina said Josh stood near the doorway.

Her thumb slowly rubbed the side of my hand, the skin tingling with every swift stroke. Her body shifted slightly as she used her free hand to wipe the falling tears from her eyes, "Um." The word shook, "I don't even..." Her voice trailed off, and she sniffled.

"Babydoll, I love you so much." Her words were more firm now as she tried to keep her composure, but they still dipped in and out with the tears that filled her throat, "And, you...you make my day, my life, brighter just by being a part of it. You were my little angel in a world where that didn't even seem possible, and-"

She took a trembled breath to force back the tears, "And I

can't imagine living without you. It's every parent's worst nightmare to outgrow their child. But that won't happen. It can't," she said, and she coughed to steady her voice, "Because I know you. And you won't let that happen. You are strong, and you're a fighter.

"You will make it out of this room alive. You will finish school and get the job of your dreams, because you push, and *you never stop fighting.*"

Her hands tightened around mine, "That's what I love most about you. Ever since you were young, you knew what you stood for, and you wouldn't let wrong happen. You have patience and pride and a hell of a better judgment than I do." She let a small laugh leave her body. One hand held onto my palm while the other rubbed the top of my hand gently, "And that's why you can't go.

"Allison, you," she started, but her voice broke and faulted, "you are my world. I would die without you. And I can't-" She stumbled and found her ground, "I can't lose you. I can't - another person can't leave me.

"So, if you can hear me, just know, I'll be right here by your side, waiting. I know you won't let me down. Because you are the most wonderful thing in this world, and no matter what happens in my life, you will always the best part of it. Because the day I got you was the day I got a daughter and better yet, my reason for living."

Her hand still held mine as she stood. She bent over the bed, her free hand holding her hair out of her face. Her lips were soft, wet with tears against my skin. She let her forehead fall, resting it on my face, "I love you, so much." Then, as she turned, her hold onto me weakened and I felt her hand slipping away. I felt her slipping away.

And whether it was involuntary, or my subconscious unable to let her go, the muscles in my hand clenched, holding tightly, gripping tightly, onto hers.

She froze, her heel hovering above the floor. Then there was a shuffle and a sudden screeching. I jumped, just barely, as the machine screamed in my ears, "Her heart rate is dropping!" Josh yelled and pushed past Aunt Nina, "Nina, you have to go."

"No," she said. Her voice didn't cry, it cracked. Her hands lifted and hovered in the air. One landed on her chest, "Josh, no."

"Nina, you have to go," Josh repeated sternly. I heard the shuffling of people entering the room, and Aunt Nina was pushed farther away from me, forced towards the door. She tried to move in closer, "Someone get her out of here!"

"Ma'am, I'm going to need you to step outside," a husky female voice said. I heard the scrape of Aunt Nina's heels against the linoleum flooring.

"No! I can't!" my aunt cried, "No, you don't - Allison!" I felt every ounce of my being, what I was, fall apart as her voice shook and croaked, and I had to fight to not run to her, "Allison!"

"Ma'am," the nurse repeated, but Aunt Nina still fought back, ripping and tearing through as several nurses tried to drag her out of the room. She screamed and yelled. But what was happening proved too overwhelming for her to bear, and eventually she hit the breaking point. And after she fell into a sob, she turned around and collapsed in a nurse's arms, an unhinged mess of heartache and fear.

I watched, my head hovering just above the pillow, as they took her away and down the hall. She was doubled over, her forehead resting in her hand while the other lay on her chest. Her plum satin shirt, tucked into a tight black skirt and sheer black pantyhose, shimmered under the hall lights. Someone, a tall and lanky man, pulled the door shut. As the handful of people inside of the room still shuffled, Josh turned to look at me, "What the *hell* was that?" he yelled.

"I know-"

"No, you don't!" he shouted over me, "I could've lost - and still can lose - my spot here at the hospital because of this, Allison. I could never be allowed to graduate or get my license! And, now! Ugh!"

He turned and kicked the wall, "Josh, calm down!" I said, standing from the bed, "Listen, I know I messed up," I said. Josh scoffed, "But nobody died, right?" I rubbed his arm, and he nodded, "It's going to be okay."

His breathing was heavy, and his chest heaved. But as I rubbed his back, a control came to his breaths, and he spoke, "So."

"So..." I said, "What do we do now?" I honestly hadn't thought of what would happen if I failed; I had been so sure I wouldn't. I looked up. Through the blinds in the window, I caught glimpses of the waiting room at the end of the hall.

Aunt Nina sat in a chair, a shapeless heap weeping in Patricia's arms.

"Now, you go home," he said, "You make a recovery, and we try again."

17

Aunt Nina was *suffocating*. Having taken the next two weeks after the 'accident' off of work, she had nothing to occupy her days but drown me in endless hugs, deafen me with incessant conversation, and choke me under an unceasing presence, "Aunt Nina!"

I pushed her hands away, "What?" she asked.

"I love you, but you have to stop." I spoke softer now, "I know you're just trying to help, but seriously, you're smothering me. I'm not going to die just laying here."

She finished fiddling with the comforter on my bed, "Aunt Nina."

"Okay, okay. I know," she said, holding her hands up in defense, "I'm sorry." She backed up and clasped her hands together, resting them on her front. Still, an innocent smile was spread across her face.

"It's alright," I said, "But really, you need to do something with your time besides wait on me. Josh swings by on his lunch breaks, and if you'd go to work, you'd be home around six. I can handle myself. It's been almost two weeks now, you need to move on, get back to your life."

She let out a breath, "I know," she said, "It was just really scary, you know?" I nodded. I did know. That was the thing I had worried about most, "I just realized that sometimes, I will be a jerk, or give you the silent treatment, or just be busy." I was going to interject, but she spoke before I could, "But, being busy is a part life, I know. Which is why I'm going back to work tomorrow."

"Wait, really?"

"Yeah," she said, sitting next to me on the bed, "That's why I'm so touchy today. I just wanted to make sure you were good before I went back."

Wow, do I feel like a jerk. "Oh, I'm sorry. I didn't know," I said, "Thank you."

Aunt Nina smiled, "It's alright. But, I'm leaving early this week," she said, pointing, and I knew there was no point in fighting her, "But *next* Monday, I'll start back on my regular schedule."

Aunt Nina worked in private practice with her own hours, but keeping a schedule was always something she had to do. An OCD thing, I guess, "Well, that's good."

There was a click downstairs then the screeching of the front door. Footsteps clonked up the stairs and Josh appeared in the doorway, "Sorry I'm late," he said, "How are my two beautiful ladies?" He walked over and kissed Aunt Nina on the cheek then came and sat down beside me.

"We're hanging in there," Aunt Nina said, "I was just telling Allison that I'm going back to work this week."

"Well, that's great!" Josh said, "I was wondering how long it was going to take." He looked down at his watch, "When will

Aaron be here? You said six, right?"

"Yeah, regional vice manager decided he wanted to tour today," Aunt Nina said, "He's supposed to have Sundays off. That's the only day he gets off. Now, they've even taken that away from him!" She shook her head and flailed her hands, and her fists clenched.

"Hey! Sorry. I'm here!" I heard someone yell from downstairs. There was the shuffling of feet and the scraping of paws as Cooper ran to see who was at the door, "Hey, Coop!"

Aunt Nina stood from where she leaned against my vanity, and Josh and I got out of the bed, "Here," Aunt Nina said, grabbing my arm, but I gently pulled it free.

"I got her," Josh said, "You go see your boyfriend. God knows he's dying to see you." Aunt Nina rolled her eyes and walked out of my room. Josh and I followed.

Aaron stood in the foyer with Cooper's front paws up on his chest. He looked up when he heard our steps on the marble above, "Hey!"

Aunt Nina trailed quickly down the stairs to her boyfriend, her hand gliding down the rail delicately. When she reached him, he gripped her arms and kissed her, "How'd he get in?" I asked Josh. But in the echo of the large house, the two lovebirds downstairs heard my question. Aaron stood at the foot of the stairs, holding up his keys, "She gave you a key?"

"Yes," Aunt Nina said, huddled up against Aaron, her hand on his chest, "I did." I looked at Josh and smiled, fighting a laugh. Aunt Nina rolled her eyes again, "Just shut up and come downstairs."

With him, Aaron brought Olive Garden to go, and we all ate in the living room. Aunt Nina lay with Aaron on the couch, curled up in the pocket of his body, and Josh sat in the loveseat with me on the floor at his feet, "So, Aaron," Josh started. Aaron stopped eating and both he and Aunt Nina looked our way, "I hear you're the reason Walmart is no longer a trash hole."

Aaron laughed, "Well, I guess I could say yes, that's true." He shook his head while twisting a strand of pasta, "Oh, but it was a nightmare today."

"Aw, what happened?" Aunt Nina said, rubbing Aaron's chest with her hand.

Aaron pushed himself up, forcing Aunt Nina to readjust her body to fit again, "Well everybody was just lazy today. Like, lethargic deadbeats. They moved at snail's pace and wouldn't get anything done. There were forty palettes in the back when I got there, and ton more were brought in when the truck came.

"The backroom was just a complete mess. Shit everywhere. The shelves were not full." He paused for a moment looking down at Aunt Nina, "I walked the store today - Home and Office had four aisles that desperately needed stocked, and one had nothing on a whole side!

"Then Ed came, and that was just a complete mess. So I had to be the boss that I hate being today. I had to pull everyone in a room and tell them. I said, 'Listen, if you don't get your shit together, we're going to have a bigger problem than Ed's unexpected visit on our hands'. But, it was just not a good day."

Josh and I just sat there. Aaron had seemed so sweet and conservative, and I could never imagine him yelling at anyone, "Well," Aunt Nina said, "Just be glad it's over. Are they giving you tomorrow off?"

"Nope," Aaron said, "Bright and early seven a.m. I'll be there."

"That's complete bullshit," Aunt Nina said, "They can't keep doing this. You haven't had a day off in four and a half weeks now. It's ridiculous!"

"Yeah," Aaron agreed, "But it's the job. We both knew it; we're both the job. It's something we just have to get over." He was clearly irritated but tried to be positive. He lifted the bowl of pasta he had set on the coffee table during his moment of rage and started eating again.

"I know, I know," Aunt Nina said, standing up from the couch, "It's still ridiculous. But get this - well first, I have to cancel for Wednesday. Why? Because my client decided she was going to wake up one morning and suffocate her husband, and now I have to make it look like she didn't. Yay me!" She stood up, sarcastically waving her hands in the air in 'excitement', "I have to go to the bathroom, I'll be right back."

Aunt Nina side-stepped through the tangle of people and disappeared down the hall. I watched the movie on the screen, but when Aunt Nina came back, her face was pale, white, like she had seen a ghost, "Allison, can you come here for a moment?" she asked.

"Yeah, sure." I stood from my spot on the ground and followed her down the hall. I turned around to see Josh staring at me. He silently asked what was going on, but I just shrugged, mouthing 'I don't know'.

When we reached the kitchen, Aunt Nina started pacing. She walked form the counter to the back door and back again. Her nerves got the best of her already torn and bleeding nails. I asked her if she was alright.

"No, I'm not," she said, throwing her hand into the pocket of her robe. Then she pulled something out, "Look at this!"

In her hand was a navy box, lined in velvet. She didn't have to open it; we both knew what was inside, "Oh my God," I said. A smile spread across my face, "Aunt Nina!"

She made a face, "You're excited?" she asked.

"You're not?"

"No!" she said, running her hands through her hair, "I mean...I don't know. I don't know if that's what I want."

I shook my head, walking up to her, "Why wouldn't it be?" I asked, "Aunt Nina, you are strong and smart, but you are too difficult." She opened her mouth to speak in protest, but I put up my finger, "Out there is a man whose whole heart is devoted to you and only you. And from what I see, you feel the same. You get all giddy around him, and it's hilarious, actually. My point is, why won't you even consider it?"

Aunt Nina shook her head and looked the ground, her eyes avoiding my gaze, "I don't know, I just- after-"

"Don't say it's because of Uncle Peter," I cut in. I closed my eyes. When I opened them, Aunt Nina looked at me, appalled, "Listen, I understand he hurt you, and it sucked, but it's been almost 14 years. You have to move on. You can't let one jackass run the rest of your life."

"I'm not," Aunt Nina protested.

"You are," I said, "And you have to stop. It's not fair to Aaron, but more importantly, it's not fair to you. You downgrade yourself, and for what reason? Because some guy was too stupid to see how amazing you really are?"

"Easy for you to say!" Aunt Nina shouted back, "You're smart, and funny, and beautiful." She walked to the island and dropped into a seat, "I'm none of those things."

"Are you kidding me?" I said, walking over to where she

sat. I fell into the stool next to her, "Do you know what one of the first things Aaron said to me when we met at the hospital was?" I asked.

"*Wow, she's an idiot,*" she replied, picking at her nails.

I grabbed her hands, forcing them to stop, "No," I said, "He told me you were the most beautiful thing he had ever laid eyes on."

Aunt Nina scoffed, "Yeah, right," she said.

"He did," I said, "Then he talked about how smart you are - how you can see through any, and every, little thing."

"Really?"

"Yeah," I replied, "And I told him I already knew that, *trust me.*" Aunt Nina laughed, "Do you know how hard it is growing up with a lawyer? Someone who professionally hears lies and yanks the truth out of you? It sucks." I said.

We both chuckled at this, "So, you really think I'm...well..."

"Beautiful. And yes, I do," I said, "And you can say it. You *should* say it. Because you are. You are beautiful and smart, and that's something you should be proud of." Aunt Nina smiled, but something still bothered her, "What?"

"Oh, nothing," she said. I just looked at her. She was so dramatic, and it was so obvious, "I just - what if he's just here for the money?"

"Wait, what?" I was shocked. Genuinely shocked, "Is that what you really think?"

Aunt Nina nodded, "Yeah," she said quietly. A small tear slipped down her face, "I mean, that's what happened with your uncle."

"No, it wasn't-"

"Yeah, Allison, it really was," she said jarringly, "How do I know?" she asked, looking at me. She looked destroyed, "I read the messages." She let her chin fall into her hand. "What messages?" I asked. But I had a feeling I already knew.

She didn't look at me when she spoke, "Between him and - *her.*" She paused for a moment, *"I only married her for the money anyway,"* she said, staring at the cabinets, *"Her parents had just died, and she was alone. They left her and her sister everything. It was perfect."*

Wow, "Aunt Nina, I'm so..." But there were no words. More tears streamed from her eyes, her face pinched. I took her in my arms, and she leaned her head against my shoulder.

"So, I have issues," she said. We both let out a short laugh, "But you think he really does, like..."

"Love you?" I asked. She nodded, "Yeah, I do. With the way he looks at you when you're not looking." I stopped for a moment, but asked, "Do you love him?"

Aunt Nina turned to look at me, "Yeah," she said, "Yeah, I really think I do." I smiled, "I love the way that he never yells at me or pins the blame for things out of our control on me." I could only assume these were things my uncle did, "And I love the way he always has something good to say. About everyone. And he's always so sweet and gentle. He makes me feel...special. Like, when I'm with him, I actually feel like I matter, you know?"

I nodded, "Yeah."

"And, every morning when I wake up, there is a message waiting, telling me how much he loves me and how he can't wait to see me." Her smile was brighter now, and she looked genuinely happy, "And, with him, I forget. I feel like *me* again. I don't feel lost or cheated or *broken*. I just feel like *me*."

Aunt Nina looked down, shyly, at the box in her hands, "If he asked would you say yes?"

She bit her lip, suppressing a toothy smile, "Yes." I beamed. She giggled, and I couldn't have been happier for her. I took her hand.

Then there was a knock at the door. I stood up, "I'll get it," I said, "You go put that back before Aaron finds out you have it."

Aunt Nina smiled and left the room. I followed. As I walked under the staircase, through the windows I saw something shift outside.

I laid my hand on the door's handle. I pulled it open, only to reveal nothing. Just as I was about to close the door, something, something that shined, caught my eye. *Something gold.*

I bent over, shivering with the cold outside and that that ran through my veins. With the dreadful envelope in my hands, I straightened, only to find myself looking down the ashy barrel of a gun.

18

"In the house," the man said. The gun aimed at the spot right between my eyes. My heart raced, "Now."

I backed slowly into the house, raising my hands in the air. Each step echoed through the empty foyer, followed by the shuffling of the man's shoes.

I recognized the man. A flutter in my chest sent chills up my spine, and I couldn't think clearly. *This is it. This is how I'm going to die.*

After backing through the doorway and into the house, I turned around, slowly, and walked into the center of the foyer, feeling the gun against the back of my head. I stood directly between the two staircases, "Get down on your knees," the man said. I hesitated as my breaths staggered with building tears, "Now!"

I dropped hard on my knees, the marble crushing my skin between the bones. I left my hands in the air and remained deathly still. Until a shrill voice turned my head, "Oh my God!"

Aunt Nina stood in the opening beside the left staircase, her hands covering her mouth. The man turned away from me, his eyes flicking between the two of us, "You too! Beside her, now!" Aunt Nina lifted her hands in the air, and as her eyes filled with petrified tears, she walked over to where I kneeled on the ground.

The man's gun trailed her the whole way, and followed her downwards as she slowly bent down to her knees beside me. She looked over at me, but I couldn't meet her gaze. I closed my eyes and tilted my head backwards. We both were going to die - right here, right now - because of me. Because of my stupidity in New York.

I heard the echo of footsteps, and my eyes tightened, "Holy shit," Josh said as he entered the room and brought his hands to the air. The man didn't have to ask - Josh kneeled next to me, no protest. I guessed protesting wasn't something to do when being held at gunpoint.

But Aaron didn't go down as easily, "Oh my - are you insane?" he shouted when he walked into the foyer. He looked like he was about to charge the man with a pistol risen to his chest, and the man with the gun snapped his fingers.

Another man walked through the front door, which still stood ajar. He walked over to Aaron and wrapped Aaron hands behind his back. He was stronger than Aaron, throwing him down next to Aunt Nina. Aaron tried to fight, but froze when he looked up.

The man with the gun now moved closer to us, the tip of the gun against Aunt Nina's temple. Still fixed in her position, Aunt Nina did not move and showed no emotion on her face, except a single teardrop that ran down her right cheek. If this man was going to kill her, she wasn't going to let him have any of her fear.

Aunt Nina, always so strong, so proud. With the four of us lined up, the two men examined us closely, one by one. I recognized *both* of the men. *The men were strong, and they could be brothers.* And I knew why they were here. I wasn't making it this time. This time, I wasn't going to escape, "Do you know why we're here?" the man with the gun asked.

"To kill me," I whispered. I had locked gaze with the marble floor below and couldn't look up.

"Excuse me?"

"To kill me!" I yelled. The two men did not wear the sunglasses that covered their eyes the night I last saw them, and I could see the green irises glowing under the light.

"That's exactly right," he replied, "But we're going to have some fun first." He smiled a twisted smile, and his brother paced behind us. With nothing in his hands, he was able to walk over to Aaron, grabbing his collar and throw his iron-ringed knuckles into his jaw.

Aunt Nina shuddered, the gun still to her head, as Aaron fell to the ground, "Get up!" the man with the gun said. Aaron tried, but he collapsed. Blood dripped from his mouth, "Up! Now!" He struggled, but he was eventually able to hoist his body up, "Good," the man with the gun said, "Now, why don't you tell your girlfriend who you've been talking to?"

Aaron's eyes widened. The man no longer held the gun against Aunt Nina's temple, but had taken a few steps back and pointed the gun at Aaron, "I…"

"Go on," the other man said.

Aaron looked at Aunt Nina, "I've been talking to Rosaline."

Aunt Nina cringed at the name, her body caving inwards,

and her eyes slamming shut. My brow furrowed, "Wait, Aunt Nina, who's Rosaline?" I asked.

"His ex-wife."

Her words were cold and bitter, and she looked straight ahead, "Nina," Aaron said, "You can read the messages. She contacted me. I told her no, that I was happy, that I was with someone. I told her I didn't want to deal with her crap anymore, that I wasn't going to. Believe me, please."

Aunt Nina looked at him, her lips pressed together. She looked like she was about to fall apart. But she took a deep breath and impassively looked forward. The man behind us began pacing again, until he stopped behind Josh, "Josh…"

He said the word with a twisted satisfaction.

"Why don't you tell - no, show - Allison what you've been up to?" Josh's lips pinched together and he looked up at the man with the gun, enraged. Then he reached for his sleeves.

Dozens of slits, some scarring, and others just beginning to heal, lined his forearms. I gasped and Aunt Nina let out a short breath, bringing the back her hand to her mouth, "I thought we were past this," I said.

"We were," Josh said, pulling the navy blue sweatshirt's sleeves back over his arms, "But…"

"But what?" I said softly, "You can talk to me, to us…"

I looked to Aunt Nina, "Yes," she said, "Josh, I know it's been…"

"Listen, it's over, alright?" Josh cut in. His eyes drilled into those of the man with the gun.

"But it's obviously not," I said, "Some of those are not even a day old and-"

"Just stop, Allison!" Josh yelled. His gaze locked onto the

wall, "This wouldn't even be a thing if you hadn't put our lives constantly at risk."

I didn't know what to say, "Wow. Okay."

The two men smirked; this is what they wanted, "And Nina," the gunman said, "Don't you think you should tell your boyfriend what you've been doing lately?" he asked. He smiled and looked at me, "Maybe Allison would like to know, too."

"Aunt Nina, what is he talking about?" I asked. She looked away, but was faced with Aaron's anxious stare. Her eyes watered, and she tried to speak, but couldn't.

She glared up at the man with a gun pointed at her, "Go on," he said.

Aunt Nina face grew cold, "Fuck off."

"Oh," the man said, "I was going to kill him first," he nodded towards Aaron, "But maybe I'll just shoot you instead."

My heart stopped, "No!"

"Alright, fine," Aunt Nina spit. She looked at Aaron, her mouth opened. Whatever this man wanted her to say…

"What is it?" Aaron asked, "Nina, you can tell me anything."

She gave him a timid and fearful glance, "I…" She let her eyes shut and shoulders drop, "I've been using again."

"*What?*" The word shook as it left Aaron's mouth, "Which ones?" he words dripped with a cry.

"Prozac and Celexa." She licked and pulled in her lips. Her eyes blinked as she looked up at the ceiling and fought to suppress a cry. She sucked in a staggered breath and leveled her head. She wasn't going to let them win.

"Where are you getting them?" I asked. Her therapist had stopped prescribing them eight months ago.

Aunt Nina said no words, but just looked down the line at Josh. My eyes followed.

"No," I said, "Josh, please tell me you're not..."

But there was nothing he could say. He couldn't defend himself. Because it was the truth, "I'm sorry."

"Why?" I asked. I spoke through a sob, "Josh, why?"

"Because," he protested, "She *is* clinically diagnosed with anxiety and OCD." He shook his head and looked at the floor, "I didn't know she'd abuse them again. I should've, but I didn't. I just figured if she was on her meds, she couldn't drink. And I know how you hate it when she drinks - how it worries you. You check on her every night while she sleeps for God's sake." His tone was biting and icy.

"That's no excuse," I said.

"Is that true?" Aunt Nina asked. I snapped my head to face her, "You really worry that much?"

I nodded, "Yeah."

The other man stood next to the man with the gun now, "Well," the man with the gun said, "While we're doing this, Allison," he pointed the gun towards me, "How about we tell dear Aunt Nina the truth about what went down at the hospital?"

Oh no. The thud of my heart grew and the hair on the back of my neck stood on end.

"Allison, what happened?" Aunt Nina asked. She was no longer in tears or afraid. She was a parent, a lawyer, speaking firmly, "Tell me, now."

But before I could speak, something buzzed in the pocket of the man behind me. He pushed past Aunt Nina and me to his brother.

A small cough barely ruffled the silence.

I glanced at Aunt Nina. She caught my gaze and raised her eyebrows. I tilted my head slightly, *what?* She flicked her eyes at the man. My eyes widened. But she looked down at herself then at the gun. Then she looked at me and at the man's legs. She wanted us to jump him.

"Well," the man with the gun said, and we were forced to look at him, "I'd love to stay and chat, but Boss wants us back, so we're gonna have to cut the conversation short." He adjusted his stance to face Aunt Nina and Aaron, "Who's gonna die first?"

"You, asshole," Aunt Nina said and lunged. I leapt from my spot on the floor, diving at the man's lower body. I wrapped my arms around his calves. But as I did, I heard a shot fired.

I looked up. Aunt Nina's hands were wrapped around the man's hands and the gun, pushing them away from the rest of us. Her face was tight. She shot out her leg, kicking the man in the gut and striking him between the ribs.

She took ahold of the gun, her hands all catawampus - obviously never having held a firearm in her life - and pulled the trigger. Two shots sounded, each one followed by the dropping of one of the two men.

Aunt Nina dropped the gun, almost throwing it onto the marble. There was a grim silence that followed. She looked at me with the wide-eyed innocence of a child. Then she turned her head.

The sound that left her body next was a cross between a *no* and an ear-splitting shriek. Three shots had been fired. Two struck the men. One found itself a dreadful, unwanted home in someone else's chest.

19

Her whole body trembled, "No!" The word was more a screech than anything else. Her hands shook violently as she raised them to her face.

She ran across the foyer, dropping to her knees, dropping in the blood, and took his face in her hands, "No, no, no, no. Please!"

Aaron sputtered, and as he did, specks of blood littered his face. Drops of the coppery, deep red pumped rhythmically out of his body. The wound wasn't a perfect hole, but more torn and caved, like a knife had been shoved into his chest and twisted, trying to make a circle but leaving nothing but a mangled star behind.

Aunt Nina threw herself over Aaron's body, her chest heaving. Josh stood from the ground and swung around the corner and into the kitchen. When he came back, he held a white towel in his hands. He rushed to Aaron's side, handing Aunt Nina the towel.

She took it from him with her free hand, pulling the other from Aaron's chest. Her skin was dripping with blood, the red a thin layer sliding like water between her fingers.

She tried to work quickly, calmly, sliding her hair behind her ear with her bloody fingers, leaving it to clump together and streak traces of red across the skin around her face as it fell out again. But the strong woman I'd always known was gone, only a weeping, crumbling mess left to show.

Josh stood up and pulled his phone out of his back pocket. I heard it ring and the *click* when someone picked up, "Hi, this is Josh Montgomery. I need and ambulance at..." He walked out of the room, trying to escape the shaking cries and illiterate words of Aunt Nina.

I could understand why. Simply watching her was devastating. It was like watching someone slowly go mad, becoming more and more frantic, paranoid, by the second, "Aunt Nina-" I started, resting a hand on her shoulder.

"No!" she screamed. She hurled me off of her body. Her eyes were swollen and red and her hands and clothes were drenched in blood, "This is all your fault!" she barely said through a quivering lip.

She turned back to look at her dying boyfriend and rubbed the tears and sweat from her face with the back of her hands, uncaring of the blood that they left behind. She lifted his body from the ground, triggering an agonized moan, followed by a cough and more blood, and rested his head in her lap, "You're okay," she said as more tears trickled down her face and fell onto Aaron's, "You'll be okay."

She said it so reassuringly, but the way she looked at Josh when he re-entered the room showed the raw fear that hid behind her eyes. She had no idea what would happen. She looked back down at Aaron and smiled through the tears, through the weeping, and laid a hand on Aaron's face. He brought his, slowly and shakily, up to rest on hers.

And then we waited.

Until I heard the sirens in the drive, I hadn't realized that the front doors were still open. The paramedics raced through the doors to the steps where Aunt Nina sat, leaning against the iron railing, with Aaron's blood slowly eating the colors of her clothing.

She backed away when the three men moved Aaron to the gurney, but was right back at his side as they rushed him outside. I followed behind.

Aunt Nina held Aaron's hand the whole way. But once it was time to load him, she was forced to let go. And for her, it seemed, that was the end of the world.

She ran her hands through her hair, and her hands began shaking, even more violently than before. It hurt so much to see her that way. I walked up to her, hoping to calm and comfort her, "Hey-"

But she whipped around, "No! Just, get away from me!" She knocked me into the car behind her, "This - you - why are you such and *idiot*? You have no thoughts about your actions, or their consequences! And now-" Her words faltered, "Now, he's going to die because of *you*. I'm going to lose the one thing I love *because of you*." Then her face dropped, turning to bitter ice, "I wish I would've let you go when your parents died. Because you're just a screw up, and that's it. And, I don't care what I said before. *I hate you.*"

The words cut like a sharp blade to the heart - stung like a shock of lightning that burned my insides. I watched in petrified horror as Aunt Nina crawled into the back of the vehicle with her boyfriend, stroking the hair from his face and clasping his hands between her soft fingers.

I sat in the stiff chair, biting the skin around my fingers until they streaked with blood. My foot fidgeted like mad, tapping the floor below. There was a certain adrenaline, a certain fear, that I could actually *feel* coursing through the blood in my veins, through my body, pumping through my heart.

I heard the sound of footsteps enter the waiting room. I looked up to see Josh walking over to a chair next to me, "He's not doing well, Allison," he said.

I let my head fall into my hands. The feeling of something running through me returned, something unnerving, something that seemed to upset every little thing inside of my body. My muscles clenched, "How is she?"

"Pshh," Josh hissed. He shook his head, "That's not going well, either." I dropped my face and hands to my lap, "But, hey," Josh said, rubbing my back, "That's absolutely no excuse for her to have said what she said. There is *never* and excuse to say that. *Ever.*"

"It's all my fault, Josh," I said, "I'm the one who started all of this. And now, Aaron is going to die. Because I'm an idiot."

"You're not and idiot," Josh said, his hand softly running through my hair.

"I am," I said, "I'm an idiot, and weak. If I had just 'died' in the hospital like I was supposed to, or even died in New York, none of this would've happened."

"Allison," Josh said. He pulled on my arm, trying to remove my head from between my knees. I fought to stay down, to just shut out the world, but in the end, Josh was stronger, "You have to stop blaming yourself for everything. Everything isn't your fault; this isn't your fault. Well, it is a little," he said with a small laugh, wiping the tears from my eyes, "But you weren't supposed to die in New York."

I was going to speak, tell him I should've, but he held his finger up, "No, you weren't supposed to, you know why?" he asked, "Because you're young and have so much more you're going to do in your life." He held my face within his large palm, "And you have a purpose, something you're meant to do.

"Sometimes we feel like we aren't meant for anything. But let me tell you, we are. You're special; you are here for a reason."

I smiled and looked at him, "Why are you telling me this?" I asked.

"Because I don't want you to do anything stupid," Josh replied, "And, it's true." I rolled my eyes, "Think about it," Josh continued, "Imagine what would've happened to Nina if she hadn't had you when your parents died, or when Peter left her. She would've drunk herself to death years ago. You," he said, pointing his finger into my chest, "You are the sole reason she's still alive. An amazing lawyer, a kind woman, and a compassionate friend, is still alive because of you."

"Yeah," I said, "How *is* she, though? How's she holdin' up?"

Josh looked at me, "Honestly, she's a mess," he said shaking his head, "I've never seen her like this. When I was back there with her, she could barely stand...and it's just not good. I finally got her to calm down, now she's passed out in the lounge with Patricia."

"God," I said, standing up, "If something happens to him-" I felt the tears welling up in my eyes, "She's going to fall apart. What if she drinks herself to death?" I asked, "She *will* drink herself to death. And it will be all my fault!"

I threw my hands in the air and let them fall to my sides. I slid them into my pockets, feeling something crisp in the right one. I wrapped my fingers around whatever rested in the pocket of my jean shorts. I pulled it out.

Then I saw the gold shimmer in the light.

"What's that?" Josh asked.

I stared blankly at the black envelope, "It was on the porch. When the doorbell first rang," I said, "I bent down to pick it up, then I stood up and saw a gun in my face."

I ripped at the crisp paper with my stiff fingers. The only thing inside was a folded piece of paper.

You don't want to play by the rules? That's fine. But in the end, you still lose, Allison. Come out; there's nowhere to hide.

I looked up at Josh. He looked down at the paper in my hands. Then I felt something on my shoulder.

I jumped. When I turned around, I was faced with a tall man in uniform, "Allison Schwartz?" he asked.

"Um, yes," I replied, shaking the exhaustion from my head, "May I help you?"

"Yes, but first I need to speak with your aunt, Nina Schwartz." He spoke firmly and I wondered how he stood so tall and awake at one in the morning.

"She's asleep," Josh cut in after the silence stretched with no answer, "It's been a rough night for her. May I ask why you need to see her?"

"I'd really like to discuss it with her."

"Listen," I said, "She just saw her boyfriend get shot, and now he's in surgery with slim chances of living. Is having her here really necessary? Whatever you have to say you can say to me."

The officer raised his brows, "Fine. I need to take you all down to the station for questioning, because as far as law enforcement is concerned, there are two dead men in your foyer and another that is in surgery. So, I'd say yes, having her here really *is* necessary."

We all turned as footsteps trailed down the hall.

Aunt Nina walked into the waiting room. She was completely trashed. There were darkening red stains littering the white lining around the pockets and edges of her robe. The black, silk sleeves that usually hung flowingly pulled down heavily on her arms, the lace at the ends had hardened with blood.

Dark rings hugged around her eyes and blood crusted her face, "He's still in surgery," she said, not looking up, "I don't know what I-" Her words ceased when she laid eyes on me. She looked back at Josh, "I'm going to get something to eat."

She stormed off, not looking back or giving me a second glance.

"Actually," the officer said. Aunt Nina turned around, her brows furrowed, "I'm going to need to take the three of you down to the station for questioning because, as I've told your niece, there are three men that have been shot, and we need to get our stories straight."

I could tell the moment the words left this mouth this wasn't going to end well. Aunt Nina was exhausted, beat, "Wait, questioning for what?" She glared the officer down. Then her eyes narrowed, *"You think I did this?"*

Her voice rose in pitch and I looked down at the ground, "I'm not going anywhere," she spit, "I'm *not* leaving, because my boyfriend is in surgery, face-to-face with death. And yes, I did shoot the two men in my foyer, but last time I checked, that was alright when you open the front door with a gun in your face. It's called self-defense." She straightened, regaining all of the pride and dignity I knew, and she folded her arms over her chest, "So you can ask me whatever you want, but I will *not* leave this hospital."

20

The room was unsettlingly cold. The metal of the table-top was like ice beneath my folded arms. A small recorder rested on the table. The person who sat in front of me was not the officer from the hospital, but a woman in a pantsuit. Her chocolate brown hair was up in a tight bun at the back of her head. It complemented her olive skin well. She was fairly young - thirties, maybe.

I had first seen her when we arrived at the station. Until then, it had just been the officer, Josh, Aunt Nina, and me. Yes, eventually Aunt Nina's pride had broken, and she had agreed to get into the car. But boy, did she put up a fight first.

Now she sat in the front room, waiting for her turn to be questioned, "Ms. Schwartz, I'm Detective Vitali with the LAPD." Vitali pulled out the chair opposite of me and sat. There was something about her voice that reminded me of Aunt Nina; it was firm yet almost friendly, "Last night around 10:45 p.m., your house was broken into, and you along with your best friend, aunt, and her boyfriend were held at gunpoint, is that correct?"

"Yes."

"And, did you know the two men that had broken in?"

Yes, "No."

"Okay," Vitali said. She jotted something quickly and illegibly on a notepad, "You didn't know them or their motives?"

I did, "I have no idea."

"Well," Vitali said, folding her hands on the table, "I'm going to ask you to revisit the events that occurred last night. Sometimes, this will give us a better insight on what went down, and sometimes you'll notice things you may have missed, or lost in the adrenaline."

I oddly trusted her. Was it crazy? Probably. If *anything* spilled out about New York or the past month and a half, Aunt Nina and Josh would be dead in a minute, "Okay," I whispered.

"Okay," Vitali said, "I'm going to need you to close your eyes and go back to last night."

I see something shuffle outside. The doorbell had just rung, and I'm going to answer it. But when I open the double doors, no one, nothing, is there. Then something on the porch catches my eye. I bend down to pick it up.

When I stand, there is a gun in my face. My heart immediately quickens. This man, a large man the size of a barge with the muscles of Hercules, is standing in front of me. I catch a glimpse of someone over his shoulder. Someone thinner and almost-

"Wait, someone else was there?" Vitali cuts in. I jump and open my eyes, startled, "And not the other guy?"

"What?"

"You said you saw someone thinner over the man's

shoulder. The two men your aunt shot in the foyer were identical twins - Ethan and Evan Hoalgin. They were both equally large men; if you saw someone thinner, that means there was someone else there."

I thought about what she was saying. I knew who it was, "It was probably a trick of the light, like a streetlamp or something."

Vitali eyed me closely, but let it go, "Alright, you were saying?"

He tells me to get into the house. I back up slowly into the foyer. I fall hard to my knees. Then Aunt Nina walks in.

He turns, keeping the gun on me. He tells her to get down next to me, and Aunt Nina nods and walks over. He followed her with the gun the whole way. Josh came in behind me and got down instantly without being asked. Then Aaron came in.

He wasn't going down as easily, and that's when the other guy came in. He forced Aaron down and punched him in the face. Then the man made us start admitting horrible truths.

"Wait, horrible truths?" Vitali asked.

"Yeah," I said, trying to think of how to explain, "Like, he made Aaron tell Aunt Nina he had been talking to his ex-wife."

"What did he make you say?" Vitali asked, scribbling furiously onto her notepad.

Oh, shit, "I had known my uncle was cheating on my aunt before he told her."

Was this true? Partially. Had I actually admitted this to Aunt Nina? I'd never. But had I known? I'd had a sneaking suspicion.

"Oh, wow." Vitali looked at me, "And when was this? Your uncle cheating?" she asked.

"Um, sixth grade," I said.

"And what happened after that?"

"He left that night - haven't seen him since," I said. And that was the truth.

"Alright," Vitali said. The word was drawn out as she finished writing, "What happened next?"

I closed my eyes and took a deep breath.

Then the man without a gun's phone buzzes and he runs to his brother. Aunt Nina coughs to get my attention, and though she doesn't speak, I can read her face for the crazy idea. She wants to jump the guy.

So we do. I go for his legs - as Aunt Nina instructed - and Aunt Nina goes for the gun. I hear a shot fire. That was the shot that hit Aaron. Then Aunt Nina wrests the gun from the man's hands and shoots them both.

Then she sees Aaron lying in a pool of blood by the stairs. She runs to his side and holds onto him until the ambulance arrives. We come to the hospital while Aaron is rushed to surgery. Then an officer comes. At first, Aunt Nina protests, but eventually she complies and gets into the car.

I opened my eyes. Vitali stared at me, her eyes sharp and narrowed, "Okay," she said, she started to get up, but before I was able to stand, she looked back as if remembering something, "One last thing," she said, "There was a tension between you and your aunt when you got here. What was that all about?"

"What?"

Vitali smiled, "Sorry," she said, "It was just so obvious." She walked to the other end of the room and slowly back again, "She was glaring you down, and you looked like a beaten puppy."

My eyes were on my stubby fingernails, "Oh," I said,

"Um." There was no easy way to say it, no way to say it so that it didn't hurt, "She blames me for what happened. I mean I did-"

But I caught myself before I could say something I regretted, "You did what?" Vitali asked. Her eyebrows were raised and she crossed her arms over her chest.

"I did open the door," I said quickly.

"Well," Vitali said, "That's not really your fault. Any normal person would open the door if the bell rang."

"I know, but-"

"Allison," Vitali cut in, "*This*," she gestured at her notebook and around the room, "isn't your fault. It happens to people in LA all of the time. But from what I understand, there have been several...*incidents*...that have happened to your family lately, is that correct?"

I nodded. And I'm not sure why, but her words triggered something inside of me, and I felt the tightness of tears in my throat and nose. I brought the sleeve of my maroon Vans hoodie to my eyes.

Vitali pulled a few tissues from her pocket and handed them to me, "Here," she said, leaning against the table, "Why don't you start at the beginning?"

"Well, it all started when I came home late from a trip I took for the New Year," I started, "I had missed my flight and was 16 hours late – and I didn't call or message. So, Aunt Nina was *livid.*" I flicked my eyes up to meet Vitali's, "I live with my Aunt Nina. When I was eight-months-old, Aunt Nina and my parents were in an accident. Aunt Nina was the only one who lived." I felt a slight choke to my words and swallowed.

"Oh," Vitali said, looking at the table, "I'm sorry to hear

that."

"Yeah, it's alright. But I had mentioned my mom, which has always been a touchy subject for Aunt Nina. She got mad at me and stopped talking to me for a few days. Then she was in the hospital, and -"

"What was she in the hospital for?" I noticed that Vitali had put her notebook away, folding over its cover and sliding it to the far end of the table.

I tried to think of a way to say it without revealing what happened in New York, "She was attacked in the middle of the night. She was asleep and said that she woke to see a man over her. Then before she could do anything, he stabbed her. Josh and I rushed her to the hospital, and she ended up being alright."

Vitali shook her head, appalled, "Wow, that had to have been hard for you two," Vitali said.

"It was, a little, I guess," I mumbled. There was a pause that stretched, and as a few more tears ran down my face, I continued, "Then the house caught on fire, and -"

"Wait, your house caught on fire?"

"Yeah, well it was *set* on fire. By someone," I said. I just saw her eyes widen, "The firefighters found a flare in a pool of gasoline in the garage." Vitali rested her chin in her hand and I continued, "Then things went quiet for a few weeks, but then Josh was shot."

"And you two are close, right?" Vitali asked. Though her notebook wasn't out, I could tell she was making a mental note about this specific question, and waited for my answer.

"Yes," I said, "His parents died when he was in high school and he has been a part of the family ever since. He didn't have any aunts or uncles and his grandparents were dead. But he was old enough to take care of himself, so he did. But he leaned heavily on Aunt Nina for a while. He's like a son to her. She can't have kids, and Josh and I are all she has."

Vitali nodded, "So after your friend was shot, what happened?"

I had to think to find my spot. But, when I found it, my mind froze. *I tried to fake my death.* Do I tell her? Or just skip it completely? "I was in the hospital. I had been in an accident, but I'm alright now."

"When was this accident?"

"Two weeks ago," I said, "Then, yesterday Aunt Nina said she was going back to work tomorrow, well today now, I guess." I let out a short laugh, "Then I opened the door and almost got us all killed."

I felt the tears fall helplessly from my eyes, but made no effort to stop them, "Hey," Vitali said. I felt her hand wrap around mine, "Listen, it's not your fault."

"But it is!" I said, "If I hadn't opened the door. If I hadn't screwed up. If I hadn't made careless decisions." I was no longer talking about last night.

"Well, this is how I see it," Vitali said, looking me in the eyes, "You are a girl that is too hard on herself and has had a lot thrown her way over the past few weeks." She stood up to get me a cup of water from the table against the wall, "And you're probably exhausted. It's, what, three or four a.m.? We have more to talk about with this new information. Because, it doesn't seem all of these things happening to your family in such a short time period is a coincidence. It seems like someone has it for you. So you should go home, get some rest, and we'll pick up tomorrow, okay?"

I nodded my head and stood from the seat, feeling the sting as my bare thighs peeled from the chair. There was something about this woman; she was nothing like any officer I've ever met before.

Vitali opened the door to the room, waiting for me to exit. I did and she followed closely behind. We walked down the hall and to the room where Josh and Aunt Nina waited.

Aunt Nina sat in a chair, the tears back. The bridge of her nose pressed against the side of her hands below her thumb, and her other hand was in her hair. Josh sat next to her, holding her arm and rubbing her back, "Josh Montgomery."

Josh stood when Vitali called his name. I started to walk away when Vitali grabbed my arm, "Go easy on yourself, Schwartz," she said with a smile. When Josh reached the doorway she looked at him, "Follow me," she said and the two disappeared down the hall. And I sat in a seat two down from Aunt Nina.

"Hey," I said, "I'm really-"

"No." The word was cold, "Do not talk to me."

It was a long 20 minutes, but after what felt like ages, Josh returned and it was Aunt Nina's turn to leave. Josh sat on the edge of his seat, eagerly waiting for Vitali to leave the room, "What did you tell her?" he asked when the door finally shut.

"What?"

"About what I had to admit," he said, "She said you'd mentioned something about that. What did you tell her I said?"

"I didn't mention it," I said, "I knew it could get you in trouble, so I kind of skimmed over it." I leaned back in the chair. I was so tired, nothing even registered anymore. Until one thought came to mind, "Wait what did you tell her I said?"

Josh shook his head, leaning back as well, "Same," he said, "I just skipped it. Didn't want to cross stories."

I nodded, "What did you tell her you had to admit?" I asked, "In case they ask us." But really, I was just curious.

"You're just curious, admit it," he said, and I smiled, "I just told her I had started drinking pretty badly."

We sat in silence with the occasional small talk until Aunt Nina was finished with her interview. When she finished, we could leave.

But I did not expect what happened when she came back.

Thirty-eight minutes crawled by, and I had fallen asleep on Josh's shoulder. He nudged me, shaking me until I woke. We stood as we heard Vitali stride down the hall in her heels. She pushed the door out, holding it open for Aunt Nina.

Who came running through.

She marched towards me, gripping tightly onto the back of my neck when she reached me. Her fingers dug into my skin, and she threw me against a wall, shoving her forearm into my throat, "You *knew?*"

I choked, trying to find words. But there were none.

"Hey!" Vitali grabbed Aunt Nina by the arms, and Josh ran to my side. When Aunt Nina was pulled off of me, I fell to the floor below. I had been lifted off of the ground, pinned in the air by her arm, and unable to catch a wisp of air.

Josh crouched down next to me, and I rubbed my throat, gasping for air, "Are you okay?" Josh asked.

I nodded, and stressed, forced tears clouded my eyes. I didn't look at him. I watched Aunt Nina fighting as Vitali pushed her into a room attempting to calm her, "You *knew!*" Aunt Nina yelled over the detective's shoulder, pointing at me with teary, narrowed eyes, "You knew he was cheating and didn't tell me about it! You let him-"

Before she could finish, she was finally forced into a room, a sob washing over her - one I can only assume was caused by the memory of that night.

"Is that true?"

I turned to look at Josh.

"Did you know he was cheating?" he asked. His eyes were widened, hurt almost.

"Yes."

Josh shook his head and stood up, "But, not exactly," I said, "I just had a feeling that something was up, that something was wrong. I didn't know he was *cheating*, or I would've told Aunt Nina, for sure." I had to chase Josh out the doors, "Josh, I didn't know." I reached for his arm.

"You did," he said, whipping around, "Whether you knew *exactly* what was wrong or not, you knew something was wrong. You should've told her. Instead you kept it hidden and let him hurt her." He lifted his hands, resting them on top of his head, and began pacing.

Josh looked up and I turned around as the sound of the opening door creaked in the night. Vitali walked outside, "She's sitting in a conference room," she said, walking over to me, "slightly calmer than before, but I wouldn't go in there for a solid hour, at the least." I looked up at the sky. How many more times was I going to screw up? How many more mistakes would I make before I made a fatal one? Had I already? "Listen, Schwartz, I like you."

I looked up at her, astounded, "What?"

Vitali sighed, shoving her hands in her pockets, and her

breath vaporized in the cold February air, "You seem like a sweet girl who is just caught up in a mess she doesn't understand," she said, "And, from your aunt's reaction, I'm assuming you *didn't* tell her what you'd told me back there."

I let out a laugh. I just didn't feel like doing this, "Your friend told me what your aunt had said to you back at the house." I looked up at her, "No parent, or parental figure, should ever say something like that to their child." Vitali raised her eyebrows and looked at the ground, "*Ever.*"

"But it's all true," I muttered, kicking a stone across the sidewalk.

"It's not," Vitali said, "Your aunt's obviously going through a tough time, and she's just taking it out on you. Which isn't right." Vitali rubbed my arm, "But you're not a screw up. There *is* something screwed up here, but it's not you. And I promise I am going to try my best to find whoever's doing this to you and your family, and won't rest until they're behind bars."

I looked into her eyes. They were a soft forest green, not harsh like those of the men in the foyer, "But for me to do that, I'm going to need you to be honest with me. No more lying, alright?" Vitali asked. My face pinched in a cry, and I nodded. Vitali pulled me in close, wrapping her arm around my shoulder, "It's freezing out here, you two wanna come inside for some coffee?"

Vitali drove us home. I sat in the front. Having someone like Vitali in my corner made me feel slightly safer, especially when it came to whatever Mick was planning next. Josh sat with Aunt Nina in the back. Aunt Nina stared out the window the entire ride and was the first one out of the car when we pulled into the drive.

She hurried to the front door, the rising sun revealing the matte, blood stained spots on her otherwise shining silk robe. When Vitali looked up at the house, a look of amazement washed over her face.

But we both snapped our heads at the front doors when we heard a blood-curdling scream shatter the early morning's stillness. We ran to the house to see Aunt Nina the doorway, a hysterical mess in Josh's arms.

There was blood in the foyer - more than when we left. It wasn't in puddles as Aaron's had been either, but in a streak that came from the living room, wrapping in the direction of the kitchen. Small drips lined the bloody path.

A splatter of bright red blood shot up the cream wall on the right of the front doors. There were several trails, as if something had repeatedly sprayed against the wall.

There was an even more horrific smell than before, too. I looked past Josh, who held Aunt Nina in his arms, shielding her from the grotesque sight in the middle of the marble entry. When I saw what had caused the new mess, let out a shrill cry and turned, burying my face in Vitali's chest, who was already there and ready to hide me from gnarled body in my foyer.

21

Vitali gasped, "Oh my God." Her body barely budged when I turned and fell into her arms. She wrapped one arm around me, using the other to cover my eyes.

Josh ushered Aunt Nina past the gnarled flesh, her back facing away from the center of the foyer. Vitali's eyes, on the other hand, were glued to the scene in an appalled stare. She lifted her phone from the pocket of her jacket, "Hey, yeah, Vitali here. We have a much bigger problem than we thought."

As she turned, I looked back. There, in the middle of the foyer, laid the bloody, mangled corpse of my dog. Cooper's blood trailed as far as I could see. His insides, a swamped mess on the marble, spilled onto the floor, and every artery in his body had been sliced open.

"Come on," Vitali said, pulling my gaze from the painful sight. She walked me to the kitchen, taking the side closest to the blood.

When I entered the kitchen, I saw Josh sitting with Aunt Nina at the counter. Her head was tucked in her arms, and Josh rubbed her back. I looked up at Vitali. She nodded towards the dining room, making her way towards the long table. I followed. Vitali sat in a chair on the right side of the dining room table, "This..." she said, trailing off. She shook her head, "I'm so sorry."

"It's not your fault," I said, sitting in the seat at the head of the table, "It's mi-"

"And it's not yours, either," Vitali cut in, "I'm gonna find who did this." She took my hand in hers and squeezed it tightly, the drive of an Italian in her eyes, "I promise."

We both jumped in our seats when a shrill cry followed by the screech of a barstool on the marble shattered the quiet air. Vitali and I stood when Josh entered the room in a worried stride, the crying still echoing from the kitchen, "We have to go, now," he said.

Patricia was waiting for us at the entrance to the hospital. Aunt Nina, still barefoot in her bloody robe, ran past her with the speed of light. Josh, Vitali, and I jogged behind, trying to keep up. The halls were fairly quiet, slowly awakening with the morning.

Josh hadn't told Vitali or me what had happened, only rushed Vitali to the car to drive us to the hospital. The whole car ride was filled with dead silence other than the chokes and sobs of Aunt Nina in the back. She had rested her elbow on the window, her face lying in her open hand with her fingers shielding her eyes.

But as soon as we entered the hall that held Aaron's room, Vitali and I knew what Josh hadn't told us. Josh had caught up to Aunt Nina outside of Aaron's room. She stood, unable to look through the glass, into the room.

Her hands clutched Josh's arms, which were holding her face.

"Clear!"

Aunt Nina's eyes slammed shut, and she fell into Josh's chest just as he pulled her in, "No pulse!" the doctor screamed. Aunt Nina's entire body shuddered, and Josh struggled more to hold onto her.

"Clear!"

Aunt Nina and Josh froze, her face buried in his shoulder and her eyes barely peeking over his back. Her face was nearly expressionless.

"No pulse!"

Her body shuddered again, and the whole hallway was filled with a heartbreaking wail.

"Clear!"

Aunt Nina's forehead pressed against Josh's chest, her eyes closed, and she held his hands and hers deathly still in front of her abdomen.

"No pulse!"

Josh had to dive to catch her, to keep her from hitting the ground. I only caught a brief glimpse of her face. It was harrowing. Blood dampened by tears slid across her skin and a thin line of saliva stretched from the top of her lips to the bottom.

When he was able to pull her up, Josh grabbed her waist, and she threw her arms around his neck, "Clear!"

The whole earth was silent. There was the jump of the defibrillator, and the nerves in Aunt Nina's body clenched, "We have a pulse!"

Aunt Nina's body dropped to the floor, and this time, Josh went down with her. They both leaned against the glass that separated them from Aaron, and Aunt Nina bawled into Josh's strong chest.

She laid her hand over her chest and brought the other to her forehead. An uncontrollable stream of tears followed, and she looked lifeless, like she had been stripped every ounce of everything she had.

Josh saw Vitali and me standing at the end of the hall and nodded for us, telling us he would keep an eye on her. I looked up at Vitali, "Wanna grab something to eat?" she asked, "Because, I'm absolutely starving."

There was a misting rain that fell as Vitali and I left the hospital doors. The car was still along the curb, and I crawled quickly inside. Vitali did the same, and we pulled out of the parking lot, listening to the crisp sound of wet pavement under the tires.

Contrary to the hospital, the McDonald's was buzzing. People ran in and out, spilling coffees, tipping teas, and dropping egg Mcmuffins. Vitali and I had found a semi-quiet place near the back wall - a booth tucked in a corner.

"Vitali?" I asked, sipping my vanilla coffee.

"Yes?"

"You were right," I said. For a moment, she looked confused, "About being honest. What I told you at the station; that's not what the men wanted me to tell Aunt Nina."

Vitali nodded, and then her brows furrowed, "Wait, wanted? So you didn't actually tell her?"

I shook my head, "No. The man without a gun's phone buzzed and they said they had to cut the conversation short."

Vitali nodded again, "Oh," she said. She took a sip of her latte and looked around the room, "So, what did they want you to tell her?"

I pressed my eyelids together. I knew this was going to happen eventually, no matter how much I had denied it, "When I was at the hospital, I was trying to fake my death."

"*What?*" Vitali had spit the coffee in her mouth, barely catching it with her hand. She rubbed her palms on napkins and closed her eyes, perplexed, "Start from the beginning."

I looked down at my cup and began picking at my nails.

"Schwartz, you gotta tell me what happened, or I can't get the guy," she said. She leaned in and folded her hands on the table, "I can't find something when I don't know what I'm looking for."

I looked up at her, and she raised her eyebrows, as if saying, *It's true.* I sat my cup down on the table, "Well, I went to New York for New Year's," I said, reluctantly starting the story, "And while I was there, I met a guy."

It was all coming back to me, "We had walked into some club that he knew; that's when I met *Mick.*" I said the name so quietly, as if just saying it would draw him near.'

"Mick?" Vitali asked, "Is that who's doing this?"

"Yes," I said, "He was hitting on me, and I obviously wasn't interested, but he wasn't getting it. So the guy I had met, Leo, told him I was engaged so he would leave me alone. Then we walked over to a table that had Blackjack and played for hours.

"And when I say hours, I mean *hours.* I had counted at Harvard, so I was pretty good. Over the course of the night, I had racked up close to a mil."

"Wow," Vitali said, choking on her coffee, "Just, wow." She shook her head with wide eyes, "So what happened with you and the guy?"

"We had been talking all night," I said, "And when the countdown ended, he and I kissed."

"Let me guess," Vitali cut in, holding her hand in the air, "Mick saw you two." I nodded, "Nice going, Schwartz."

"Yeah," I laughed, taking another sip of my coffee, "Then he came over. He brought all of the money I had won, and then he made a comment on how my luck was going."

"Uh oh."

"Yeah. Then I said something along the lines of 'I guess I'm just really good of keeping track of numbers'. And let me tell you, people don't like it when you count," I said, "And I knew this, so-"

"Do *not* tell me you ran with all that money," Vitali said, looking at me with *that look.*

"I did," I forced out, cringing at the words, "I know, I'm sorry."

"You don't have to apologize," she said, "But that was *very* stupid. Anyway, continue."

I thought about what came next, "Then they beat me and gave me this scar," I said pointing to the fair line of skin that trailed my face, "But then I woke up the next morning, and there was an envelope slipped under the door."

"An envelope?" Vitali asked.

"Yeah, I've been getting them since. There all in a shoebox at home."

"What was in the envelope?" Vitali stared at me with a deeply unsettling intensity. I didn't think she meant to, figuring it was just habit after years of interrogations.

"There was a note and a picture," I said, "The picture was of Leo; he was dead. And the note said something about how this is what happens to people who count.

"Then I came home and Aunt Nina found out. I got more and more letters and pictures. With everyone, they seemed to be getting closer. Then the night Aunt Nina was stabbed, I had found a one stuffed in the wound."

"That's sick," Vitali said, "Just sick."

"That's what I thought," I said, "Then I had the crazy idea of faking my death because the note they had left threatened Aunt Nina and Aaron.

"At first Josh wouldn't go for it, but after they set the house on fire, he realized it wasn't too insane after all." *But it was*, I thought to myself, "Then I tried it, and failed; I couldn't do that to Aunt Nina."

Vitali sighed, "Well," she said after a pause, "It seems like you love your aunt very much."

I smiled and looked down at the table, "More than anything."

"Well, then, let's get to it," Vitali said, gathering her things, "So, they wouldn't be in a motel - too risky. They're probably working out of a car. Van, maybe? Can I check out those photos and envelopes? I want to see if we can find out where they're from."

"Uh, yeah, sure," I said. I felt a buzz in the pocket of my coat. *Josh,* "I'll be right back. It's Josh."

Vitali nodded and I turned and stepped away, "So, looks like I'm just staying here," Josh said when I answered the call.

"What, why?"

"Because, Nina refuses to leave, and I'm not leaving her." He sounded exhausted.

"Well, Vitali's going to come look at the house, ask me

more about last night," I said, looking back at her. I heard Josh's tone change, but I didn't hear what he said.

Instead, I was looking at Vitali. She was on the phone, her heels clacking as she paced the floor, "I mean - just - be careful, alright?"

"Yes," I said firmly, "Now, I have to go. Thank you for staying with Aunt Nina."

"Yep."

I hung up and walked over Vitali, who had just hung up her call as well, "Ready to go?" she asked. I nodded and we left the building.

As we walked to the car, something ate at me, and I had to say it, "Vitali?" she turned and looked at me as she opened the driver's door of the car, "You can't tell anyone," I said.

She smiled, "I know." She sat in the car and waited for me to buckle before pulling out, "That would get us nowhere but you and your aunt in jail."

When we got to the house, we made a direct shot for the guest bedroom and the notes. They were right where we had left them; tucked between a few boxes on the top shelf. The notes were neatly piled on the side, the photos on the other. The envelopes laid folded in a corner of the small box, "I'm going to take these, see if I can find who distributes them."

I nodded and watched as Vitali dug through the contents of the shoebox. She shuffled through the pictures, her face more and more horrified the more she turned over. Then she paused, taking one from the stack, "Is this…?"

The picture drew a slight sting from within me. It was the picture of Copper and Aunt Nina on the bed, "Yes," I said.

Vitali shook her head. Then she tucked the box under her

arm, "I'm gonna look at these." She noticed the look of fear in my eyes, "Downstairs. I'm going to look at these, *downstairs*." We made our way slowly down the grand staircase, "I was thinking," Vitali started, "If you showed me what order they came in, and if I find where the pictures are coming from, we can track where they're coming from, and more importantly, where they're heading."

We turned the corner into the kitchen. I felt ready, determined to put this whole thing to rest. Because with Vitali, I felt like I finally could. Then I heard the box drop from under arm.

I looked up, startled. Vitali stood completely still, her eyes widened and locked on something. I followed her gaze to the counter. To the gold that shimmered.

"Shit," I said. Vitali inched towards the counter. I stood there, staring down at the envelope, and she did the same. She looked up at me, and then lifted the envelope from the marble surface.

Even with the shuffle of the envelope's contents, the drop of a pin would've been heard. Vitali's shaking hand pulled out three pictures.

She and I standing in the doorway when Aunt Nina found Cooper.

The four of us at the hospital, Aunt Nina collapsed in Josh's arms.

Vitali and I sitting in a booth at McDonald's.

Vitali lifted her hand to her mouth, throwing the pictures to the floor, "If..." But she was at a loss for words, "I...how?"

"I don't know," I said, "But this is how it's been." And it was, "Getting pictures barely an hour after something happened."

We both stared at the images on the ground, neither of us having the courage to lift the letter. Finally, Vitali caved, sliding the printer paper from the envelope.

Wrong move, Allison.

22

"What the hell is that supposed to mean?" Vitali's breaths were short and quick, sharp inhales if air followed by strong gusts of exhales.

"I don't know," I whispered. *Wait.* I ran to the box Vitali had dropped.

The papers shuffled between my fingers as I sifted through the letters. Then I found what I was looking for. Unfolding the paper, I read the note aloud, "Did you really think you would get away that easily? And here, we thought you had to be smart to count. Oh yeah, and the police…I wouldn't if I were you. See you in LA, Allison."

Vitali took the note from my hands, "I told you what happened," I said as she skimmed over the note again, "I told the police."

She looked up at me with horrified eyes. Somehow, her olive, Italian skin had washed sickly pale. Then her face turned, and her breaths became heavy again. She stomped over and lifted the box from the ground. When she reached the counter, she slammed the box down on the marble surface and dug furiously through the contents.

She pulled out every note, "Which one was the first one?" she asked quickly with irritation.

"Uh, *This is what happens to people who count.*" I said.

She filtered through the letters until she stopped on one, "*This is what happens to people who count,*" she said, setting it at the far, left end of the counter, "Next?"

"The one about telling the police."

There was the sound of paper against paper, followed by, "*Did you really think you would get away that easily? And here, we thought you had to be smart to count. Oh yeah, and the police...I wouldn't if I were you. See you in LA, Allison.*" She set it next to the other, "Next."

I had to think for a moment. *Which one came next?* "Um, something about saying hi to Josh," I said to the grounds, trying to remember, "And Aunt Nina, how she was alone."

Vitali searched with determination for what I was describing. She had a silent *ah-ha!* moment, and walked back to the end of the counter, "*Nice place, Allison. Nice guy you have there too, tell dear Josh I said hi and who's you aunt? She looks pretty. And drunk. And alone.*" The words came out rushed as she read, setting the letter in the timeline, "What came after that?"

I remembered clearly now, "Josh had stayed the night. So something about how I should have him stay again."

Vitali found the note and laid it on the counter. She didn't ask, but looked up at me, "Um," I said, "Oh, you probably won't be able to read it; it's the one covered in blood."

As I had guessed, the paper was a dark, hardened piece, crusted in dried blood, the words unable to be read. Vitali laid it in line, shaking her head, "Just sick."

She returned her gaze to the letters, "Next I think is the one about Aaron," I said, then paused. I nodded, "Yeah, that was the night I met him. So, yes, *Aaron seems like a nice guy*, or something along those lines."

"*Aaron seems like a nice guy. I would hate for him to get hurt.*" She read it, nodding, "Nice memory, Schwartz." She dropped the paper on the counter, the line reaching a third of the way across, "Next."

"Well, after that," I said walking over to the box, "Was the day our house caught fire." I dug through the box, pulling out the casing of the flare. I handed it to Vitali, and she put in the line, "Did anything else *happen* before anymore letters?" she asked.

"Yes," I said, "They took my phone." Vitali rubbed her eyes with a combination of fatigue and impatience and dug a black crust of mascara out of the inner corner of her eye, "But the next letter I think is the one where he called me Tiffany."

"Wait," Vitali said, setting the last two letters in their spots on the counter, "Why would they call you Tiffany?" she asked.

"That was the name on my ID, which they had stolen," I said.

Vitali brought her hand back to her face and sat at the counter. I walked over and sat next to her, "So," she said, her hands tapping on the counter and eyes looking around the room. Her eyes fell on a drawer along the wall in front of us, "May I?" she asked.

I nodded, "Yeah, go ahead."

She walked over and opened the drawer. After digging through, she pulled out a pack of sticky notes, "This'll do." She came back to her seat at the island and scribbled out several notes. She stuck one under the bloody note I found in Aunt Nina.

Nina was stabbed.

She stuck another under the flare.

House was set on fire.

She slid the next two notes down a space and slapped her note in the newly made spot.

Phone was stolen.

She put one about the ID under its note, and others about Josh getting shot, me attempting to fake my death, and the two men in the foyer in their spots in the timeline, "So," she said again, "This is what we are working with."

We both looked down the line. Vitali stared at the notes - old and her new - with her arms folded.

Both of us turned as the front door opened. I held my breath.

But only Josh walked through, followed by Aunt Nina. I let out my breath, and Vitali did the same.

But I breathed quickly again when I saw Aunt Nina. She held onto Josh's arm tightly. Her eyes were empty and lifeless, and her entire body trembled. She moved slowly across the foyer, her eyes not focusing on one thing, as Josh coaxed her forward. He had to lower her gently to the couch, where she sat staring straight ahead, her elbows on her knees and her folded hands hanging in the air.

Josh walked over to us, glancing over his shoulder as if taking his eyes off of Aunt Nina would cause her to spontaneously combust, "It's not good," he said, "Aaron…if he makes it, it would truly me a medical miracle."

I brought my hands to my mouth, looking to Aunt Nina. A small tear rolled down her cheek, but she didn't move. She just sat there, a cold corpse with no purpose. I couldn't begin to imagine what this was doing to her.

"What's all of this?" Josh asked, looking at the counter, "She knows?"

He eyed Vitali closely, "Yes," I said, "But she's not going to tell." I looked at him, "She's going to help. And if she does, if she finds him, I won't have to go."

Josh's eyes widened for a moment, and he looked at Vitali, "So, how're we doing?" he asked, walking over to where she stood in front of the counter.

"Well," she started and took the box from my hands, "We need to see what all, or who all, is involved." She lined the pictures up with their notes. Then she wrote something on another sticky note and stuck it at the beginning of the line, "Allison goes to New York," she said as she wrote. Then she backed away, looking at the string of information on the counter as a whole, "Alright, as shown obviously by last night, this Mick guy isn't working alone. The two brothers are dead. Do you know if anyone else was working for or with him?"

"I have no idea," I said.

She walked to the beginning of the line, and Josh followed closely behind, "Well, we know there were the two men from last night," she said. She whipped around and looked at Josh, "Who shot you?"

"The two men from last night," he said.

Vitali looked at the counter again, studying every event, every picture, "Wait." She looked at Aunt Nina then at me, "Who stabbed her?" she whispered.

I looked back at Aunt Nina, "I don't know," I said, "She wasn't talking to me."

"We need to find out," Vitali said, "Because the more people that are involved, the higher the chance that someone will slip up - which gives us more to look at."

I looked at my aunt, so fragile, sitting there on the couch, "Vitali - no, we can't."

"We have to," she said, walking towards the living room.

I grabbed her arm firmly as she passed, "Wait," I looked down at the ground, "Let me."

I took a deep breath and stepped into the living room, "Aunt Nina?" I said meekly. She didn't look up, or even acknowledge the fact that I spoke, and I wondered if she had even heard me.

I sat on the couch next to her and grabbed her hand. But she pulled it away and shifted her knees so that I was looking the back of her head. I raised my hand to lay it on her back, but brought it back to my lap.

I stood and walked back to the kitchen, and as I did, Josh passed me, "Nina?" he said, dropping next to her on the couch, sitting on the opposite side I had so that she looked at him.

She looked at his chest, but only because it happened to fall in her natural line of unmoving vision. Josh looked at Vitali and me, then back at Aunt Nina, "Hey," he said softly taking her hand, "I need to ask you something important." She didn't move, and Josh tried again, "It's about us," he said, "It concerns our lives - yours, mine," he paused, "and Aaron's

Her face creased with pain and she blinked, her eyelids moving as if they were locked in a slow motion film, "Shoot."

The word came with no emotion, but Josh looked at us, "Well," he said, "It's about the night you were attacked." He shifted in his seat and took her hands in his, "Do you remember the guy that attacked you?" he asked, "Or maybe something about what he looked like?"

We all waited in a deafening silence, "Anything helps," Josh said.

Aunt Nina looked up at him and swallowed. Then she looked back at the ground, "Um." She cleared the endless tears from her throat, "He had dark hair, like *really dark*. He was fairly tall. And scrawny. Really scrawny." She closed her eyes, the memory cutting her like a blade and she stood abruptly, "I need to use the restroom."

We all watched helplessly as she took off, the back of her hand raised to the bridge of her lip. Josh walked back over slowly, "Well, there you go."

"Does that sound like Mick to you?" Vitali asked, looking at me.

I shook my head, "No," I said, "No, Mick is buff, and he has light hair. That's not him."

"Well, we need to find out who that is," Vitali said, looking for her phone in her pockets as it buzzed, "Shit," she said when she found it, "I have to go." She reached for the sticky notes, but changed her direction last second and grabbed my phone from the counter. After a few seconds she handed it back, "Here."

I took the phone from her hands. There was a newly made contact on the screen. *Catarina Vitali*, "Call or message if you see anything or hear anything," Vitali said, grabbing her jacket from the back of the stool, "I don't care if it's as minute as a knock on the door, alright?"

I nodded. She walked to the door, letting in the rays of late morning sunlight, "Stay safe, Schwartz," she said, already outside, her hand on the door's handle, "And don't let anyone in."

The minutes were frozen and slow. Josh and Aunt Nina had come home around ten. It was nearly eleven, "Josh, she's been in there a long time," I said.

"What?"

"Aunt Nina," I replied, looking at the bathroom door, "She's been in the bathroom for almost an hour."

Josh looked at me, and I walked across the room to the bathroom door, "Aunt Nina?" I asked, knocking lightly.

No answer.

"Nina, are you alright?" Josh asked, knocking harder, "Nina!" He looked at me. His hand fell to the door handle, but it wouldn't budge. *The door was locked.* Josh yelled her name again, and when she didn't answer, he threw his shoulder into the door.

It flew open. I gasped, a screeching cry leaving my lips, "Aunt Nina, no!"

Josh ran to her as she lifted her hand, a palm full of pills, to her lips. Her eyes were even emptier than before, red and, almost, dead. There was a slam, followed by a sound like marbles skitting across a floor.

I couldn't look.

On the vanity, three pill bottles rested, empty. Why? *You know why,* I thought. She was going to lose him, and she'd rather be dead than do so.

I looked at the ground. I watched in horror as Josh held her arms tightly to her sides and she fought to move towards the pills on the floor. But every time she got a hand free and reached, Josh shot it down and brought it back to her side. Eventually she exhausted herself, and she sobbed, looking up at Josh.

He took her in his arms, and a feminine cry left his body. It was small, and had almost gone unnoticed.

Aunt Nina shuddered. She was a child, small in Josh's arms. She cried into his chest, gripping his shirt between her fingers, and the most distressed, grief-stricken cries rang out repeatedly in the cold room.

I didn't know what to do. *What could I do?* I bent down to clean up the pills that spread across the floor. There were two different kinds, small blue ones and slim white ones. *Wait, two?*

I stood, all of the pills in hand and put them on the vanity. I sorted them into their bottles. I had been right; there were not enough to fill all three of the empty containers, "Josh!" I said, looking at them both. Aunt Nina lay in Josh's arms, calmer now, staring into space, "Josh, she already swallowed a bottle before we came in!"

"Oh my God," he said and sat up, pulling Aunt Nina to her knees. She was pale, wan in the natural light that poured into the otherwise dark bathroom.

I was frozen. *Oh my god, she's going to die. I'm going to lose her.* I couldn't move but, but inside of me was mayhem. I watched as Josh cried and shook her, asking her how many were in the bottle.

It seemed like everything was far away. *Oh no. Now is not the time for a panic attack.* My breathing quickened. *Call someone!* I stood from the ground and ran to the kitchen. My phone, sitting in the middle of the counter, was charging, and I unplugged it and called 911.

"Nine-one-one, what's your emergency?"

"My name is Allison Schwartz. My aunt, she's trying to kill herself," I said frantically, "She swallowed a bottle of pills. My best friend is with her now, but-"

My voice cut off, and my chest tightened. I couldn't breathe, "Ok, Allison, I need you to tell me what pills she took." I heard the clicking of keys in the background.

"Uh, I think it was Zoloft, her antidepressants," I said.

"You think?"

"I know," I spit.

"Alright," the lady at the other end of the line said, "What is your address?"

"903 Alpine Dr., in Beverly Park."

"Okay," the operator said, "Help is on the way."

I nodded, as if she could see me. But I couldn't get out words. I needed Aunt Nina. Needed her to calm me, tell me everything would be okay. I tried to breathe.

In - one, two, three, four.

Out - five, six, seven, eight.

I needed to calm myself, take care of myself. Because after this, I just might've had to.

When I was sure I could breathe and my vision began to clear, I walked back to the bathroom. I pushed lightly on the door, peering inside.

Aunt Nina was curled up in Josh's arms, still choking on the acid in her throat. In front of the two on the floor was a puddle of vomit, and I could see the individual pills inside.

Josh looked up at me, "Based on when I gave them to her," he said quietly, rubbing her arm as she pressed against his side, "There should be around 30-40 in there. If she got them all up."

I began to count, visually. When I finally finished, I let out a sigh of relief and began to cry.

Thirty-seven

"Thank you for coming," I said, "I didn't know who else to call." I stood in the cool air, bouncing between my two feet, which were cold on the stones of the driveway. Aunt Nina sat in front of us in an ambulance, a blanket wrapped around her shoulders. Josh sat next to her.

"No problem," Vitali said, "I'm glad you did."

We both looked forward as a paramedic walked over, "We think that they all were removed from her body," he said, "But we are going to take her in, just to be sure. They'll probably keep her there overnight, once again, just to be sure. But it looks like your aunt will more than likely be okay."

I smiled, tears flooding my eyes. And, impulsively, I turned and hugged Vitali. Her body was rigid at first, and I began pulling away. But she gripped me tighter. And for some reason, this just made everything seem okay, even if it was only for a moment. I began to cry, and I felt Vitali's hand stroke my hair, "It's okay," she said, "She's going to be okay. It'll all be okay."

I took a step back and looked at Vitali. Her forest green eyes were warm and bright, and we both walked towards the car as the ambulance pulled out of the drive.

23

The moment Aunt Nina passed through the front door, she walked directly to the music room. The French doors closed softly with a small click, and I saw her lower herself onto the piano bench, her back to the piano. Natural light from the grand window behind her glinted on her hair and back, and she rubbed sweaty palms along her loose, black yoga pants. Her hands ran over face, wiping the tears that had fallen. Her gaze fell to the Scott Cao violin in the corner. She drifted delicately towards it, lifting it gently from its stand.

Re-adjusting herself on the piano bench until she was in the ideal position, she leaned the violin on her leg and reached for the ponytail holder on the piano behind her.

She pulled her soft, brown hair back into a low pony, as she always had whenever she played. Her bangs drifted like feathers away from the rest of her hair, resting against the right side of her face. There was no care or neatness, just a natural swift motion, bunching the hair together where it naturally fell.

She lifted the violin and laid it perfectly in her right collarbone. Her right arm was outstretched, holding the violin, and her dominant hand held the bow. Just before the bow hit the strings, she looked up, as if sensing someone was watching her.

I quickly left the foyer.

I met Josh in the kitchen. He looked up as a muffled *Largo e pianissimo sempre,* a slow piece from *Spring* of Vivaldi's *The Four Seasons,* echoed throughout the house, "Hey," he said as I sat down next to him.

I smiled at him, and then dropped my gaze to my fingers, "What if you weren't here?" I asked, looking up at him with tears in my eyes, "She would've died. I would've just stood there while she lay on the floor and died. I-"

"Hey, hey, hey," Josh said and rubbed my back as my breath staggered.

We both jumped when my phone rang, "Alright, this is what I got," Vitali said, "All of the pictures, except the Polaroids and ones from New York, of course, were printed at the Photo Center on Beverly Blvd."

"Okay, so…"

"So, I went down there and talked to the people working there. It turns out this one girl was working there the night that they printed the pictures of you three at the hospital the first time."

I knew what she meant. The pictures of Aunt Nina being taken away, of Aaron and me in the waiting room, and of a blurry Aunt Nina and Aaron behind my defined curl, "Apparently she remembers thinking they were weird," Vitali said. I heard a shuffle of material as Vitali shivered on the other end of the line, "Anyway, I had her describe the man that had printed the photos."

I sucked in a breath, "Yeah?"

"Yeah, and she described Mick perfectly," Vitali said, "Down to the sterling grey eyes and everything." I heard a car door open, "I asked for the surveillance footage in and around the building, I'm going to skim through it, see what I can find."

"Alright," I said, "Are you going back to the station?" I asked.

"No, home. Why?" Vitali asked.

"No reason," I said, "Be careful, Vitali."

There was a short laugh and the start of an engine, "You got it, Schwartz."

I hung up the phone and walked back to the foyer. Aunt Nina still played, and *Spring* had faded to *Summer*. I turned my head, watching her. There was a grace, a grace almost too powerful to name, with which she played.

Her eyes were closed, rarely opening, and every stroke, every move, was one, fluid motion. The lower half of her body remained completely still other than the tapping of her foot, keeping the tempo, and the upper half moved ever so slightly with the music.

I shuffled, side-stepping to the left staircase, never taking my eyes off of her. I sat there on the eighth step, propping my arms and chin on a swirl in the iron railing. I had discovered this spot as a young child. It was the perfect spot to watch the refined musician, but to stay hidden yourself.

She could play for hours. And I could've watched her for hours.

I jerked awake, smacking my head against the top of the iron as I did, "Nice going, slick," Josh said. He sat next to me, "This has been going off nonstop."

He handed me my phone. The metal vibrated in my hand. *Vitali.* There were eight missed calls, and one came in now, "Vitali?" I asked, "Is everything alright?"

"No!" she hissed. Her breathing was hard and deep, "Allison, I-"

Then the line went dead.

I looked up at Josh, "She called me Allison," I said.

"What?"

"She called me Allison," I repeated, "She never calls me Allison. It's Schwartz. Always Schwartz."

He looked confused, and he brought his hand to his chin. Then he snapped his head towards me. He ripped the phone from my hands, and I scooted closer to see what he was doing.

He opened *Contacts.* His finger swiped at the screen, scrolling until he found *Vitali.* I knew what he was doing. It was a long shot, but…

"Here," he said, handing me the phone and standing up.

I looked at the screen. Under the *address* bar, there was a house number and street name typed. Josh ran out the front door, keys in hand, and I followed.

Josh's car flew down the highway at almost 30 miles over the speed limit, but it still didn't seem fast enough, "Hurry!"

"I'm going as fast as I can, Allison," Josh said.

When we pulled into the driveway of the house, the car hadn't even stopped, and I was already out. I ran to the door, reaching for the handle.

But the door hung cracked open. I pushed on it lightly.

A small hall met me at the front of the house. An open concept living and dining room sat to my right, everything a shade of grey, gold, or teal. Dark wood floors laid below my feet as I slowly made my way down the hall. I could see the base of the stairs, and the ceiling dropped off, climbing another fifteen feet at least.

A small pool of blood grew with a steady drip in the opening next to the stairs.

When I reached the large, tall stairwell, I looked up slowly, praying I wouldn't see what I feared I would. But when I saw her, a shrill cry echoed throughout the ascending staircase.

There, swinging from the light fixture that hung from the ceiling was Vitali, a lifeless corpse drifting from side-to-side. I brought my hands to my mouth. A steady stream of blood trickled down the front of her body from her throat. The spongy redness of her tongue hung limply from the opening.

But the blood that dripped from the tips her shoes came from somewhere else. I looked, horrified, the remnants of a sob on my face, at the body dangling in the air.

Her eyes were gone. Only empty, pink sockets holding blood like teaspoons remained.

The center of her body was nothing but a mass of blood and tissue. Her organs hung from the gaping wound, sliding against the torn skin of her core. In the mix of gore and flesh were hints of white - the bone of cracked ribs that poked through her chest.

She still wore her suit, the burgundy collared shirt under a black blazer. But it was destroyed. Not only by the blood, but a blade had slit the inner arms and legs of the material, as well as deeply lacerating the skin beneath.

Her arms, still dripping with bright, fresh blood, peeked

from behind the dark clothing. A watch wrapped around her wrist. That's when I noticed there was something tucked beneath.

I drifted towards the body. I had to close my eyes, raising my hand to my mouth and using the free one to grab whatever lay between Vitali's watch and her skin. The paper was wet and unsettlingly warm.

Dots of red bled from the back of the white paper to the center. There was something scribbled across the sheet of paper.

Look behind you.

Josh stood, looking over my shoulder, "Look behind you?" he said and turned around.

A man with sickly pale skin and jet black hair stood, smiling twistedly up at us. He was a scrawny little thing, and had to have been no older than his late twenties. *This is the man who attacked Aunt Nina.*

He lunged forward.

I ducked under Josh's arm and ran for the door. As I did, Josh kicked the shining blade from the man's hands and began to run. I hurried down the hall, flinging the door open and running out. Just as I was about to open the car door, I looked up at Josh.

Only, he wasn't there. I heard a grunt from inside the house and ran back in.

The two men wrestled on the floor. Josh had gotten on top of the scrawny man, but the man pulled another, smaller, blade from his pocket and swung at Josh.

Josh ducked, and the blade sliced through his arm. He let out a moan, and the man took advantage of this moment of weakness. He flipped Josh over onto his back, pinning his arms down, and lifting the knife above his head.

I looked around the room. A plaque rested on a bookshelf in the corner. I grabbed it and ran towards the two men.

A crack rang out and the man fell onto the floor. I stood over them, Josh laying on his back and the man on his stomach, and heaved. Blood slid down the side of the man's face, but his chest rose and fell.

"He's still breathing," I said, "Let's go."

I reached my hand out for Josh to grab. He took ahold of hit and I pulled him to his feet. His arm bled, and I reached out to look at it. When I fingers touched the tender wound, Josh winced and pulled back, but eventually let me examine it, "It's not deep. Probably won't need stitches," I said.

We turned towards the front door, and I took one last glance at Vitali swinging from the ceiling. I felt a sharp clawing in my throat, and Josh wrapped his arm around me, pulling me away from my only way out of this mess.

Josh had dropped me off at home. I couldn't bear going with him to report what had happened. When we had gotten outside, before we got into the car, I had thrown up, leaning my forehead against the hood, trying to calm my head.

Now, I sat in Aunt Nina's music room. She had gone to the back patio to read, and without her to scold me, I walked through the doors with ease.

I laid my fingers on the keys of the piano, and they drifted lightly up the scale. But I cringed when I reached the seventh note of D Major. The natural C played like nails on a chalkboard to my ears, which have been trained by the endless amount of times Aunt Nina tried to force the scales into my memory.

"Again," she says. I roll my eyes and groan, "It's the only way you'll get better."

I take a deep breath and crawl my way up the scale again. And I don't know why - maybe it's the nerves of Aunt Nina watching me, or of the fact that she could do this in her sleep, but when I reach the seventh note, I press the wrong key.

Aunt Nina lets out an irritated sigh, "C sharp, Allison," she says, "It's not that hard. Again."

I hadn't noticed, but my hands had begun climbing their way up the scale once more. It wasn't the notes that pulled me back, but the sweet harmony in which they played. I looked down at my fingers; I had gotten through the whole scale - correctly.

I couldn't help but smile, letting the pain from the day's tragedy slowly melt away. I began going through all of the scales as I had with Aunt Nina as a child, hearing her voice in my head as I went.

"Good. Next."

I followed the pattern in which I had learned them: chord, scale going up, scale going down, chord again, next chord. I repeated this until I had gone through three octaves.

When I finished, I was quite pleased with myself, and I looked up. On the black wood of the grand piano, a picture frame stood in front of me. Within it laid a picture of Aunt Nina and Aaron. She had come up from behind him, wrapping her arms around his neck and resting her chin on his shoulder.

I heard a strong sound, an abrupt stop, and took a quick breath in, looking at Aunt Nina. She stood in the doorway, her arms out to her sides, not expecting anyone to be in the room.

Her feet pounded the floor as she marched towards me,

"Aunt Nina, I'm sorry. I-"

But I had no time to finish, for I was forced to stand or be crushed by Aunt Nina, who pushed in the piano bench, with me still on it, and slammed the top that covered the keys shut without warning. I backed slowly from the room, and she barreled past me, closing the doors behind her.

I watched as she turned the corner towards the kitchen. My phone buzzed in my pocket, and I looked down. A message from Josh.

It's done. I'm on my way back now.

And suddenly, that feeling of a suffocating sorrow came flooding back. I knew I'd to have to be questioned. Shoving the phone back into my pocket, I walked up the grand staircase and to my room. The warm, heavenly smell of oranges was comforting. I walked to my bed, dropping myself on the corner, lying on the pillows.

When Josh walked through the front doors, I heard his steps as they trailed through the house. When he finally realized I had gone to my room, his steps beat the stairs, hopping two at a time.

He appeared in the doorway. I had been staring out the window. From my bedroom, I could see Aunt Nina in the backyard, arms folded across her chest - holding her robe together over her front. The shiny black material flew vigorously in the strong winds that blew her hair around her face.

She stared out to the miles of open land that stretched forever, rolling into hills and spiking into mountains, sliding into streams and dipping into valleys, "She hates me, Josh," I said, "She *really* hates me."

He walked over to the bed, forcing me to scoot over and make room, "She doesn't hate you," he said, brushing the hair from my eyes.

"She does," I said looking back out to her. Though I could not see her face, I could tell she was crying, and I remembered Josh's words from the other day.

Aaron…if he lives, it would be a medical miracle.

24

I looked into the mirror as I smoothed the skirt of my dress. It was black laced and had a certain level of elegance to it. I only ever used it for funerals.

I heard the sound of footsteps coming up the stairs, and a hand slapped on the door frame, "You ready to go?" Josh asked.

I nodded, "Yeah, just a minute." I reached for the gold hoops lined with diamonds on my vanity. Clipping them into my ears, I stole one last glance into the mirror. My eyes were already beginning to puff, and my nose had reddened.

A single tear slipped from the rim of my eye, and I wiped away, grabbing my small black purse and leaving the room, shutting the door behind me. Josh smiled, and I followed him down the stairs.

My black heels left a high pitched sound as they clicked against the marble. The smell of a late breakfast cooking in the kitchen made my stomach clench; I hadn't eaten since Josh and I went out yesterday morning - I did not want to face Aunt Nina. I had given up on her. Simply going near her was like having a negativity placed on your shoulders, weighing you down.

Josh opened the front door, and I walked outside, the air cooling my body. We walked to the car. I watched as the light glinted on the glass. Despite the coolness of the day, the sun shined, shimmering through leaves on trees. But it was dulled by the clouds that rolled inwards overhead.

The rain had begun before we pulled into the parking lot. My hair, up in a ponytail at the top of my head, began to feel heavy by the time we reached the doors of the funeral home. I had gotten to the doors first. I looked back at Josh, and took a deep breath before opening the door.

Inside, there was a sign perched on a stand which read: *Catarina Vitali*. I felt a choke in my throat and looked at the ground, and Josh grabbed my hand, leading me into the parlor.

It was warm in the room, an almost suffocating swarm of heat sliding over me like a glove. We found ourselves seats near the back of the room. Other detectives, officers, and people on the force filled the seats in front of us.

The room was a light shade of beige. Large, stained glass windows lined both of the walls, and colorful rays of light poured in onto the floor. A group of people, all of which were significantly darker than everyone else in the room, sat in the front corner. I was able to catch small bits of conversation, all of which were in what I assumed was Italian.

The funeral was closed casket. Because of this, every time I thought of Vitali, the last memory I had of her was her limp body hanging from the ceiling. I closed my eyes at the memory, pushing through, digging deeply to remember what she had looked like before they had done that to her.

I saw her green eyes and her olive skin, still warm and full of life. I saw her dark, chocolate brown hair and her tall form. I remembered her smile and how there was the smallest hint of an Italian accent in her voice.

I coughed, clearing my throat, still looking down at my hands. Then I heard a voice from my left side, *"You!"*

I looked up. A tall, young woman in all black stood over me. Her face was nothing but pure fury, and her eyes were puffed and swollen. She was young. She had the same forest green eyes and olive skin as the woman I was here to mourn, "You're the one who got her killed! You're the reason my sister's dead!"

Her accent was thicker than her sisters, "I-" I began and stood.

"No!" the woman yelled, causing everyone in the room to turn their head, "Our mother is back in Italy, sick and dying, and the last thing she needed was to hear that her daughter was killed because she worked with the wrong case."

I was appalled, but I couldn't blame the woman, "This is what always happens," the woman continued, "to people with big hearts. They get involved, trying to help someone, and it always comes back to bite them in the ass."

"Christiana!"

Everyone looked up when the deep voice boomed, "It's not this young lady's fault," the man said. He was older, with white hair that contrasted with his dark skin.

"It is!" Christiana yelled, only an inch from my face. I felt the pressure in my nose, "I thought you of all people would understand. Your daughter is dead, and it's this bitch's fault!"

"Christiana!"

"Listen," I said, "I'm really sorry about your sister. And you're right, it's all my fault. Catarina was kind and-"

But I was cut off by the loud smack that shattered the silent room. My face was thrown to the side, and I brought my hand to the reddening patch of warm skin on my cheek, "You know *nothing* about my sister," Christiana said.

"Christiana, look at me, *right now*," her father said. Christiana looked back at him, whispering something in Italian, "Christiana!"

Christiana looked at her father and began shouting in Italian. But her father was louder and bolder, and began to do what I could only guess was scold her. He shouted over her, and the people of the room that were able to understand the two gasped, "Now, go take a walk and calm yourself!" Christiana's father shouted, waving his cane at the door.

Christiana glared at her father, but turned and stormed out of the room, knocking me off of my feet as she passed. Her father shot his arm out and gripped mine to steady me, and his grip was firm and strong for an older man, "I'm sorry about her," he said, "I know it's not your fault. She's just been having a hard time with her mother's illness and inability to come here."

I looked back at the doorway, a long stretch of silence filling the room, "No," I said, "It is my fault."

Vitali was dead, and now a sister, a father, a mother will never see a part of their family again, and it was all my fault.

The rain hadn't stopped by the time we reached the cemetery. I stood in the second row of people as the rain poured over us all. There was a pitter-patter as the falling water hammered the dozens of umbrellas all around me.

Several people walked to Vitali's casket and spoke. But I couldn't tell you what they said. The voices were far away and distant, and I just stared at the casket blankly, imagining Vitali inside.

What would she look like? I pushed the thought of her empty eyes out of my head and looked up at the sky as the water fell in a heavy downpour from the clouds above. They were a shadowy and a warm grey, like the sun was pushing its light through. But the rich darkness won, concealing all of the sun's efforts except for the thin rays that peeked from between their captor's fingers, only just visible.

I had known better than to put on makeup. I allowed the rain beat relentlessly against my flesh, letting myself feel every drop. Josh looked at me. He had given up on keeping me under the umbrella ages ago.

I was one of the last people to leave. I stared down at the headstone. It was a beautiful black, with the words *Catarina Vitali, beloved sister and daughter* engraved into the stone. I stood there, staring at the newly upturned soil that covered the ground in front of the headstone.

Christiana saw me standing there and glared daggers my way. She shifted her weight towards me, but her father dug his fingers into her arm, "Christiana, please!" he hissed. I could feel all of the eyes on me. But that's where they belonged. I was the girl that got Catarina killed.

When the sun crossed from noon to afternoon and on, Josh pulled on my arm, "Come on," he said, nodding towards the car, "I know you haven't eaten, let's go."

After a moment of excruciating silence, I turned, inexpressive, and started for the car. My heals fell into the mud, and I had to pry them out with each agonizing step. The shoes were completely trashed, and I was going to have to soak them when I got home.

I wiped my eyes before opening the passenger door of the car. The rain had caused any warmth that had been in the air to dissipate, and only a chilling, wet February was left. As I lowered myself into the car, the warmth that had cultivated inside thawed the frozen ice in my joints and bones. I let my gaze fall one last time to Vitali's grave, "I have to go," I said.

Josh's head snapped around, "What?"

"I have to go," I repeated, "I have to leave LA. For good. Just like we had planned."

"Allison, no," he said, shaking his head.

"Yes, Josh," I cut in, "It's the only way."

He shook his head, "It's the only way to what?" he asked. The engine started, and the car rolled across the pavement.

"It's the only way to protect everyone," I said, looking at him.

"Alliso-"

"No!" I yelled, hurling my fist down on the dash, "People are dying, Josh! Innocent people are dead *because of me*." My face was hard, and I threw my gaze to my lap, "I won't let another person die because of me."

Josh turned onto the main road, "They won't," he said.

"They will."

He let out a frustrated breath, "So you're going to do that to Nina?" he asked. The words cut like a serrated blade through the heart, "She's going to lose Aaron, and you're going to take her niece from her to?"

All of the emotion - all of the pain that had built up inside - I let it all out, "It won't matter, Josh!" I screamed. My face flooded with a flush, and the muscles tightened, "She hates me anyways! Told me so herself!"

I felt the anger rise in my throat, "I'm done being this weak little thing," I said, "I'm done sitting and waiting while other people take care of my problems! I wouldn't only be hurting others of I stayed, I'd be hurting myself! I'd wait for Aunt Nina to calm herself, if she ever did, and then I'd let the two of you fix this." I clenched my jaw, "I'm done. I'm a better, stronger, person than this, than what I've been."

"Yes, but having other people help you isn't weak, Allison," Josh said.

"But crying and letting mommy take care of your problems is," I said. I had relatively calmed, but my voice was still sharp, "Even if my mother died years ago, Aunt Nina has played mommy and fixed every mistake I've ever made. I've never done anything for myself."

I took a breath and swallowed, "But, I am doing this. Because I am going to be the strongest person I can be. I'm going to fix things, even if it means I have to leave my family. At least they'll be alive." I crossed my arms over my chest, slowly, and looked over to Josh, "So I'm leaving, whether I have your help or not."

Josh slowly pressed the brakes as we approached a light. He sighed, staring at the wheel. Then he looked up at me, "You really want to do this?" he asked.

I nodded my head, "I have to."

He was about to speak in protest, but swallowed his words, "Are you sure?"

"Yes."

He looked back at the road, pulling out at the green light, "Alright."

25

The house was no relief to the icy air outside, "We'll talk when you get out of the shower, alright?" Josh said as I walked up the staircase. I turned and nodded. I had this feeling of emptiness inside, and it was piercing.

I slipped off the black dress, letting it fall lightly to the floor and stepping out of it. The tiles chilled to the bone, and the room was instantly misted with fog when I turned on the hot water.

When I stepped into the warm shower, the water seared my skin, leaving behind a pricking sensation from the heat on my cold body. There was a tiredness pulling down on me, and I held onto the ledge of the shower as I lowered myself to the ground.

I let every muscle in my body relax, on-by-one, running each under the warm spill of water. The tenderness in my scalp had finally gone away, and I massaged the shampoo deeply into my skin, not letting one inch get looked over.

The weariness tugged harder at my body, and I began to slowly drift away as my mind wandered.

But only moments after I slipped consciousness, the water ran cold. I shivered and scrambled to the door, pushing on the glass with my fingertips. I crawled out of the shower, taking a moment before standing.

Even after doing so, though, a tidal wave of lightheadedness washed over me, and I had to grip the vanity for balance. I raised my hand to my head, and blinked the dizziness from my vision. After I steadied myself, I reached for the faucet and turned off the water. I silently opened the closet door, removing a towel from the stacks within. I wrapped it around my body and opened the door.

In my bedroom, I was met with the sound of running water, which filtered through my open bedroom door. I wrapped the silky black robe that hung on the back of my door around my body, tying the thin strap tightly around my waist. Clothes just felt like a chore, and the robe was soft and convenient.

I leaned over the rail that overlooked the living room and spotted Josh beneath. I floated slowly down the stairs and pivoted towards the living room. Josh looked up when he heard me come in, "Hey."

"Hey." I walked over to the large couch and dropped myself in the little pocket between his chest and his arm. I laid my head on his chest, and his hand pulled me in by the arm. Looked out the window. The day was dull, even with the setting sun spraying hints of color over the mountaintops and through the trees and valleys, "So…"

"So," Josh said. He looked down at me, and I looked up at him, "We obviously can't do an accident again. So what're we gonna do?"

I had to think about it. There were so many possibilities, but only one seemed to make sense, seemed to fit best. I racked my brain for an idea better than the other, but there was no getting around it; it's what worked, "Suicide," I said after a pause.

"Really?" Josh asked, "You think you can do it?" His brow creased upwards. He looked at me, then at the stairs, and I knew what he was thinking.

"Yes." I said, "If we do this right, we can make it so she never sees me alive." I could tell this confused Josh and continued, "If you come over and find me already dead, she wouldn't come see me in the hospital - because I would be dead. Then we could have Rebecca do her thing, and you'll talk Aunt Nina into a closed casket funeral."

Josh nodded slowly, eyes squinted as he ran through all of the points in his head. Then he finally spoke, "Okay."

Later that day, we had decided to visit Aaron in the hospital. From what we'd heard, he was doing remarkably well. When we pulled into the hospital, Josh looked at me, "They said he might be well enough to go home next week," he said, "As long as Nina stays home with him. Which, she will."

We walked inside. I held the flowers we had picked up on the way there in my hands. The halls were quiet as the day winded down, and our footsteps were easily audible throughout the way.

When we turned the corner, my heart skipped a beat. Aaron laid there, his eyes shut. There was a shooting pain in my chest, and I couldn't help but scold myself for putting him here.

I walked over to the nightstand and laid the flowers down. I pulled a chair to the bedside and grabbed Aaron's hand. But as I did, his eyes fluttered open.

For a moment, he looked startled, but then he focused on me and smiled weakly, "Allison," he croaked, "Hey."

"Hi," I said smiling, "I didn't mean to wake you."

"No, you're fine," he said with a smile.

I felt the tears already in my eyes. I had been so worried he wasn't going to make it, that he was going to die and, eventually, take Aunt Nina with him. But he was here, alive and well, "How're you feeling?"

"Pretty good," he said, "Just tired. But it'll go away, eventually." He looked around the room, "Is Nina with you two?" he asked.

I closed my eyes, "Uh, no," I stuttered, "She and I aren't in a really good place right now."

Aaron's brow furrowed and he looked sympathetic, "It's not because of me, is it?" I didn't answer, and he dropped his head, "It is, isn't it?"

I smiled, "No," I said, "It's about the whole thing, all of the lying and the hiding things. I think she just snapped and needs time, that's all." I wouldn't let him think this was because of him, "Aaron, I am so sorry."

I felt the words choke in my throat as another wave of tears flooded my eyes, "For what?" he asked.

"For this," I said, looking around the room, "I, it-"

He lifted his other hand and wrapped it around mine and his, "Allison, what did we say about you blaming yourself for everything?" he asked. I smiled, and he said, "This isn't your fault."

"But I opened the door," I said looking to the ground. I was mortified - of my actions, of how naïve I was.

"Yes," Aaron said, "But any normal person would've." He lifted a shaking hand to my face, placing it on my cheek. I rested mine on top of it and smiled. Then a buzzing in my pocket pulled my eyes down.

"I have to go meet Rebecca," I said to Josh, standing.

My back was to Aaron, but Josh had noticed the look on his face, "A friend from school," Josh said to Aaron.

Aaron nodded, "Have fun," he said and smiled.

"I have to admit," Rebecca said, shaking her head, "I was surprised when I saw you at the Starbucks the other day." We both laughed, and I sipped my coffee, "But seriously, though, what happened? You were so ready when I left, and then..."

"...And then I choked," I said, "Aunt Nina was saying something about how she couldn't lose me, and when she stood to leave, I grabbed her hand."

Rebecca just clapped a slow, staccato applause. And I laughed, rolling my eyes, "So you need me to do you up again, huh?" she asked. I nodded, "Yeah, you only talk to me when you need something."

"That's not true!" I said, setting my coffee down, "I just...last..."

"Uh huh," Rebecca said. She brought the warm cup of tea to her lips, "So are we going accident again, or...?"

"Suicide," I answered.

A crooked look of pleasure twisted onto her face, "Ah," she said, "Suicides. My favorite." She looked at me and narrowed her eyes. After a moment of scanning me up and down, she said, "Okay, so I'm thinking slit your throat. What do you think?"

I was shocked, "Uh." That sounded like an absolutely horrible way to die. But then I remembered it wasn't real, "Yeah. I mean, you're the expert. If that's what you're thinking, then it's good enough for me."

I looked around the coffee shop. It was a small little place with a warm vibe, and only a few people worked the counter.

Rebecca and I were two of the few customers in the building. Some would walk in and order at the counter, but then hurry on their way, "So, how much is this gonna cost?" I asked.

Rebecca licked her lips and stared at me, "Nah," she said, "You're good." My eyes widened, and she held up her hand, "You paid me a lot last time, a little more than you should've but, hey, I wasn't gonna fight it. But now, I got you covered."

I smiled, "Thank you."

By the time I had gotten home, the sky was and inky velvet, and the moon shone full in the night. Josh's car was no longer parked in the driveway, and I pulled up through the grass, as close to the house as possible. Partially because it was freezing, and I didn't feel like walking very far to get into the house, but also to spite Aunt Nina.

I unlocked the door, and closed it hard enough to let my aunt know I was home without having to see her. I climbed the staircase, tearing into the muffin I had picked up before I left the coffee shop. Because Lord knows I couldn't go into the kitchen with Aunt Nina.

When I reached the top of the stairs, something seemed off. The marble, as well as the air around me, was cooler than usual beneath my feet. My eyes fell to my bedroom door, which hung wide open.

I walked to my room, passing through the doorway. When I entered the room, I found where the frigid winds were coming from.

The windows were open, and the coral curtains swayed in the breezes that drifted in. I ran over to the bay window and shut it. Moonlight poured through the window, falling onto the floors

82

ANASTASIA SMITH

and surfaces. Then a shimmer in the corner of my eyes caught my attention as I moved away from the window.

In the middle of my neatly made bed, which had been a complete wreck before I left, laid a gold-lined envelope.

I shuffled towards it slowly. It was still cold in my hands, and a shiver ran up my back. I tore open the flap, feeling the cool gold against my skin.

Inside set three pictures as well as a thin piece of printer paper. I sat on the bed and pulled out the pictures, spreading them across the comforter.

Josh and I at Vitali's funeral.

Aunt Nina, home alone playing the piano.

Rebecca and I at the coffee shop.

I lifted the note from the bed, unfolding it. The paper was whiter than snow, and as I lifted it quickly, the edge ran across my thumb, slicing through the skin. I raised my finger to my lips and sucked on the cut. Then I let my gaze return to the note.

Watch you're back, Allison. We're coming.

I sat for a moment in the silence. The frozen air caused my arms and legs to shiver. I looked back down at the note.

We're coming.

Then I heard the shatter of glass from downstairs.

I leapt from the bed and raced down the staircase. Holding onto the railing, I swung around, almost running into the wall as I rounded into the kitchen.

Aunt Nina stood between the island and the wall of cabinets, fractured fragments of a salad bowl spread across the floor, "Dammit," she whispered to herself and bent down.

I began to walk over to help, but she looked up at me with thar look that sometimes made me think she was directly related

82
- 278 -

to Satan himself, and I backed out of the room.

I went back upstairs, letting the fatigue that fell over me be the motivation to climb to whole way. I stepped onto the landing and trudged to my room. Not changing out of the yoga pants and sweatshirt that covered my body, I crawled under the covers of my bed.

They were cold and, for a few minutes, only made me colder. I shivered until the blanket warmed, and it held in the heat.

There was a rustling sound that pulled my attention, and I fought to ignore it. But in the end, my curiosity, as it always did, won, and I rolled over in bed.

The window was wide open.

26

Aunt Nina could be a demon at times, but she had the voice of an angel. I sat, curled up on the eighth step, watching her through the French doors. Aaron rested in the corner, lying back in a recliner Aunt Nina had brought in just for him. Aaron loved every little thing about Aunt Nina, but he loved her music the most.

She played and sang for him for *hours*. Anything that he wanted, anything that distracted him, she'd do. The first week after he had come home was the hardest. Being that he couldn't be left alone, he had come to stay with us instead of going back to his apartment in the city. The poor man couldn't do anything for himself, and Aunt Nina never left his side.

But as the time went on, he began to heal - slowly. The discoloration on his chest was horrifying. He had spilled something on himself, and when he lifted his shirt for Aunt Nina to take, I caught a glimpse of the bruising that lined his tight, slender body.

He began walking again, with Aunt Nina's help of course. Every day, she would take him around the block, or at least try to. And every day, they had gotten farther than the day before. Hey, it's progress, right?

It was around 11 a.m., and Aunt Nina was being talked into singing, *"Just one more song,"* before she took Aaron for his daily walk before lunch. She rolled her eyes and smiled, steadying herself on the piano bench and thinking of what to sing next. She took in a breath.

Then there was a muffled request from Aaron, and she smiled brighter as he handed her a book, and she turned around to face the piano. He loved it most when she played and sang. There was a soft chord, and then, "When I was a child, my eyes were clear," Aunt Nina sang.

This was one of her favorite songs - *Fly, Fly Away* from *Catch Me If You Can*. Her fingers glided swiftly across the keys, and the notes poured harmoniously from her lips, together a heavenly melody.

Aaron watched her as she did, and he sat up. He watched her with the most loving and affectionate eyes, and you would've thought God had given him the world. But to Aaron, he had.

When Aunt Nina finished, she turned around and stood, pushing in the piano bench. Aaron begged for one more song. But despite the pleading, she forced him up, promising one when they got back. He reluctantly agreed, gripping Aunt Nina's arm and shuffling towards the doors. When they reached the doorway, Aunt Nina steadied him and quickly opened the doors.

She walked him through and into the foyer, but when she glanced up and caught me in the stairs, her warm and radiant face fell. She took her glaring eyes off of me and returned her gaze to Aaron, forcing a smile back onto her lips. Aaron fiddled with the handle, and they walked through, leaving for the next half hour.

I walked down the marble steps and turned into the music room. Aunt Nina had never known this, but ever since I was young, I used to watch her, listen to her sing, and I would try to do it myself. When she was at work, I would sneak into her room, digging through her dozens of piano scores and finding songs to learn.

I wanted to learn one, like *really* learn one, and play and sing it for her. But I always ended up getting frustrated and quitting. Reading music was not really my forte, and it was something I had always struggled with - especially in bass clef.

I slowly made my way to the bookshelf that stretched nearly to the ceiling. My fingers slipped across the spines of the books of sheet music. But my hand stopped trailing when it fell on *Funny Girl*. That was one of her favorite musicals.

When I was first able to lay my fingers on the keys, my aunt tried to teach me pieces from the show. Barbra was her Goddess, and she wanted nothing more than to see her niece play songs from the musical. But I had always messed them up, pressing the wrong keys and forgetting chords and lyrics.

I slipped the book from the shelf, walking slowly back to the piano. I shimmied myself onto the bench, propping up the book and flipping through its pages. I stopped when I reached the piece I was looking for.

My hands sweated, making the keys slippery beneath my fingers. I played the first few notes, but my finger slipped, pressing a completely wrong array of keys.

I took a deep breath and tried again. I played the first measure without error. Then the second, "Funny." The word was drawn out, ending in vibrato. I'd had some help from Jillian at school, who was a freaking musical genius, and she was helping me surprise Aunt Nina for her birthday in August, "Did you hear that?"

The more I played, the more natural it felt. Like it was this thing I had fought for so long, but now embraced. I practiced, starting and restarting again and again, and I hadn't even heard the front door open when Aunt Nina and Aaron got back. I just played. I let the last notes flow from my mouth, "Funny girl." My fingers trailed the piano with the end of the melody.

As the last of the notes faded, I looked up. Aunt Nina stood in the doorway. Her arms were crossed, but there was a small grin on her lips. But she pushed it away when I caught her eye, "Took you long enough," she said and left the room. I couldn't help but smile.

There was something folded in the back pocket of her jeans that hadn't been there before she left. She walked to the kitchen where Aaron waited on a barstool, sipping a bottle of water from the fridge. When I walked in, he smiled, "Hey," he said, pulling the barstool next to him out from under the counter, "I heard you playing back there. Not too bad, kiddo."

"Thanks," I laughed, "I've only been trying with that song for almost twenty years now." Aunt Nina fixed a Caesar salad for herself and Aaron, then pushed the bowl my way. She didn't look at me, but still had the slightest hint of a glare on her face.

I wasn't going to fight it. It was a step up from her putting the food away, and I not eating at all, "Thank you," I said.

She wiped the counter off, "Mhm."

I stabbed clumps of lettuce, moving them to a plate Aunt Nina had left in the middle of the counter. After I finished making my plate, Aaron shifted, painfully, in his seat with a wince, "Hey," he said, facing Aunt Nina and I, "I still haven't seen that one movie you're always trying to make me watch," he looked at Aunt Nina, "What is it? Beaches? Wanna watch it?"

Aunt Nina beamed, "Why the change of heart?" she asked.

Aaron smiled, looking at her sweetly, "Honestly," he said, "When - *the accident* - happened, one of the things that was going through my head was how all you wanted to do was watch that movie, and I always put it off and said later." He paused, looking down at his fingers, "Then, I thought that there wasn't going to be a *later*. And I felt so guilty. Because all you wanted was to watch a stupid movie, and I said no."

Aunt Nina teared up and walked over to her boyfriend, kissing him, "So, is that a yeah, you wanna watch the movie?" Aaron asked. Aunt Nina laughed and glided into the living room, sifting through DVDs.

When I entered the living room behind Aaron, Aunt Nina didn't react. I took the loveseat farthest from her spot on the couch - didn't want to push my luck. But during the entire movie, I caught Aunt Nina's stares, her eyes burrowing into me with looks of sorrow and longing. She would pull her eyes away, but minutes later, they would be back.

The whole day was like this. Stares from both she and Aaron as we moved past each other and went through the day.

When the evening had fallen, Aunt Nina took Aaron upstairs. I held onto Aaron's right arm, Aunt Nina holding the left, as we walked him to the staircase. I moved his hand to the railing, and he and Aunt Nina climbed the staircase, one step at a time.

I stayed downstairs, loading the dishwasher and just trying

to make things easier on Aunt Nina. After I had swept and did every chore I could think of, it was around 8:30, and I finally surrendered to the upstairs. But as I walked up the stairs, I heard Aunt Nina's and Aaron's worried voices drifting from the master bedroom.

"Nina, it's not your right," Aaron said, "You have to give it to her."

"I know, but," Aunt Nina stopped mid-sentence, "I can't. You've seen her lately. Ever since that detective died, she's fighting things, facing them without fear. I can't, Aaron. She'll go, and I'll lose her."

What? "Nina, listen-"

The ring of metal sounded as I stoved my toe on the railing that curved at the top of the stairs. I silently screamed and cursed under my breath, "Allison."

The word was firm and strong. I walked over to the doorway and looked at my aunt, "Yes?"

She looked at Aaron with a look of hurt and regret. But he arched a brow and nodded in my direction. Aunt Nina looked up at me, and she looked like she was about to cry, "Here," she said.

She stuck her arm out, holding whatever had been folded in her pocket earlier. *The black and gold pierces my insides.* I sucked in a breath and took the envelope form her hand, "It was on the front porch when we got back. I-"

But I wasn't listening to her, and she knew it. Instead, I tore into the envelope. Whatever it was, I was ready to take. The thin sheet of white paper was the only thing inside. But Aunt Nina and Aaron already knew that; the envelope had already been opened.

I unfolded the paper.

Mt. Carmel on W 71st, 9 o'clock. Alone. We'll settle this - for good. Anyone else comes, and you can kiss everyone you love goodbye.

W 71st. That was in downtown. I remembered Aunt Nina pulling me close and clutching tightly onto my hand in that part of town, even though I was 14-years-old.

Wait.

I flicked my eyes up at the clock on the wall - 8:38. I had 22 minutes, "Why didn't you give me this earlier?"

Aunt Nina let out a small laugh, "You're not going." She looked at me like I was insane, a condescending smile on her face, "You're nuts if you think I'm letting you."

I felt that fury I'd felt towards her these past few weeks tighten in my chest, "I am going," I said firmly.

"Allison, you're not going." She stood from the bed, "You just aren't."

My eyes narrowed, and my pounding breath was the only sound in the room, "Watch me."

I turned and left the room and stormed down the hall. But Aunt Nina was quick to follow, and she dug her nails into my arm and pulled me backwards just as I was about to grab the railing, "Allison Grace," she said viciously, "Stop, now." I didn't, but tried to pull my arm from her grasp, and almost succeeded. But she was too quick, "I said stop!"

Her face was hardened in a cold-blooded scowl. But I was feeling rebellious, "*Or what?*" I asked dangerously.

She huffed, "Allison, I don't know what's gotten into you, but you do *not* walk away from me when I'm speaking to you, and you do *not* talk to me this way."

I laughed bitterly, "Why? What are you gonna do?" I asked,

"Because, as far I can tell, the only thing you've been good at lately is drinking yourself to death and swallowing pills trying to kill yourself. And you can't even succeed in doing that."

Aaron looked horrified.

He had no idea what Aunt Nina had done. He was going to say something, but I wasn't finished, "You're weak," I said with merciless venom, "You can't - or just aren't strong enough to - get your shit together. You're just a drunken-"

But this time, I was the one who didn't get to finish. My face stung where Aunt Nina's palm had left its mark.

She brought both of her hands to her mouth, gasping. I was trapped in my own body. I couldn't move, and I didn't know what to do. In all of the years I had lived with my aunt, she had *never* laid a hand on me.

My breathing quickened, and I whipped around fiercely. I darted down the stairs. I could hear the clap of Aunt Nina's feet behind me, "Allison, wait-"

But I didn't. I flung open the front door. I was going to do this, I had to. Because I had to put an end to this. If not for her, then for me.

I had almost gotten to the car when a pair of hands wrapped around my arm, "Allison, no. Wait, please," Aunt Nina said through choking tears, "Don't - you can't go. You'll die. Please - just-"

"No!" I ripped my arm from her fingers, "I'm done with you. You're over-dramatics - all of it. Do you know why you're husband left you? Because you're a heartless bitch. And hell, I would've left you too."

I heard a sharp intake of breath. When I turned back around, her hand was over her chest, and Aaron was at her side, holding onto her arm, "And you were right. You should've let me go," I said quietly, with no remorse, "Because you *aren't* cut out to be a mother."

There was a shaky exhale, and a sound like everything on the earth had died, and all motion stopped completely. I walked to the car without looking back. When I turned the key in the ignition, the headlights shined brightly on the two in front of me.

Aunt Nina looked up as the tears in her enervated eyes overflowed. She was cold, lifeless. She stood there for a moment, looking into my eyes. I had crushed her heart.

She looked at me with an evilly exhausted glare as something welled up in side of her. Her fists clenched at her sides. I watched them, the muscles folding in one by one. Then they came undone and a spastic burst, and she collapsed to a heap of crying and tears curled up on the cement.

27

My heart is pounding. My fingers clutched the wheel, and the foot that didn't push down on the accelerator like a lead weight was tapping furiously. *This is it; this is finally going to be over.*

I slow at the red light. *8:52.* I glance at the handgun on the passenger seat then back at the light. *It's still red.* I shoot my hand over, grasping the gun and tucking it in the waistband of my leggings. The metal was cool on my back, sending a wave of goose bumps over my skin.

The gun is heavy in my hands, and, unlike anything I'd ever expected about a gun. There was no rush of adrenaline, but a surge of fear that sends goose bumps trailing my arms, "Stop shaking, Schwartz. It's just for peace of mind - mine more than yours."

Vitali's eyes are wide and reassuring. I nod, clearing my throat, "Do you think I'll…"

She looks at me, "Let's hope not."

There was the blare of a horn, and I looked up, finding the light green. I stepped on the pedal, peeling onto the road. I turned left onto W 71st St, sliding into a spot along the side of the road.

I crept slowly down the street as I did, and when I parked, I opened the door slowly. I held my breath, slipping the door shut, pushing on it with the bottom of my shoe after laying it in place. Then I tiptoed to the sidewalk.

I walked onto the basketball court, my steps echoing in the night despite my efforts to remain silent. It was only a half court that I stood on, "Hello?" I called into the night, "Mick?"

I looked around the darkness, the fence of the ball field fine, blurred lines in the night. Wind rustled the branches of trees that lined the sidewalk, and the city hummed in the distance. But other than that, the world was silent, "Mick? I'm here!"

Then I saw my shadow on the concrete in front of me.

I whipped around. A glaring light blinded my eyes, and I raised my arm to shield them, squinting in the brightness. There were two glowing beams against the black background, "Well hello, Allison."

A door slammed shut, and a figure walked in front of the headlights. Mick's hands rested in his pockets, and he walked leisurely, one foot in front of the other, in my direction. I didn't move as he circled me. His hand drifted along the skin at the nape of my neck. I felt his breathing, warm against my skin, and he whispered, "I'm going to kill you."

A thump bashed my head, and I was sent to the ground. Mick stood over me, and I looked up at him. I began a shaky attempt to stand, but a dropkick struck the hollow between my ribs, followed by another, and another, and another, and I was left choking on the ground.

I rolled onto my back, and as I did, Mick lowered himself over me, straddling my body. I wrestled under his grasp, throwing punches, but he was stronger, and one throw of his fist stunned my movements. Involuntary tears, stirred by a strangling pound, clouded my eyes, and I clenched my jaw. There was no air in my lungs, and Mick's hands pushed down on my chest.

A tightened cry left my mouth as Mick's hands relayed his body weight onto my ribs. His legs straightened, and I seized the opportunity, shooting my foot up between his legs.

He let out a squealing yelp, dropping to the cement. I hauled myself from the ground. Lurching for my car, I took off in a sprint, but a clenching grip tightened around my neck, lifting me from the ground. I kicked and thrashed with rage, swinging my arms around my back, hoping to hit something.

But I couldn't it was useless. I was thrown into a tree, feeling the familiar sensation of blood trickling through my hair. My hands trembled with fury as I reached for Mick's hands around my throat. His brow dripped with sweat and his arms bulged as he threw me into the mossy roots of a tree.

I staggered, lunging towards Mick, and he turned to the side, watching as I dove past him and fell to the sidewalk, "Oh, oh, oh," Mick laughed, "Just give it up Allison. Accept that you have lost. Make this quicker and easier on all of us, and just stop now."

I looked around. But Mick wasn't finished; he was just getting started. The bone-crushing steel toe of Mick's boot pummeled my face. A thick, coursing stream of blood streamed from my nose, the skin around it torn.

It throbbed. The bones in my face shattered, and I croaked. Mick laughed, and he stared down at me.

I lay on the ground, my back flat against the concrete. My

left arm hung limply on the ground, and the other held the pools of blood streaming from my nose. I pounded my foot into the sidewalk below me. My toes clenched and my fingers tightened into a white-knuckled fist as Mick stepped on my forearm, pinning me in place.

I struggled to pull my arm from its clip beneath Mick's boot, but he just pushed down harder. I tried to find a way out, something I could do.

It was so dark, I couldn't see anything. *Light, I need light.* I looked around. Above the ball field were stadium lights. *But how would I get them on?* I followed the pole until I found an open box hung on the wood.

But my arm was still secured to the ground. I rolled my neck, searching for a rock, a stick, a - *a needle.* A needle lay only a few inches from my head. I asked myself why it would be there, but then again, it was South LA.

I stretched my hand toward the needle-tipped syringe. It was *just* out of my reach. I felt the strain on my muscles as I pushed my arm farther. Then I felt the plastic between my fingers.

I swung my arm around, plunging the needle into Mick's shin. He pulled back his leg, grabbing the syringe. I leapt to my feet and bolted for the pole. My steps beat the ground, and I huffed for air. I wiped the blood running from my face and down my neck, the stickiness gripping onto my jacket and hair.

After what felt like forever, I reached the pole, throwing my hand into the switch. The whole field illuminated with a thunderous click, and I ran for the gate in the outfield. Behind center field was a building with lights still on in the offices. I ran across the clay as fast as I could.

But a sharp drum turned me around as an object came thrashing down on my head. I fell to the dirt, which stuck to the crusting fluid on my skin. Mick stood over me, a rock dripping with blood clutched in his hand, each drop falling with a clink in the silence.

His chest heaved. I held the gash at the top of my head, and backed away frantically. I tried to stand, but stumbled, and I had to watch my feet to keep them from tripping over each other.

Mick walked my way, around my side, and I backed away, inching towards from where we came. I fought the fear that pushed on my chest, and Mick smiled, "It's over, Allison," he said. She took a step towards me. I stepped back, "I win. Because there's nowhere to run; nowhere to hide."

I coughed, the sandy ball field sticking to the back of my throat. Mick's malicious laughed crackled through the night, "You lose. You should've listened to Aunt Nina."

Aunt Nina.

I told her she was heartless. I told her that her husband was right in leaving her. What was wrong with me? All she wanted was to keep her niece alive.

And now I am over. My vision is fading, and I can't breathe. I can't think, and a wash of dizziness is drunkening my movements. Mick stands in front of me, and I am trapped. If I run, he will catch me. If I fight, he will beat me. And if I stay, he will kill me.

It's me against him. If I win, I can go home. If I lose, they'll kill her. I should've listened. Aunt Nina told me not to come, that I'd die, and she was right.

She was right. She always was. Always so smart, so prepared. I was never prepared. Not for New York, and definitely not for this. The only way that I could even be considered prepared was given to me by Vitali - she gave me the gun.

The gun.

I let my hand slide from the back of my head to my waist. My fingers, slickened with blood, slipped under my shirt and wrapped around the gun. I lifted it slowly from my back, pulling it around my side. Then a click froze me in my tracks.

The rigid tip of metal shoved into the small of my back, "I wouldn't if I were you."

The voice was high-pitched. My neck rotated to the side, and I could see pale skin and dark hair out of the corner of my eye. *The man who murdered Vitali.*

He murdered Vitali. I felt a rage bubble in my chest, and my heart quickened. I lifted the gun anyway, completely disregarding Mick in front of me.

But the weapon was thrown from my hands in an instant and I was hurled to the ground. I watched from the side as Mick lifted my weapon, my only hope for survival, from the dirt, twirling it between his fingers. He watched as the man sat on me, keeping his aim at my chest.

The man used his free hand to pin down my shoulder. But I had another arm, and swung with it, dragging my nails across his flesh. I clawed at his face and neck, but he kneed me between my legs, and I faltered.

He scooted closer to my face, using his knees to hold my wrists to the ground. The man's brown eyes looked into mine, and he lifted the gun, shoving the barrel against the center of my forehead, "Game over," he hissed.

I watched his finger wrap around the trigger and sucked in

a breath. I closed my eyes. Then a shot deafened my blood-crusted ear.

But I was not the victim.

28

I opened my eyes. The pressure on my arms and chest had released. I pressed my chin to my chest, looking at where the man had sat only moments ago. But there was nothing there. Then I looked to my right.

The man's body lay in a pool of blood, his eyes still open.

I looked around. There was nothing but trees and lights and Josh.

Wait, Josh?

Sure enough, even after blinking to be sure it wasn't a trick of the mind, Josh stood in left field, a gun still aiming at the man on the ground. *Where did he learn to make a shot like that?* Then I remembered: his father was an officer before he had killed himself and Josh's mother.

Josh looked at me, and I smiled. Then hands were around my throat.

Mick pulled me into his clutch, and a gun - *my* gun - pressed into my temple, "Take another step towards us, Josh," Mick said, "And I shoot." Josh snapped his aim towards Mick, but yielded at his words, "Drop the gun," Mick ordered.

Josh raised his hands in the air, and slowly lowered the gun to the ground. Just as his hand reached the dirt, another loud echo shattered the night, and I was let go, "Allison, run!"

I sprinted across the dirt and to the grass. When I stole a glance back to the field, I saw Mick on the ground, holding his leg as blood poured through an open wound. I looked up at Josh, and he turned and took off.

But as we turned, two more sets of headlights flicked on, followed by the relay of slamming car doors. The group of men hopped the fence and marched towards us. Josh lifted his gun as the men began to circle around us, but as he did, there was a click right behind him.

Mick breathed down our necks. Then, as if on instinct, I whipped around. I grabbed Mick's arm, shoving it towards the sky as he fired another shot. I had the better grip, and after twisting his wrist with a strain, I pried the gun from his hands, which were slippery with blood.

Josh's back pressed against mine, our arms out in aim, and I could feel the heaviness of his breathing, "Calm down," I whispered.

"Calm down?" he barked, "There are, like, five guys trying to kill us!"

"Actually, it's more like eight."

"Oh, my bad for not being specific enough!" He huffed and spoke again, "So, what's the plan?" he asked more calmly.

"Plan?"

"Oh. My. God, we are going to die." I looked around the circle. There were seven men other than Mick. They all looked similar - the same muscular build in black suits. But none of them had weapons that could fire. I side glanced the road and time slowed, "Hey, Josh," I whispered.

"Yes?"

"Run."

I took off for the street, not looking back. I heard Josh's pounding steps behind me. Josh helped me over the fence and followed closely behind. When we reached the car, I hopped into the driver's seat, barely leaving Josh time to get into the car before pulling out.

I flew down the midnight streets. Three cars followed as we turned down alleyways and wove through lanes on highways. I pulled off of an exit in Hollywood. The streets were narrower, and I watched in the mirror as the cars filed into a line. A light up ahead turned yellow.

I gassed it.

I sped through as the light changed to red, looking out the back windshield. A black car that held two of Mick's men was demolished as it clashed with a larger van going in the opposite direction, "Oh, shit," Josh muttered. Then two more black SUVs, identical to the last, appeared from the sides of the crash, racing down the road, "Crap, go, go, go!"

I hammered the pedal, weaving through cars. When I made a sharp turn, slamming the breaks as the tires skidded a half-circle, the black SUV behind us had flung itself into the wall of a brick building on the side of the street.

Only one more car followed us; the car that held Mick. A buzzing sound drew both my eyes and Josh's to the center console, "What the hell?" Josh asked picking up his phone.

The call was on speaker, "Hello, Josh," Mick said, "Allison, can you hear me?" he asked.

"Yes," I said, "I can hear you. And when I-"

"Oh, hey, hey, I just asked a simple question," he said. There was a stretch of silence as I breathed furiously heavily. Then Mick spoke, trying to fight a demonic laugh, "We have her."

And then he hung up.

"What does he mean, Josh?" I asked, panicked. But I knew what he meant. My phone buzzed - *Aunt Nina*. I answered the call, "Aunt Ni-"

But I was cut off by a blood curdling screech, "Allison! Help me, please." The words weren't even words. They were sobs that had been given syllables. There was a deep breath over the line and another scream.

A scream that was cut off by the death of the line, "No!" I cried, "No! Aunt Nina!" I punched the wheel. Josh grabbed my arm as I tried to watch the road.

They're going to kill her.

"Allison," Josh said, "Breathe. We are going to find her." He reached for my phone, "She called from her cell right?" I nodded, still keeping an eye on the last SUV that trailed behind. Then Josh tapped my arm, "Here."

He had pulled up Find My iPhone. The location of Aunt Nina's phone was shown by a pin on a map. *W 63rd St*. Literally, where we just came from. I made a U-turn, ignoring the thousands of blaring horns and curses.

But as we drove down the highway, I noticed that Mick's SUV no longer followed us. *Had we lost him?*

I pulled onto 63rd. Parking along the road, I raced to the empty lot that held my aunt captive. Josh and I jogged to the cracked cement, only to find... *nothing*. I kicked the gravel on the dirt, frustrated. *She's not here - we're too late*, "Wait,

Allison," Josh called, "Come here."

I walked over. We weren't too late after all. But, we never would've been. In the sandy dirt laid Aunt Nina's phone, next to it, a recorder, "What the…"

"It was a trap," Josh said, looking up, "It was trick. She was never here. She never called, it - it was a tape. But now…" Our eyes widened and we ran back to the car. There was an unspoken understanding.

They were going for her now. They just needed to get us out of the way first.

I was in a full panic. I knew my way around the city, and I knew shortcuts that would shave off time, but not enough. Then it hit me. *The ridge.*

The road leading to the ridge opened right onto my street. But there was another road that you could access the ridge from. I switched lanes and pulled off of the exit before mine. The gravel road was just ahead.

My Ferrari, low to the ground, was not built for climbing the ridge so quickly, and we bumped the whole way. But as we came over the top of the hill, I saw headlights. *Mick.*

I flew down the hill. When I reached the road, the ride smoothed, and my tires were able to grip the pavement, letting me catch up to the SUV. The rev of the engines sliced through the silence of Beverly Park.

The SUV tried to speed up, outrun me, but it couldn't - it was no match. I served to the right, pushing the black SUV into the railing that lined the road. On the other side was the drop off. The SUV pushed back, the sheer size of the car giving it power over me. But I jerked the wheel, pushing the large vehicle back into the metal.

Sparks flew from the rail against the SUV. I let my eyes look ahead. There was straight road with a bend. At the end of the bend, the railing cut off. So I sped up.

I forced the SUV to keep up with me as I raced towards the bend with no intention of turning. Instead, last second, I slammed the breaks, and the car came to a halt with an ear-splitting squeal.

The SUV continued forward, on the other hand. Josh and I watched as it soared through the air, flying off of the edge and into the night. There was the shuffle of trees, and then the car was gone.

I stepped onto the road, walking slowly to the edge of the ridge. There, at the bottom, crushed and destroyed by the rock's jagged edges, was the flaming SUV. The fire lit up the night and I looked at Josh.

He stared in awe. I jumped when his arm pulled me into his chest. His eyes looked into mine, "It's over," I breathed, "It's finally over."

I closed my eyes as a single tear ran down my face.

29

I slid down the front door once in the foyer, sitting on the cold marble. Looking up at the stairs, they seemed too grand to climb. My body had nothing left in it, and I decided on the couch for the night.

But when I walked into the living room, I saw the back of Aunt Nina's head. In her hand was a bottle. I felt an instant stab of guilt and walked to the kitchen in desperate need for water. I could feel her eyes following me as I crossed the room.

I let out a breath upon entering the kitchen. It was dark, and I flicked the light switch. There was a glass in the sink - the one I had used earlier. I rinsed it out and stuck it under the ice maker in the fridge. After the glass was packed with ice, I pressed it against the back, filling it with water.

It was cold against my lips, and I held it against my sweaty face and neck. I tilted my head backwards, letting a sip of ice-cold water sit in my mouth. I let my mind drift, though I knew where it would go.

My eyes caught a glimpse of Aunt Nina through the doorway. I knew what I had said was wrong and awful. And there was no excuse. But she wasn't going to listen to me and I knew it. I watched her, her empty face, and wanted so badly to curl up in her arms.

But I had really screwed up this time. What was I thinking - to have let myself say that? She had every right to never speak to me again. But I was sick of missing my aunt, of her shunning me. I was going to go in there, make things right, I had decided. Then I dropped to the ground.

I choked on the blood filling my lungs and soaking my shirt, the glass slipping from my hand and shattering as I fell. I held my hands over the slit, but it was hopeless - the blood seeped through my fingers and onto the marble. I clutched my throat, lying on the ground, and as I did, I saw a man standing over me.

There was a rustle of trees, and then the car was gone.

Mick had escaped.

Mick stood over me, a bloody blade in hand. He threw it to the floor, bending down to grab me by the ankles. And he began to drag me away.

I was rolled onto my stomach. My fingers grabbed at the floors, but slipped with the blood. I tried to call to aunt, only feet away, "Aunt Nina!" But nothing other than a hollow, whistling wind came out, "Aunt-"

I was pulled through the back door. The freezing cold seemed more intense, more biting than it had only a half hour before. I heard the *click* of the back door locking. A sound similar to water spraying against a window drew my attention towards the house.

Blood splattered the glass, pulsing from my throat. It pumped and pumped and *pumped.* I felt the cold seeping its way through my flesh, settling into my body. It started in my fingers and toes. Like ice was slowly eating, freezing, cementing my muscles and nerves. Eventually, I couldn't move them at all.

It spread to my arms and legs next. I knew this when I tried to lift my arm to bang on the glass - tried to grab Aunt Nina's attention. But I was too weak. My arm hovered an inch from the ground, then I had to let if fall with exhaustion.

The moon was full and bright. It had shimmered on the water's reflection on the glass, and I rolled my head to find it. It was bewitching. My lips trembled with the frigid air, and my eyes only barely blinked, but my gaze could not be torn from the moon.

It lit up the night, showed me that life Aunt Nina had shown me before. I saw the life of the mountains and the stars. I heard them whispering my name, "Allison," they hissed sweetly in my ears, their voices carried by the soft winds.

Beauty is not found in a mirror, on a person, but in what is naturally around us. I could feel the pulling of the stars, drawing me to them. Telling me to leave the world behind, "Allison," they whispered.

The blood around me had ceased to run, but stuck in icy, viscous clumps to the patio. I had to tug, several feeble tugs it took, to pull my sleeves from the stones beneath me.

I laid my fingers on the glass. I laid them over her face, "Goodbye…"

My neck rolled back out to the beautiful scene of the garden, then the mountains of secrets and truths that stood behind it. *"They see all…"*

A breeze blew a stray curl from my face. My chest ached, the love inside too much to bear. It was silent, it was peaceful, and it was *remarkable*. I took it all in for the last time. And as I lay there taking my last, burning, struggling breaths, I realized a truth. Even out here, all alone, with all of the eyes of nature on you...

You're never alone.

There's nowhere to hide.

EPILOGUE

Aaron stands at the front door. He hesitates and lays his finger on the button, the bell echoing through the dark and empty house. He knows it's useless, but presses the white button once again.

The key chain rattles as he pulls it from his pocket. He twists the key until the lock clicks. No movement greets him as he enters the house. This morning, like all in the past weeks, is filled with a stiff and brittle silence. The air is heavy, so heavy that Aaron can feel the stillness in his heart and lungs. His breath is vapor, and the floorboards are cold under his feet.

His hand brushes along the iron railing as he climbs the stairs. He feels the heaviness thicken as he remembers Nina running down the steps, chasing after Allison. Saying the last words she would ever say to her.

The air is even colder upstairs. Her door at the end of the hall is cracked open, only barely. Aaron's hand gently pushes the door open. He sees her lying there in the bed, and his heart falls.

The golden brown hair sticks to her face and neck. A tissue is clutched between her fingers. Her eyes stare at the wall and tears roll slowly from her eye sockets. There is no light in the room; black curtains are drawn over the windows and the fire inside of her has burned its last kindling.

Nina is in so much pain, her complexion has ashen. Her naturally golden skin has sunken to a lifeless tone, so much it scares Aaron just to look at her. She has sucked herself into a deeper place, a place so deep and dark only few can understand. All Aaron can do is stroke her graying hair and hold her frozen hand. Her bony, frozen hand.

The skin hugs her bones. Her face is hollow under her cheekbones and her silk, black robe hangs off of her body.

The blanket is stiff; it hasn't been moved in days. From time to time Aaron's eyes drop to the bed sheets, but mostly they are fixed on her face in a soft stare so that whenever she looks his way, he's the first thing she sees.

Bottles and bottles, all empty, lay on the bed, on the floor. Wine stains the bed. Aaron grabs Nina's arm, and it takes almost no strength to pull her into his embrace.

Her empty, lifeless eyes look up into his. She looks up, and her frail body falls into his arms. The weeps are howls as her body shakes violently, uncontrollably. A light tear slides down Aaron's face as he holds his aching, heartbroken girlfriend's trembling body.

The pain must come in waves. There minutes of sobbing, broken apart by short pauses for recovering breaths, that stretch before she's hurled back into the outstretched arms of grief. There is a raw quality to her cries, the realness of a person consumed by a pain that knew no end or limit.

Her hand quivers over her mouth, the tissue still held within it. She remembers clutching Allison's cold body in her arms.

The despair overtakes her whole body, her whole being. The shaking worsens, and Aaron has to hold onto her tighter. Then the silence returns, deafeningly.

ACKNOWLEDGEMENTS

I would like to send my deepest regards first to all of my supporters and beta readers that helped, motivated, and cheered me on through all of the ups and downs of writing a novel. Thank you Alexis, Mom, Dad, Grace and my dearest Shelby. You all are the reason I didn't go insane – or why I didn't get caught in the act, really!

Another thanks to all of my supporters back home, including – but definitely not limited to – Sydney, KK, Sidney, Lexi, Jana, PK, Mrs. Taylor and Mrs. Venick. Thank you to Eileen, the woman who started my love for writing at a young age.

And my deepest gratitude to Janine. Thank you for teaching me what it was to not only be a successful student and writer, but an amazing woman as well. Thank you for *everything.* Thank you for being the first person to believe in me as a writer, and most importantly, thank you for teaching me how to be brave.

ABOUT THE AUTHOR

Anastasia Smith is a 15-year-old author originally from Uniontown, Pennsylvania. In December, she moved to Fernandina Beach, Florida, where she currently resides with her mom, dad, brother, and two dogs. She plans to graduate in the year 2020, and after high school, wishes to pursue writing as a student in Princeton's Creative Writing program. Anastasia is the author of *Nowhere to Hide*, a suspense novel coming this fall, and is currently working on her debut novel's sequel.

Anastasia began writing when she was in the first grade through the gifted program at her school. There, she was encouraged to write short stories and poems, as well as submit them for local contests. She continued writing through elementary school and took Creative Writing classes all through middle school. Her eighth grade year, she wrote many short stories for her class, and finding that it was something she enjoyed - and was good at - she decided she wanted to be an author. But she never really knew where to start.

She on-and-off attempted writing books her eighth grade year, but nothing seemed to stick. When she got into high school, she took up many new activities and classes and took a break from writing for a while. But when she moved to Florida in December 2017, her schedule had cleared up, and she decided she was going to sit down and finally write that novel. She started writing towards the end of February and finished her first draft on May 4, 2018.

Besides writing, Anastasia enjoys reading, playing softball and volleyball, theatre, pageants, and marching band where she hopes to be a drum major. She has held several state titles, including Miss Preteen Pennsylvania and Pennsylvania State Miss. She has played at the World Series for her softball team, and she won an MVP award at age 14 playing for a 16u team.

Anastasia loves connecting with new friends, and you can message her through her website!

CPSIA information can be obtained
at www.ICGtesting.com
Printed in the USA
BVHW082345251218
536330BV00012B/1344/P